THE BOX

A BRUDER HEIST NOVEL

JEREMY BROWN

WOLFPACK PUBLISHING
— EST 2012 —

WOLFPACK
PUBLISHING
— EST 2013 —

The Box

Paperback Edition
Copyright © 2021 Jeremy Brown

Wolfpack Publishing
5130 S. Fort Apache Road 215-380
Las Vegas, NV 89148

wolfpackpublishing.com

Paperback ISBN 978-1-64734-573-0
eBook ISBN 978-1-64734-572-3

THE BOX

THE BOX

PART ONE

CHAPTER ONE

When the armored car came into view just past nine in the morning, Bruder and Kershaw and the other two in the crew were ready for it.

They were on a windblown straightaway of two-lane asphalt called Pine Lane in the northwest quadrant of Iowa.

An overnight dusting of snow rippled sideways across the road like flat white serpents and disappeared into the ranks of brown cornstalk stubs.

It wasn't enough snow to bring out the plows and there wasn't any ice to require salt trucks, which was good. Either one of those might have caused trouble.

Bruder and Kershaw waited in the concrete tunnel beneath a railroad overpass, the only feature of note in any direction. They wore heavy winter work clothes and reflective vests and hard hats with the symbol for the Iowa Department of Transportation on them.

Under the hard hats they wore insulated balaclavas with the mask part tucked under their chins to leave their faces exposed. Under the balaclavas everyone wore electronic earbuds connected to radios. The earbuds also amplified ambient sounds and speech but clamped down to protect the wearer from sudden noises above eighty five decibels, like gunshots and explosions.

Surveying equipment and hard plastic cases were piled outside the tunnel, where they could be seen from the road, and Bruder and Kershaw walked around beneath the railroad and pointed at the concrete and nodded or shook their heads.

The road and the railroad crossed each other at exactly ninety degrees, like an X, with the road going northwest to southeast and the tracks going southwest to northeast.

The tracks ran on a low berm, like a wrinkle in the otherwise flat landscape, and the road beneath it was dug out slightly below ground level.

The old concrete tunnel was too narrow for two modern-day vehicles to pass each other. The entrance looked like a World War II bunker, with thick concrete retaining walls starting wide and narrowing like a funnel. It was too low for anything taller than ten feet, even with the road dug out, so all the big rigs and buses used different roads.

It was also much too small for any road work equipment, and the road under the overpass was scarred and pitted concrete that turned to newer asphalt as soon as possible on the slight inclines coming out from under the tracks.

Permanent signs with flashing lights warned drivers to stop about one hundred feet from the tunnel, where they were supposed to verify no oncoming traffic was already in the chute. It was a straight shot from both stopping points through the tunnel, plus the rest of the road all the way to the horizon, so there wasn't much guesswork involved.

The armored car coasted to a stop at the northwestern sign, then crept forward to Connelly, the man standing out there with another stop sign on a pole. He was dressed the same as Bruder and Kershaw, with thick canvas coveralls and a reflective safety vest and a DOT hardhat.

Connelly also had two Glock 17s inside the coveralls and his balaclava was pulled up, allegedly to keep his face warm, but mostly to keep anyone from recognizing him.

A pair of safety sunglasses hid his eyes.

His radio had the talk button locked down so the others could hear his conversation.

Bruder and Kershaw listened, and waited.

***

Aiden Connelly was thirty years old and liked to think of himself as a breacher.

He had an open, Irish face with a resting smirk that acted like an inkblot test for other people.

For those who wanted to enjoy life, looking at Connelly's face made them say, "What's so funny?"

Those who had a piss-poor outlook and went around in search of examples to reinforce their misery looked at Connelly and said, "What's your problem?"

Connelly enjoyed both reactions, because they either led to fun or a fight, which to him was also fun.

He liked the word *breacher* because it described him personally and professionally. He prided himself on his ability to chat with almost anybody and put them at ease, make them feel special, like he was cracking their emotional and intellectual defenses. He mostly used it on women, but it came in handy when he was working and had to establish a rapport.

He could also blow just about anything up or open, a more literal application of the breacher tag.

When the armored car stopped next to him, he was looking up at the blue morning sky, unblemished from horizon to horizon except for a few contrails being slowly scattered and erased from the tail forward.

He turned and smiled, letting it show in his eyes, and looked through the thick, hazy window at the bearded man inside. He didn't recognize the man but knew the vehicle as a 1987 International, probably purchased at auction or pulled out of a scrap yard and brought back to life.

It was painted flat black and looked more like a military or S.W.A.T. assault machine than a cash-in-transit vehicle, but considering who was inside, it was probably a bit of both. It had newer run-flat tires but that wouldn't matter.

Connelly said, "Good morning!"

He turned his free hand in a cranking motion to get the man to drop the window.

The man shook his head and frowned at Connelly, who was apparently too stupid to realize armored windows don't roll down.

Connelly said through his balaclava, "Is it broken?"

The man shook his head in irritation and leaned down to the gunport centered just below the window.

He moved the interior steel plate aside and said, in a thick Eastern European accent, "No roll! No open! What's happening here?"

Connelly knew where the men were from and he was tempted to say, "Is that a Romanian accent I detect?"

Just to mess with them.

But Bruder was listening, and he didn't like improvisation unless it was absolutely necessary, so instead Connelly knocked the stop sign pole against his hard hat and rolled his eyes.

"Oh, duh! Of course it doesn't open. This thing is like a tank, right? Anyway, you can go on through, nobody's coming. I don't even know why they have me standing out here, there's already a freaking stop sign, you know?"

The man turned and said something to the other man in the passenger seat, who also had a beard, then opened the gun port again.

"What is happening here?"

"Oh, we're surveying. Surveying! They want to see if it's

possible to widen the tunnel. Wider!"

Connelly looked down the road behind the armored car, then through the tunnel. He had to shield his eyes against the sun, about a hand's width above the tracks. No other vehicles were in sight, just like every other time they'd scouted the road.

He listened and didn't hear any approaching freight trains, which was also according to schedule.

"You can go through! It's fine!"

The man said something to his passenger again and frowned through the thick glass at Connelly, then put the truck into gear and rolled forward.

Connelly could see his mouth moving but couldn't hear the words. He turned away from the vehicle and looked northwest along the road, seeing nothing but more drifting snow and the remnants of last summer's corn.

When the armored car's rear bumper went past him, he unlocked the radio's talk button, but before he let it go he muttered, "Ten seconds."

***

When the armored car moved again Kershaw went to the pile of surveying equipment just outside the tunnel and started messing with a laser level mounted on a tripod. Bruder left him there and walked through the tunnel to the southeast end.

The low rumble of the diesel engine was getting funneled toward him, but he could tell from the sound it wasn't in the tunnel yet.

He didn't want to look back.

He walked the twenty three steps without hurrying. When he got to the end of the tunnel, he went to the white crew cab truck sitting on the gravel shoulder with the tailgate and cap open. A telescoping rod with height measurements and a laser receiver attached were waiting on the tailgate along with a bright yellow carrying case the size of a small cooler.

The truck didn't look like anything special, but some modifications done at a Las Vegas garage would make sure the truck would do what Bruder and the crew needed it to.

So far, all they needed it to do was sit there and look like a truck.

When the sound of the armored car's engine grew and began to echo straight at him, Bruder took the equipment off the tailgate and started walking along the truck, away from the tunnel and toward Rison, the other man standing out in the wind with a stop sign on a pole.

As he walked, he counted down to himself: 3...2...1.

***

Kershaw hit the button when the armored car was exactly halfway through the tunnel.

The shaped charges disguised as lumpy concrete patches went off, a jarring *crack* that smacked out of the tunnel and rolled out into the empty fields.

The small but powerful explosions went up and out at about a fifteen-degree angle from the centerline and lifted the armored car a few inches, just enough to take the weight off the tires and shear the rims off the axles.

The vehicle slammed back down on its belly in a cloud of dust and brief splash of sparks when the old metal struck the concrete.

Kershaw pulled his mask up and lifted an AR-15 with a 16-inch barrel, suppressor, flashlight, and optics out of one of the hard equipment cases and slung it across his chest.

He found the rope tucked into the snow and dead weeds along the concrete retaining wall and moved with it toward the middle of the road. The rope popped loose of the snow and occasional bits of ice until it hung straight down from the railroad overpass and Kershaw pulled hard, unfurling the thick canvas tarp.

The far end of the tunnel was already blocked, so Bruder was ahead of him.

***

Bruder pushed through the tarp blocking the southeastern end of the tunnel.

The tarp crackled as it moved because of the reflective insulation foil lining the inside, which, along with the thick concrete walls, turned the tunnel into a Faraday box. No electromagnetic signals—like those from cell phones, in particular—could get in or out.

Bruder had a 100,000 lumen flashlight attached to his AR, and he sent the beam through the armored car's windshield.

Dust and dirt drifted through the white light but he could clearly see the two bearded men in the front seat lifting their hands and turning away from the beam, which hit like a baseball bat when you looked straight at it.

Bruder wasn't sure how muffled his voice would be inside the vehicle or how badly the ears in there were ringing, so he erred on the side of loud.

"Open the back!"

The two men inside blinked and flinched in the flashlight beam.

"Open the back now, or we will blow it open!"

Their mouths moved as they talked to each other, then the driver turned in the general direction of the flashlight with his hand held up to shield his eyes and addressed Bruder.

"Fuck you!"

Bruder heard that just fine, so he knew the men inside could hear him.

"Last chance! Open the back or we will blow it open!"

The men pointed pistols at him through the windshield.

The driver yelled, "Come on in!"

Bruder hit his radio.

"Blow it."

***

Kershaw slapped the shaped charge against the armored car's back doors and flipped the toggle switch to make it live.

No one was supposed to be in the back of the vehicle, but if they were, the sound of the magnetic frame thumping onto the steel doors ought to be sufficient motivation to open up. The frame had a piece of duct tape with #2 written in black Sharpie.

Kershaw pushed through the tarp on the northwest end and stood with his back against the concrete retaining wall. He pulled out a small black remote, which had its own piece of tape with #2 written on it.

The remote for the charges that had blown the armored car's wheels off had "*******1" on it, and it was in a vest pocket he'd designated for used charges.

The pocket for unused charges still held remotes numbered 3, 4, and 5.

He pressed the radio.

"Blowing in three, two, one."

Then he hit the #2 button.

The shaped charges were small and focused but still made a hell of a noise inside the tunnel.

Kershaw checked on Connelly, who was now about twenty yards from the entrance, still watching the road for any vehicles. There weren't any coming from the northwest, and Rison hadn't raised the alarm about anything coming from the other side.

Kershaw knew Rison would also be closer to the tunnel on that side, near the white truck, and both he and Connelly could come into the tunnel for backup if needed.

Connelly had designed and built the explosive charges, and after the second one went off, he turned and gave an enthusiastic thumbs-up to Kershaw.

Kershaw returned the gesture, dropped remote #2 into the used pocket and lifted the rifle and went back through the tarp.

***

Bruder was already at the back doors of the armored car.

More dust and dirt swirled in the beam of his flashlight, and when Kershaw kicked his light on the rear of the vehicle was lit up like a football stadium at night.

The rear doors hung open a few inches. Bruder used the suppressor at the end of his barrel to ease the right door open a little wider so Kershaw could toss a flash-bang grenade in, then Kershaw pushed the door shut.

They looked down and waited until the bang came. When it did, the windows of the armored car sent a lightning flash into the tunnel.

Bruder pulled the door on the left open and Kershaw took the right.

The storage area of the armored car had been stripped of its metal shelves and cages and jump seats at some point, and there was no partition behind the cab's two seats. Now it was just a large metal box with mismatched duffel bags lined up along the walls.

The two bearded men were both covering their heads with their arms, tipping around in their seats from the shattering light and noise of the grenade.

Bruder stepped in and went past the bags and pulled the pistol out of the driver's hand. It came without a fight.

Then he pulled out a knife, ready to slash the seatbelt, but the driver hadn't bothered with one.

Bruder hauled him out of the seat and tossed him toward the back doors, where Kershaw waited with pre-looped zip ties.

The passenger didn't have a gun or a seatbelt, but he had regained some sense of what was happening and when

Bruder reached for him the man lunged up out of his seat and clawed at Bruder's throat.

Bruder stepped back, pulling the man with him over the seat, and slapped him between the eyes with the butt of the rifle.

The man dropped to the metal floor with his legs tangled between the seats.

Bruder dragged him between the duffle bags to Kershaw, who trussed him up and put him next to the other bearded man along the wall of the tunnel, both with cloth bags over their heads.

Bruder hit his radio.

"Load up."

***

Connelly took the sunglasses off and came through the tarp carrying the hard plastic cases that had been stacked near the retaining wall. The cases held the rest of the explosives and extra magazines for the rifles.

The stop sign on a pole was in the ditch next to the corn field.

He walked past the two Romanians without looking at them and wiggled his eyebrows at Rison as they passed each other in the tunnel, then put the cases in the back of the white truck.

When he got back to the tarp, he held it open so Kershaw and Rison could get through, each of them carrying two duffel bags on their first trip to the truck.

Connelly went to the back of the armored car, where Bruder had stacked the bags, and got two for himself. He tried to do a quick count of the remaining bags and thought there might be six or eight left, maybe more.

He grinned and hefted his two and had to laugh.

"Holy shit!"

They were awkward and heavy and sagged, but Connelly

didn't mind.

When it came to cash, the heavier the better.

***

Bruder took the last two bags and carried them past the two bound and hooded men.

Kershaw hadn't bothered to gag them—no one would be able to hear them hollering until they stood right outside the tunnel, and at that point whoever was out there would come inside anyway.

Bruder saw two cell phones on the concrete next to them, both smashed.

Inside his hood the driver repeated, "You're dead for this. You're fucking dead for this."

Over and over.

Bruder ignored him and hauled the duffel bags to the truck and shoved them into the back with the others. He put his rifle into one of the open hard cases next to Kershaw's, then closed the case.

He turned to the crew.

"We got everything?"

Kershaw and Rison both nodded, and Connelly said, "All packed."

Bruder shut the tailgate and cap and got into the front passenger seat.

Kershaw drove, and Connelly and Rison got into the crew cab seats.

They drove southeast along Pine, six miles of straight road until it ended in an angled T intersection with a four-lane road—technically a highway—going east-west. This was where the vast majority of the area's traffic was, and most of it only slowed down for the one traffic light in the middle of town.

The end of Pine was a quarter mile ahead when they watched a pickup truck pull off the shoulder of the eastbound highway lanes and curl into a tight U-turn so it could take a quick right and come straight at them.

"Who's this?" Kershaw said.

Bruder said, "Doesn't matter."

The pickup came on fast, then seemed to slow when it got close to the DOT truck. The male driver frowned at them through the windshield, then through the driver's window as they passed each other.

Kershaw brought a hand up to his face to stifle a fake cough while covering his nose and mouth, as effective as the balaclava without causing suspicion.

The pickup drifted into their wake, then its engine climbed as it picked up speed toward the tunnel.

Bruder checked the passenger mirror.

"He's moving. He's looking for the armored car."

"I thought they didn't have lookouts," Rison said.

Bruder ignored that.

He told Kershaw, "Get us out of town."

***

When they got to the intersection with the highway Kershaw turned left and headed due east toward the town.

No other vehicles took the turn to head toward the tunnel.

Connelly said, "We got time. We got time."

Which was either true or not, but they wouldn't know until they got out of town.

The town was mostly a collection of old brick and wooden slat buildings around a traffic light and post-war middle-class housing spreading out into the countryside, where some newer, richer estates had been built among the ancient farmhouses.

During their scouting runs Bruder noticed the farmhouses all had barns and machines and equipment worth exponentially more than the actual house on the property, and he respected it. The right tools were important.

Kershaw drove two miles above the speed limit as they came to the first houses on the western edge of town. The land in and around the town—pretty much everywhere they'd gone in Iowa—was just as flat as around the tunnel, and Bruder could see all the way through the intersection to the other side.

They were coming up on the turn that would take them north to the tertiary hideout, a hunting camp trailer no one had used in years, tucked in the woods off a two-track.

Kershaw glanced at Bruder, who shook his head. There was no reason to hole up this close to the job—better to keep moving and put as many miles behind them as possible while they still could.

Then, in the middle of the town, right under the traffic light, a dark red van skidded to a stop and the front doors opened.

Two men got out and looked around.

"What have we here?" Kershaw said.

A blue pickup truck coming from the south slowed and stopped in the intersection, even though he had the green light.

One of the men approached the driver's side and looked in, then waved the truck through.

Kershaw said, "Turn it around?"

Bruder shook his head again.

If they pulled a U-turn and went west, it was forty miles of highway with no turnoffs. If someone came after them or called ahead, it would be like trying to escape an alley.

Going east, they had major north and south options within five miles, and motel rooms waiting in Minnesota.

Rison had parked clean vehicles at the motel and stocked the rooms with provisions, empty luggage, and cash counting machines to make splitting the cash four ways easier.

But they had to get through town first, and that wasn't going to happen.

"Make the turn," Bruder said.

Kershaw worked the brakes and turned north and kept to the posted speed.

Bruder took his pistol out and heard the two men in the back do the same.

Kershaw glanced at him again.

"You think we're burned?"

Bruder shook his head again.

He didn't know.

But whatever was happening, it wasn't good.

CHAPTER TWO

Three miles along the northbound road they turned left, sped through another two miles with fields on both sides, then cut north again.

They didn't see any other people—bearded or not—stopping traffic to see who was inside the passing vehicles.

The two-track was on the left, a mile or so along the second northbound road. It didn't have a mailbox or a gate, just two bent metal stakes with a rusty chain stretched between them a few yards off the road. Three warped No Trespassing signs were nailed to trees near the track, barely legible from the rust and pocks from .22 bullets.

The nearest house was a half mile further down on the other side of the road, and its driveway was long enough for them to need Google Map's satellite view to look at the house. From space, it was rustic with some overgrown junk in the yard and an above-ground pool full of leaves and sticks.

So possibly abandoned, and even if there was someone in residence, the road was straight and flat enough for the crew to see them coming with plenty of warning—if anyone saw them using the two-track, they were burned for sure.

The two wheel ruts went into thick woods full of tall gray trees, their trunks angling for an advantage while the branches tussled with each other. Here and there an oak still had thin, stubborn brown leaves clinging to the twigs. Thirty yards in the two-track made a hard right to avoid a mucky patch, and after that it was hidden from the road.

The chain had been attached to the stakes with wire so old it had flaked and snapped as soon as Bruder tried to unwind it two weeks earlier during a scouting run. Since then, the chain was kept in place by short pieces of bronze baling wire, the closest thing they could find to the original.

Kershaw stopped at the chain and Bruder got out, unhooked one end and carried it across.

The truck rolled forward and took the first curve and stopped. Bruder re-hooked the chain, then used a dead tree branch to fluff the dead grass between the wheel ruts and sweep the tire tracks from the dusting of snow.

He straightened up and examined his work. The tracks were still obvious to him, but he knew exactly what to look for. Any civilians driving by wouldn't notice them, he figured, but there were some non-civilians on the prowl...and folks in the Midwest were notorious for checking on their neighbor's property when something didn't look right, even if the neighbor who owned the land lived in another state and hadn't been back for years.

Bruder knew about the out-of-state part because they had checked the local property tax records. The part about not being back in years was an educated guess based on the condition of the place.

While Bruder was standing there scowling at the ground a gust of wind kicked up and pushed the snow around and did a much better job of concealing their tracks.

He didn't know of any ways to make the wind blow faster and harder, so he tossed the branch into the woods and got in the truck.

"Good as it's going to get."

Kershaw took his foot off the brake and let the truck's idle speed carry it forward. The tires jounced in and out of small pits and over tree roots and rocks. The track curved left and the trees around it grew denser, tangled with wild grape and thorns and climbing vines, some of them as thick as Bruder's wrist.

After a few hundred yards of tilting and bouncing and taking slight curves left and right the truck broke into a small clearing with a single-wide trailer, a wooden outhouse, and a burn barrel so rusty it looked more like a sieve.

Everything was overgrown, with tufts of tall brown field grass sprouting in random spots and a few brave mini-copses of sumac venturing into the clearing to see what would happen.

Kershaw drove the truck around the back of the trailer so it wouldn't be seen from the two-track and killed the engine.

Everyone got out and met at the back.

"Divvy time?" Connelly said.

Bruder shook his head.

"Not yet."

He opened the hard cases and started passing out the long guns, one for each man, then closed the back of the truck again.

Connelly said, "What, the money stays here?"

Rison, who hadn't said much the entire ride, said, "You want to haul it all back in here if those assholes come out of the woodwork?"

"I guess not," Connelly said. "I'm just curious about how much the take is."

Bruder said, "It's zero if we can't get out of here with it. Get the winter gear on and go watch the road. Rison, go inside and see what you can find out."

Rison nodded and hustled toward the trailer.

Connelly reached for the bundle of insulated turkey hunting camouflage in the back of the truck.

"What are you guys gonna do?"

Bruder said, "We still have three explosive charges left. We're gonna make a line in the sand."

***

Rison stepped up into the hunting trailer and closed the flimsy door.

The place had been gutted long ago of anything resembling comfort and looked like a subway car without any seats or poles. It was cold inside because of the thin walls and broken windows, and it smelled like mouse piss and moldy wood and tomato soup. He took a moment to turn on one of the kerosene heaters to feel a little more civilized and beat back the odors.

He'd take the fumes, as long as the broken windows could keep up the ventilation.

Stacks of boxed and canned food and shrink-wrapped trays of bottled water were against one wall, along with rolled-up sleeping bags and duffel bags full of clothes and other gear.

He went to a small card table with folding legs surrounded by four collapsible camp chairs and turned on the police scanner and the small color TV, both of them powered by an array of batteries Kershaw had rigged up; a generator would make too much noise.

The TV had an antennae, which Rison hadn't seen in probably twenty years, and he was out of practice moving the wands around to get a clear picture. Then he found something local showing a game show and turned the volume down but kept an eye on the screen for any breaking news.

He needed answers, right now.

Rison was just under six feet tall and built like a cornerback, with wide shoulders and a thick neck and narrow waist. When he wasn't working with men like Bruder he was a professional poker player based out of Vegas, and jobs like this bankrolled him for months at a time, sometimes a year or more if he hit a good streak.

He adjusted the heater while he waited for the TV and scanner to give him something.

When in Vegas he lived in hotels, either comped or as a paying civilian when things weren't going his way. Being based in Vegas gave him access to all sorts of heist training disguised as tourist attractions, like semi- and full-auto shooting ranges, tactical driving schools, and endless opportunities to observe world-class security systems and teams.

He enjoyed the driving courses the most. The crew out at the tactical driving school thought he was just a bored gambler with too much money, but over the years Rison had developed driving skills that put him on the same level as anyone on the Secret Service's presidential detail.

Standing there in the hunting trailer, he tried not to think of what he'd do when they got out of this.

A typical day would have him in the gym right about now, or at the spa, in the sauna or getting a massage, then getting his hair and beard taken care of. He dyed them both black to hide the flecks of gray creeping in. He liked the look of it, dark and dangerous and Connelly relished giving him endless shit about it.

But Rison could take it and play along. Connelly was clever but not cruel about busting chops, and even though Rison assumed Bruder thought he was a fool for caring so much about his appearance he never mentioned it.

He told himself this stress and third-world existence was temporary, and soon enough he'd be back in Vegas getting his espresso and fresh fruit juice as he left the spa, headed for the pool or the tables based on how things were going.

He glared at the TV and scanner, willing them to provide clarity.

This whole job was his idea, and something had gone horribly wrong.

***

Connelly threw the turkey hunting parka on over his coveralls and carried the rifle back toward the road.

The parka had a pattern of white and tan and gray strokes to blend in with a variety of cold-weather backdrops.

Connelly looked at his surroundings, then checked the parka, and decided Iowa was solidly within the palette.

He kept to the two-track until the final turn, then stepped off into the woods on the right side and picked his way through the scrub brush and vines, surprised to see some of the stuff still had small green leaves this time of year.

He spotted a deadfall off to his left a bit and went that way. It had a ragged stump as high as his chest and a mess of branches and bent saplings in the crook between the stump and fallen trunk. He looked back toward the two-track, maybe twenty yards away, and liked it.

He was at one corner of a rough square, with the inter-section of the road and two-track at the opposite corner. The deadfall would shield him from any traffic coming from the south, back toward town, and the camouflage and un-derbrush would be enough to hide him from anyone coming from the north, if he could hold still.

Connelly kicked his way into the spot, not caring about noise since the only other living creature he could see was a crow eyeballing him from the branches of a barren tree and sat down in the snow with his back to the stump.

He waited for the cold and wet ground to seep through his clothes, but it didn't happen.

Impressed by the canvas coveralls, he pulled his bala-clava up to keep his face warm and hide the steam from his breath. Then he made sure the AR-15 was on safe and tucked it under the parka so it wouldn't make a hard black profile and ruin his fine little nest.

***

Bruder mostly stayed out of the way and listened for trouble while Kershaw checked the remaining explosive charges and got them ready to use as perimeter defenses.

He was finishing with the second one when Bruder had a thought while staring at the duffel bags of money.

"Hold on," he said.

He dragged one of the bags out and dropped it near the open tailgate, then pulled on another.

Kershaw stepped back, confused.

"I thought we were leaving them loaded."

"That was assuming we're driving out of here," Bruder said.

He made a base layer of bags and stacked them in a tight ring, making a tower as high as his knee. He pointed at the hollow core.

"Put the third charge there."

Kershaw frowned at him.

Bruder said, "If it comes down to it, the Romanians might care more about getting the money than us. The remote for this charge might be our only way out of here."

"You think it'll get to that point?"

Bruder shrugged.

"They responded a lot faster than we expected. There's no point in having any expectations going forward, just contingencies."

Kershaw blew air out of puffed cheeks, like he couldn't believe what he was about to do, then set the small satchel of explosives in the center of the bags.

Bruder set the rest of the bags on top to tamp the explosion and make sure it destroyed as much of the cash as possible.

They both stepped back and looked at the dome of mismatched bags.

There were twelve of them, each one more than half full of cash.

"How much you think?" Kershaw said.

Bruder reached down and unzipped the closest bag. He could see banded stacks of twenties and fifties, with a few stacks of hundreds peeking out.

He closed the bag and surveyed the pile again, then shook his head.

"No way to tell until we put it through the counters. Might be the fourteen million we're expecting. Give or take."

Kershaw gave a low whistle, then held the remote out for Bruder to take.

"I'd never sleep again if I accidentally blew up fourteen million dollars."

"Give or take," Bruder said, and took the remote.

CHAPTER THREE

SIX WEEKS EARLIER

"Fourteen million dollars?" Bruder said.

Rison spread his hands, like he couldn't be held responsible for the shocking amount.

"Give or take."

He had called Lola and left a message to have Bruder call him, which led to Bruder flying to Vegas the next day.

They were sitting in the shade of a comped cabana at the Mandalay Bay pool. A DJ played music for the people in and around the pool, all of them drinking and yelling and turning red under the early afternoon sun.

Bruder and Rison sat close enough so they wouldn't have to shout, but there was no chance of anyone listening in.

Bruder took another Corona out of the ice bucket and used the opener hanging from the bucket's handle to open it.

"In Iowa?"

Rison nodded.

"Iowa."

Bruder drank some of the beer and stretched his legs out. It was hot inside the cabana, but the ceiling fan kept the air moving and the sun and colors around the pool were pleasant to look at from behind his sunglasses.

He hadn't worked since the summer, when he and Kershaw and some others had pulled two and half million dollars out of an Escalade in the Financial District. As it turned out, the money belonged to an organization called The Labyrinth, and Bruder had kept his head down waiting to see if there was going to be any fallout from crossing them.

So far so good—they knew his face but not his name, not even an alias—and even though he still had plenty of his share from the job and several jobs prior, he was ready to get back to work.

"Convince me," he said.

***

Rison said, "I was in a private card game with a group of guys, this thing we do whenever we're all in LA at the same time. It's mostly pros, but word gets around and sometimes we get some rich amateurs. Celebrities, Silicon Valley dorks, some organized crime but not too often. They have their own setups."

Bruder took another drink of the beer.

Rison said, "But at this game about two weeks ago there was a guy named Tug. He—"Bruder said, "Tug?"

"Yeah, that's right. Tug."

"Is that a nickname?"

"I don't know. He was Romanian."

"Romanian?"

Rison blinked. "Well, yeah, but that's skipping ahead."

Bruder sat back. "I'll shut up."

"So this Tug, he lost a lot of money. I mean, a lot. He talked a big game and thought he knew what he was doing, but he was coked up to his eyebrows and couldn't focus, plus he kept showing his cards. Even without that, man, he was chum in the water. This one hand, he—""I don't need the card details," Bruder said.

"Right, right, sorry. It's just, us card guys, we can geek out on that stuff all day."

"He lost a lot of money," Bruder said, getting things back on track.

Rison nodded.

"A lot. And he covered his debt, good for him, but he was torn up about it. He kept saying it was everything he had. He and I were sitting in this rooftop jacuzzi, big as a freaking bus, and we were the only ones left in the penthouse. This is like, four in the morning. Everybody else from the game had left. He would lean over and put his hand on my shoulder and in this thick accent—Romanian, like I said—'Rison, my friend, I am as broke as a joke,' then he'd laugh and cry at the same time. Over and over. I felt bad for him, but what are you gonna do?"

It was a rhetorical question, so Bruder didn't answer.

Rison said, "And then he lays his head back on the edge of the jacuzzi and closes his eyes and goes, 'Fuck, now I have to go to Iowa.' I didn't think I heard him right. Because Iowa, you know? Iowa? But then I think, oh, maybe there's someplace back home that sounds like Iowa. Like, E-Y-E-O-J...whatever. So I go, 'Where's that?' And you know what he said to me?"

Bruder waited.

"He goes, 'It's right in the middle of your fucking country, you idiot.'"

Then Rison burst out laughing and drank the rest of his beer. A server in shorts and a bikini top strolled past the front of the cabana and pointed at the ice bucket with raised eyebrows.

Rison said, "We're good for now sweetie, but can we get some food? Some of those barbecue sliders, and the fruit plate thing."

"You bet, hot shot."

The server, a pro, glanced at Bruder and saw there was no point in chatting him up for a bigger tip and moved on.

Bruder said, "Iowa."

Rison cracked another beer for himself.

"Right, Iowa. I ask him why in the hell he has to go to Iowa. And he starts rambling about his cousins and uncles and farms and I'm thinking, boy oh boy, this poor bastard is so broke, he has to go back to his family farm and shovel cow shit until he gets back on his feet. I almost felt bad about taking his money."

A group of young women with pale skin and full drinks shuffled past, looking for a place to set up camp. Bruder could see the lingering marks from an airplane neck pillow on one of their cheeks.

Rison called out to them, "Not now ladies, but come back here in one hour. One hour!"

They laughed and leaned into each other to make comments, but most of them looked back and Bruder made a note to be gone within the hour.

Rison leaned back and said, "So he's yammering on about farms and shit, and then he said something that set off some alarm bells. Maybe you have this too—it's like a program running in the background, a passive monitoring system, and it's always listening and watching. Maybe somebody says something, or you notice somebody come and go through a side door and now you know it isn't locked. Or you see a security guard with their holster all jacked up, like pushed around to the back, and you know that damn gun is welded in there with cobwebs and the person toting it around sure as shit never pulled it, let alone fired it. The monitoring system notices stuff like that and you go, huh…"

"Sure," Bruder said. He wouldn't call his version of it passive, but he knew what Rison was talking about.

"Well Tug says this one thing, and my system starts going off like a slot machine. Bing, bong, bing!"

Bruder wondered if Rison was going to get to it before the pale horde returned.

Rison said, "Tug, he goes, 'The boys in Chicago would never notice a missing bag.'"

He raised his eyebrows at Bruder to emphasize how intriguing the statement was.

"But the way he said it was kind of rueful, like he knew that was bullshit. The boys in Chicago, whoever they were, would absolutely notice a missing bag and Tug knew it. And at this point he has my full attention but I don't want to spook him. So I say something lame and distracted, like, 'A bag of what, manure? Ha ha ha.'"

Rison leaned forward with his elbows on his knees, getting into the story.

"Tug, he just laughs. Then he jerks up off the concrete ledge like he got hit by lightning and goes, 'Hey, do you know any farmers?'"

He frowned at Bruder, showing how confused he had been by the question.

"Now, I know some guys who grow a bit of weed, but if I know any real farmers it would be a newsflash to me. But I can tell saying no to Tug will close this road we're going down, so I tell him 'Yeah, I know some farmers. What's up?' Then he goes, 'Do you care if some of them get killed?'"

***

Rison held the beer bottle in both hands and stared past it at the concrete between his sandals, making sure he got the details right.

"The way Tug explained it to me, Romanian organized crime figured out a scam with farming subsidies. You know what those are?"

Bruder said, "The government pays money to farmers to

help them grow crops."

"Right, basically. Sometimes it's because the land is flooded and they can't grow anything, or just to keep them in business so we aren't relying on foreigners for our corn and wheat, you get it. So the Romanians, they find a rural area with a bunch of farms and they move in, then start spreading cash around to the farmers to get them to claim all of their land—whether it's trees, parking lots, swamps—as farmable. Then the farmers list all that land on their paperwork to the government and get paid more in subsidies."

Bruder frowned. "A bunch of home-grown farmers jump right into bed with Romanians to screw the government?"

"Well, some of them aren't so happy with Congress, or the president, or their local hack, or the post office, or whatever. Others, yeah, they have big 'ol flags waving in their front yards no matter who's voted in, and they put up a fight, which is why Tug asked me about the killing part. These Romanians, they aren't shy about getting rough if they have to."

"So the farmers get paid by the government to farm land that isn't actually arable."

"Arable?"

"Farmable."

"Right, yeah. And Tug said they also get the farmers to double-down on the land they're already claiming, sometimes getting paid two or three times for the same acreage."

Bruder said, "Nobody from the government ever comes out and actually looks at these farms?"

"Man, do you know how much farmland is out there? And how many people the government has working in these departments?"

"No, I don't."

Rison squinted out at the pool.

"Well, neither do I. But it's a lot of land and not a lot of people. If Tug is right about it, all these bureaucrats do is push paper around and listen to lobbyists and rubber stamp these claims when they come through and cut the checks once a year."

"Checks?" Bruder said.

"I know, I know, but don't worry about that. These farmers like their money in banks or in cash, usually the latter. They go in to look at a new truck and pull out a fat roll and buy it right then and there, cash money. It's pretty baller, actually. But that's not the point. The Romanians, they know when the checks are coming, and they make the farmers cash them, then take everything except what the farmer would have coming to them legitimately."

"So the farmers keep whatever subsidies they should be getting, and the Romanians take the fraud end."

"Exactly."

"And that fraud money ends up at fourteen million dollars," Bruder said.

"Give or take."

Bruder scanned the pool area, not really looking at anything, just letting his mind work through it.

"The Romanians collect it all at once?"

Rison grinned.

"You're catching on. I wondered about collecting from the farmers before the Romanians get to them, but it's too messy. All these people have guns right next to the front door, and all they'd have to do is call around after we left— assuming they didn't shoot us—and we'd be in it up to our necks. So yeah, you nailed it. The Romanians make the rounds and put the cash, get this, in an old armored car they got their hands on."

"You're kidding."

Rison shook his head.

"I know. These Romanians are crazy, man. From what Tug said, they act like an occupying army out in this little corner of Iowa. I guess the whole scam is something they've done back home and around Europe for a while, now they're trying it here. They load up all the cash and drive it to Chicago and deliver it to the big boss."

"And the job is to hijack the delivery."

"Bingo," Rison said.

"When do the checks go out?"

"In about six weeks."

Something was gnawing at the edge of Bruder's thoughts. He said, "And Tug just came out and told you all of this?"

"Like I said, he lost a lot of money. He was trying to recruit me into giving up these imaginary farmers I knew so he could start his own scam going. Or go tell his cousins about them, who knows. I told him I was going to have to see this thing in person before I went in with him. So he laid it all out, man. We set up a time and place to meet so I could watch it all go down."

"You're supposed to meet him when they collect the cash, precisely?"

"Well, not down to the minute. He said we'd meet up, maybe hang out for a few days and drink...Ah, shit, what was it...Rachiu, something like that. Some kind of liquor made out of plums, or pears, or something. He said if I survived, I'd never want to drink anything else."

Bruder frowned.

"So the Romanians are expecting you to be there? You're going on the inside?"

Rison shook his head again.

Bruder was getting more skeptical.

He said, "You're trusting this Tug guy to be your source?"

"No, no way. He's a walking shitshow. If I went there with him, or if I tried to rely on him for more info, I'd probably end up dead or a hostage or something worse. I didn't even know if Tug would remember having the conversation the next morning, you know? I go up to him and start talking about Iowa and he pulls a gun and goes,

'Who told you about that?'"

"But if he does remember, and he tells the other Romanians about you, and we take down the truck..."

Rison grinned like a wolf.

"Nah man, they don't know shit about what he told me. It
was the craziest thing. I guess Tug was so distraught, right
after he got done filling me in, he got out of the jacuzzi and
jumped off the balcony. Thirty floors up."

"Huh," Bruder said. "That's too bad."

"A damn shame," Rison agreed.

***

The food arrived at the cabana and they both picked through
it and sat chewing and watching the pool for a few minutes.

Bruder said, "We're going to need somebody with local
information."

Rison wiped his face and fingers on a thick cloth napkin
and took a drink of beer.

"Well, it won't be Tug."

"No. From what you've said, I wouldn't rely on him even
if he was still around."

"A solid bet."

"And from the sound of it, nobody in the Romanian crew
is going to be pliable."

Rison said, "Pliable. I like that. And I agree—Tug was a
crazy son of a bitch, and he made the crew in Iowa sound
even worse. None of them are going to give us an assist."

Bruder thought about it.

"These farmers. Some of them wouldn't mind seeing the
Romanians take a hit."

"Maybe. Yeah, maybe. I bet they're scared though. If
somebody helped us and the gang found out...And what
if we approach the wrong person? We see a corn-fed Billy
Bob who looks prime to work with us, and it turns out he's
filing for Romanian citizenship, you know?"

"Yeah," Bruder said.

He was looking at the angles and holes and dead ends, trying to find a spot to pry against.

"How many random strangers show up in this place?"

"Population for the town is just over two thousand. The township website calls it a village, and it damn sure ain't a city. The main drag is pretty much all there is to it. The rest is farms and a school and a big-ass train station where they load up grain and corn and whatever. Soybeans, maybe."

"Have you been there?"

Rison took a bite out of another slider.

"Nah. I found all this online."

"Let me look into it a little more. I'll bring Kershaw in if you're good with that."

"No problem. Is he in Vegas too?"

"Not yet," Bruder said.

***

That night the three of them were in Bruder's hotel room at Caesar's looking at Kershaw's laptop.

He'd flown in from Austin with a carry-on bag that afternoon and Bruder and Rison got him caught up on the ride from the airport.

The laptop showed a map of the town in Iowa. The satellite view showed what looked like a ball of yarn in the middle of a set of crosshairs. A tight grid of roads in the center, where the town was, then a mess of old, curving roads that wandered around the countryside and somehow found their way to another piece of thread that kept the wander going.

The only roads in and out of town were the crosshairs— north, south, east, and west.

Other browser tabs had the town's Wikipedia page and websites for the school and some of the local businesses, including a farm machinery dealership, the granary train depot, a motel, and a bar named Len's offering live music

Friday and Saturday nights. It also had, according to the site, the world-famous Lenburger as featured on a TV show called *Dash & Dine.*

Kershaw clicked on the tab showing the machinery dealership. The page had a sidebar with current job openings, of which there were two: Lead Account Manager and Agricultural Service Technician.

"I still like this one," he said.

Rison said, "What the hell is an Agricultural Service Technician?"

Kershaw shrugged.

"Somebody who works on tractors?"

"You ever worked on tractors?"

"No. But I bet I could sell you one."

Rison looked at Bruder. "The Account Manager?"

Bruder said, "All we need is a reason to be in town. One of us can apply for that job. One of us can do the one at the granary."

Kershaw went to that tab and read: "Second Shift Site Manager."

Rison said, "What's that mean?"

"You manage the site during the second shift."

"Thanks, smart-ass."

"It doesn't matter," Bruder said. "We look at the job requirements and build a resume that makes sense. Drop it off and tell them you're in town at the motel until the next day. Drive around, scope the town. Eat at the bar. Watch the people. If you get a call, go in for the interview or don't. Tell them you got another offer somewhere else."

Rison tilted his head from side to side, thinking about it.

"We stagger our visits?"

"A few days in between. If we see enough out-of-towners some overlap is okay. We share what we find out so the next guy going in doesn't have to cover the same ground."

Rison looked at Bruder.

"Wait, what about Lola?"

"What about her?"

"Well, I called her to get in touch with you about this, so I assume you two are still on speaking terms?"

Bruder said, "What's that got to do with this?"

"She might come in handy. I mean, a bunch of dudes rolling around town could raise eyebrows. A guy and his lady, or just a single lady..."

Bruder shook his head.

"That won't work."

Rison looked at Kershaw, who just shook his head and refused to participate.

Rison said, "Why, because she's your ex...?"

He didn't know how to finish the question—Wife? Girlfriend? Lover?—so he just let it dangle.

"No. She would do fine pretending to be with any one of us to blend in, but she won't be bait or a honeypot."

"Really? Not even chatting somebody up?"

Bruder said, "Look, if one of these Romanians tries to touch her, she'll kill him. Job over. It's not worth the risk."

Rison blew his cheeks out, then turned to Kershaw and the laptop.

"Go back to the school for a minute."

Kershaw clicked over. The only job openings were for a custodial engineer and assistant wrestling coach.

"I could put in for the custodian thing," Rison said.

Kershaw shook his head.

"I've seen your hotel room. Have you ever wrestled?"

"Not that kind. I—oh, shit."

Bruder and Kershaw both looked at him.

"Have you guys ever worked with a dude named Connelly? Aiden Connelly?"

"No," Bruder said.

"He's solid. He's a safe guy, a vault guy. Gets through doors, walls, you name it. So we could use him for the ar-

mored car. And I think he wrestled in high school. Or maybe
he just likes to fight, I can't remember."

"You trust him?" Bruder said.

"Yeah. I worked with him once, in Florida, and we agreed
to call each other up if something came along that looked
like a good fit."

Bruder looked at Kershaw, who nodded.

"Call him," Bruder said.

                                    ***

Rison called Connelly with the speaker on.

"Hello?"

"Hey, you and me, did some work together near Tal-
lahassee a couple years ago. We joked about draining
the swamp and turning it into a prison for politicians. You
remember that?"

The man on the other end laughed.

"Yeah, shit yeah, I remember. What's up? You got
something?"

"I got you on speaker with two other guys here, we're
looking at some work. Let me ask you this—you ever done
any wrestling?"

Connelly paused.

"Like, professionally?"

"I mean high school or college."

"Oh, *real* wrestling. I thought you were asking about the
off-the-top-rope kind. Um, no. I mean, headlocks and shit
like that, but no real training or competition. Have you ever
seen a wrestling practice? It's insane. Running around in
garbage bags to cut weight...So no, I've never wrestled. I've
fought some wrestlers, and that sucked. Zero stars. Would
not recommend."

He paused to take a breath.

"Why, does that take me out of whatever you got going?
Because my curiosity is piqued."

Rison looked at Bruder and Kershaw.

Bruder didn't want his voice on the call, so he just nodded.

Rison said, "How soon can you get to Vegas?"

***

Connelly arrived the next morning on a flight from Nashville.

They met in Rison's suite and after a round of handshakes and some talk about common acquaintances they got him caught up and into the planning.

Connelly looked out the window at the Strip for a few moments, then said, "I could do the resume for the coaching gig, but they take their wrestling pretty seriously in Iowa. My concern is they'll offer an impromptu interview right then and I end up sparring with the head coach or something. It'll take them about two seconds to realize I'm full of shit. And—hey, do you guys mind if we go outside somewhere? It was gray and raining in Nashville when I left and I'm dying for some sunshine."

Bruder was irritated by the delay, but they split up and met at Rison's comped poolside cabana fifteen minutes later.

When they were settled and Rison had drinks and lunch on the way Bruder asked Connelly, "What about the other options?"

"I've been thinking about it, and I like the bar. I can play the guitar halfway decent. If they're looking for jackasses to come in and play and sing covers, I can do that."

"That's not bad," Rison said. "I bet they get a lot of people from out of town doing that. You know, traveling bands and shit."

"People in bars talk," Kershaw added. "You sit next to the right person, we could get some good info."

"Show me the website," Connelly said.

No one had a phone on them, per Bruder's rules, and Kershaw's laptop was the only electronic device in the cabana. He flipped it open and got to the website via a satellite or radar dishes or something. He'd explained it to Bruder once, and Bruder said, "Is it secure?"

"Yes," Kershaw told him.

"Fine."

Now Connelly looked at the website for Len's, scanning for anything about open-mic nights.

"Oh, shit!"

"What?" Bruder said, ready for bad news.

"This place has been on *Dash & Dine.*"

Bruder, Kershaw and Rison all exchanged looks.

"That's bad?" Rison said.

Connelly shook his head.

"No, it's great. You guys don't know that show? Oh, man. They drive these crazy fast cars, motorcycles, whatever, around the country and visit restaurants to try their signature menu items. If they've been to this place, Len's, we're golden."

"Why?" Bruder said.

"Because they must have people coming in from all over to try the, what is it...Lenburger. Just because it's been on the show. So goons like us stopping in for a meal? Totally normal."

Bruder relaxed a bit.

"A meal, maybe, but what about a few days? We still need a reason to linger."

"Okay, so I'll still do the guitar thing. Kershaw still does the granary. You and Rison, you can be separate, or maybe a pair of salesmen driving through, or just some old guys checking stuff off your bucket list."

"Careful," Rison said.

Connelly grinned, then said, "Oh, what about a band?"

He got blank stares in return.

Rison said, "Huh?"

"Do you guys play anything? Or sing?"

Rison glanced at Bruder and couldn't help snickering.

"I don't think so. I can play a little piano, but it's limited to exactly the number of notes needed to get a woman naked."

Kershaw said, "How many is that?"

"About twelve, but the women are hookers, so maybe it doesn't count."

The ice bucket of beer arrived and Connelly passed them around, taking over the role of host.

He said, "Okay, so I'm on guitar and vocals. Rison plays the keyboard. Kershaw, you strike me as a bass guy—pretty steady and low-key, but you can slap it around and get chunky with it if you have to."

Kershaw accepted the beer and the compliment, if that's what it was.

Connelly looked at Bruder, who looked back at him and wondered how he'd respond to being told to shut his trap so they could get to work. Connelly seemed like the type who needed to talk everything through out loud, asking himself questions and answering them halfway through.

Bruder's method was to sit and think or move and think, mulling over the facts and variables and pinch points, and not say anything until he emerged from his cave with, "This is how it will go."

That wasn't going to be possible with Connelly running his mouth, so he made himself be patient.

Connelly said, "Now Bruder here, he's a drummer all the way. As long as every song we play has war drums. BOOM-boom-BOOM-boom-BOOM-boom. Ever onward, into the breach, keep going lads, that kind of thing. A couple months of practice and we'd be onto something."

"We don't have a couple months," Bruder said.

"Well fuck me then, forget I mentioned it."

Connelly kicked his feet up and gave a sigh of perfect contentment.

"But I'll still go in as a solo act. Stop in at the bar for a burger and beer, I'm wandering the countryside with just my wits and guitar to get me by, hey, do you guys need an opening act? Or just somebody to play something besides the four songs on the jukebox getting worn out?"

"What if they tell you to go to hell?" Bruder said.

Connelly flashed a smile.

"Well, that's when the conversation actually gets interesting."

CHAPTER FOUR

PRESENT

When Connelly heard the engine coming down the road, he moved just enough to check his watch. His ass was sore and his foot kept falling asleep no matter which way he put the leg, and it turned out he'd been sitting next to the deadfall for just over two hours.

He keyed his radio.

"I got a vehicle coming from the south."

That meant it was coming from the direction of town, the same way they'd come in the truck.

He let go of the radio and made himself become still.

The engine was the only man-made sound. He still had the shooting earbuds in, and everything else was amplified, birds flitting around and snow plopping off branches and leaves rustling when something small rooted through them. At one point a doe had wandered within fifteen yards before hearing or smelling him, then bolting away like he'd goosed her.

Connelly waited and slid his eyes to the right.

As the car, a beat-up blue Honda Accord with one person in it, came into his peripheral vision he heard the engine sound change.

The driver had taken their foot off the gas and was letting it coast.

The driver's face was turned toward the chain across the two-track and Connelly could see it was a man with a reddish-brown beard.

Connelly watched without staring—he didn't want the man to feel his eyes.

His heart started bumping a bit, getting ready for whatever might happen next.

This could be some random neighbor, or whoever delivered mail along this rural route, or the land owner—though that was unlikely—or the Romanians scouring the countryside.

The engine continued to coast with the man looking out at the entrance to the two-track, then the sound picked up again and the Honda jumped forward.

Then the brake lights flared and the Honda skidded to a stop just beyond the chained driveway.

Connelly risked a more focused look.

The man's face was pressed against the glass so he could look back. Then the window came down and he stuck his head out and said something Connelly didn't hear clearly.

The door popped open and the man stepped out. He was a little taller than vehicle's roof and had the beard and a receding hairline. He wore an unzipped hooded sweatshirt with a faded Metallica shirt underneath. The shirt was too tight, and Connelly caught a glimpse of his pale belly drooping over his pants.

The man shuffled over, muttering to himself, and bent over with his hands on his knees to stare at the ground where the road turned into the track. His head swung around, looking at everything, then he stood up and went to the end of the chain closest to Connelly.

He bent over again and peered at the wire holding the chain to the post.

He reached out and almost touched it, then shot upright and turned to look at the other end of the chain.

His head tilted to the side and his eyes moved to the two-track, scanning.

Then his hand went to his pocket and he pulled out a cell phone.

Connelly stood up, faltering a bit because of his damn sleepy foot, and got the rifle out from under the poncho and pointed it in the man's general direction.

"Stop right there."

The man jumped and almost dropped the phone, then stared at Connelly with his mouth open like he was a wraith risen from the ground.

"Drop the phone," Connelly said.

The man looked down at the phone like he'd forgotten it was there.

Then his face turned sly, just for a moment, and Connelly pointed the rifle directly at his chest.

"I already have the slack out, buddy."

The man's face twisted in disgust. He dropped the phone into the snow and let his arms hang at his sides.

"Open that sweatshirt for me."

He pulled it open from the bottom corners.

Connelly saw the butt of a pistol sticking out of his front pocket.

"The pocket, huh? Keep your hands out like that."

Connelly kept the rifle on him and hit the radio again.

"This is the man at the road."

Kershaw's voice came back: "Go ahead."

"I got one. Bring the truck."

"On my way."

Connelly let the radio go and worked his way forward

through the brush until he was on the edge of the track.

The man had his head tilted back and was watching him with a small grin, like he was the one in charge and Connelly hadn't figured it out yet.

Connelly said, "You speak English?"

"Of course."

He had a deep voice for his size, a little scratchy, and his teeth were white and straight.

"But you're Romanian, yeah?"

"Unfortunately for you, yes."

Connelly pointed at his shirt.

"I saw them at Madison Square Garden. Amazing show."

The man looked down at the shirt and shrugged.

"I don't care about them. I picked this shirt because I don't care if I get your blood on it."

That was the end of the small talk, so Connelly just pointed the rifle at him and waited for the truck.

***

Bruder was in the passenger seat of the truck with Kershaw driving.

They didn't know what they were going to find when they got to the road—it might require an urgent return to the trailer under gunfire—so Kershaw went down the two-track in reverse and swept around the final curve without slowing down.

What they found was Connelly standing next to a stocky guy holding his sweatshirt open like he was trying to cool off or flap the sides and fly away like a bat. Connelly had his rifle pointed at the man's face.

Kershaw stopped the truck and they both got out and walked to the back of the truck, wading through the disappearing exhaust. They had their balaclavas pulled up to hide everything except their eyes.

Bruder said, "Who's this?"

"I didn't get his name yet," Connelly said.

"He's alone?"

"I didn't see anybody else in the vehicle."

"Did he call anybody?"

"Nope."

Bruder picked the phone up and brushed the snow off. The screen was locked.

He thought about smashing it but didn't yet know if they'd need any information it had, so he held the power button down until it asked for confirmation to shut down. He did that and put the phone in his jacket pocket.

Connelly asked the man, "What's your name?"

The man just looked at Bruder and Kershaw like he was bored.

"This isn't an interrogation," Bruder said. "It's a negotiation. There's no reason not to tell us your name."

"Then what's your name? And show me your face."

"I didn't say it was an equal negotiation."

The man shrugged. "Claudiu."

"What do your friends call you? Claud?"

"No, but you're not my friends, so that's fine."

Bruder walked up to him and pulled the pistol out of his pocket. It was a beat-up Glock 23. Bruder ejected the magazine and put it in another pocket, then pulled the slide back to spit out the cartridge in the breech. He put the Glock in the same pocket and plucked the shiny brass out of the snow and put that in with the gun and magazine.

"Turn around."

Claud rolled his eyes and turned in a slow circle. Bruder patted him down and didn't feel anything alarming.

"Alright Claud, get in the truck. I'll drive your car, so you don't have to walk all the way back here to get it."

Claud's eyes shifted between all three of them.

"Back from where?"

"Just up the track here. Not far."

"Why?"

"I told you. We're negotiating."

"Ah. The terms of your surrender."

"Something like that," Bruder said.

***

Kershaw and Connelly switched places at the road.

Kershaw donned the poncho and kept his own AR-15, and when the truck and Claud's Honda were past the chain, he hooked it back up and did his best to remove the tracks. Then he found the spot Connelly had pointed out to him and settled in.

Once the vehicles were far enough away the birds started moving around again and talking to each other. Kershaw was a hunter, when he had the time, and he enjoyed being in the woods.

He closed his eyes and listened to the critters and trees and waited for anything louder—like a gunshot or detonating charge or fleet of incoming vehicles—to tell him things had gotten worse.

***

Bruder dumped the Honda next to the truck where it wouldn't be in the way. The interior was loud with squeals and thumps along the two-track and it smelled like stale tobacco.

When he got out, he pulled his balaclava down for a moment and spat in the snow to get the taste out of his mouth.

Connelly and Claud got out of the truck and Bruder pointed at the pile of duffel bags sitting in the thin snow and brown grass.

"That's the money."

"I recognize it," Claud said. "Good. I'll take it from here."

"Inside that pile are enough explosives to turn all of it into mulch."

Claud was horrified.

"You wouldn't do that to money!"

"There's always more money. When you go back, let your people know if they get too close they might get us, but they won't get the money."

Claud seemed ready to cross himself to ward off the blasphemy.

Bruder stepped up into the trailer and stayed in the doorway, blocking everyone still behind him.

The heaters were cooking inside and had replaced the moldy smell with the sharp tang of hot metal and an undercurrent of kerosene.

Bruder looked over at Rison, who was still listening to the police scanner and fiddling with the antennas on the small TV. Apparently the signal kept moving.

"Anything?"

Rison grimaced.

"Nothing. Not yet, anyway."

Bruder nodded.

"Keep doing what you're doing. But pull your mask up."

Rison tugged his balaclava up over his mouth and nose.

"You got a guest with you?"

"Yes."

"You want me to relocate this stuff?"

Bruder shook his head.

He stepped forward and let Claud enter the trailer with Connelly trailing him.

Bruder said, "We're just talking right now."

Claud grinned at him and surveyed the living quarters.

"So this is what it's like on the inside."

Bruder said, "You've been here before?"

Claud just gave him a patronizing look, which Bruder was already tired of. He pulled the three empty camp chairs over and put them in a small circle in what used to be the kitchen area of the trailer, judging by the severed pipes jutting out of the walls and open drain in the floor.

Claud sat in one of the chairs and put his hands in his

sweatshirt pockets.

Bruder and Connelly took the other two.

Rison said, "You want me over there?"

"Not yet," Bruder said.

Then, to Claud: "Why have you been here before?"

Claud gave a sly grin, his eyes sliding back and forth between Bruder and Connelly.

"If you knew enough to rob the delivery truck, I assume you already know what we do around here."

"Don't assume anything," Bruder said.

Connelly said, "Your English is very good, by the way."

"So is yours," Claud said.

He pulled out a bag of loose tobacco and rolling papers.

"I am going to smoke."

"No," Bruder said.

Claud shrugged and opened the bag and started working anyway, and Bruder reached over and took them away, then stood up and tossed them down a hole in the floor.

He sat back down.

"So you've been here because you and your crew run this territory. You know the land, you know the properties, and you know where to look for a group of people who are trying to lay low for a while. Your boss—I'm guessing you aren't the boss—sent a bunch of you out to check all the likely spots."

Claud held his hands out, as though presenting Bruder to the room.

"You see? You don't need me to say anything."

"How did you know we hit the armored car?"

"Like you said, we know everything that happens around here."

"Bullshit. How did you know?"

Claud grinned at him.

"You think you might have a rat on the inside? I smell mouse piss in here..."

He sniffed the air and wrinkled his nose.

"Maybe some rat too."

"No," Bruder said. "It's something else. The man we passed in the pickup truck."

Claud shrugged.

Bruder said, "So that's what happened."

"Sure, why not."

Bruder took a deep breath in through his nose.

Connelly picked up on the rising frustration.

He said to Claud, "So you're from Romania?"

"That's right."

"You have Transylvania there. And Dracula."

Claud's eyebrows went up.

"Oh, you've heard of Vlad?"

He was mocking Connelly, trolling him, like he'd told an Italian, "You have spaghetti there."

"Vlad is the best," Claud said. "Very strong communication skills. Not with the English, like me, but his actions. Impaling all those people sends a strong message. You know, the first time I went around to these farms I saw this attachment, it was on the front of a tractor. It was just a big spike, and I asked the farmer, what the hell is that for? He told me it picks up bales of hay and straw. Just pokes right through them so you can carry them around. And I thought, man, I'd like to try that on somebody. Put them on the skewer—zwip!—and park the tractor on the edge of town, letting everyone know how things are around here. Just like Vlad. A tribute, you know?"

"An *homage*," Connelly said.

Claud frowned. "That's French?"

The pop quiz alarmed Connelly for a moment, then he said, "Yeah, I think so."

"Then no, not an *homage*. A tribute. I think, maybe, I will try it on one of you."

Bruder nodded.

The negotiations had officially begun.

***

Bruder said, "The police are working with you."

Claud made a big show of thinking about it, stroking his chin and squinting up at the ceiling and finally nodding.

"Enough of them. The others just take their little cash and don't interfere, which is fine."

"Is your boss local?"

"What is local these days? We are all connected."

"Can I meet with him face-to-face," Bruder clarified.

"Not if you like your face the way it is."

Claud was proud of his wit and looked around for appreciation. He got hard looks in return.

Bruder said, "Are you high enough in your organization to make a meeting happen?"

"Of course. But it won't happen. Not for talking, anyway."

He looked around the trailer.

"You are all dead men."

Bruder ignored the threat and said, "What happens if we try to drive out of here?"

"You can't."

"Why not?"

"You already know, surely. You seem like professionals. Mostly. The ski masks are a bit much though. So how did you find out about the armored car? Did one of the farmers tell you? Which one?"

Bruder said, "Why can't we drive out of here?"

Claud sighed and sat back in his camp chair.

"There are only four roads in and out of this area. North, south, east, west. We are watching all of them right now and will keep watching them until we have you and the money."

"There are other roads," Bruder said.

"Ah, see? You did your research, like I thought. But really, roads?"

He tilted his head toward the two-track outside.

"Most of them are no better than this goat trail. And all of them go through property we own or manage."

"Manage," Connelly said. "That's what you call it?"

"What word would you use?"

"Scam."

Claud shrugged.

"That's fine too. My point is, you can't get out of here with that truck and the money. You could try to walk out, but these farmers are country people. They watch their land. They have cameras in trees to watch the deer come and go. Four assholes walking through the woods will be noticed. Then, they will call us and we will come get you."

"What's the cost of passage?" Bruder said.

Claud seemed shocked.

"That's it? You're giving up already?"

"I'm making a list of options."

"Oh, there are no options."

"How much will it cost?"

"All of it. It's our money."

Bruder shook his head.

"Not right now it isn't."

Claud leaned forward, ready to level with them.

"Look, my friends, there are truly no options. When you give up, we will kill you all and take our money back. It will be fast in return for your cooperation. If you fight, or make us come in here and get you, it will be slow. We might force you to kill each other or draw cards to see who gets their arm or leg cut off first. Have you done that before?"

Claud looked at Bruder and Connelly, then over at Rison, whose eyebrows were furrowed in disgust.

"I mean, from here it looks like none of you have had limbs cut off, but have you played the game with others? You have a deck of cards, and diamonds are left arm, hearts are right arm, clubs left leg, spades right leg. The higher the card, the more you cut off. Yes?"

"No," Bruder said.

Claud went on.

"So the two of hearts, you cut off the fingers on the right hand. Ace of clubs? Oh baby, that's the whole left leg, good-bye. And you need a good saw, because what happens if you get the four of diamonds, then the five of diamonds? Sometimes the cut is just an inch or so. You almost have to be a trained butcher to make it. But you get to draw the cards yourself, so it's your luck that determines the results. You guys, it's so much fun."

Connelly said, "What happens if both hands are gone? How do they pick?"

Bruder appreciated him jumping in to keep Claud talking.

Claud tapped his nose and bent forward.

"They do like this. Peck. Peck. Peck. Sometimes they lose enough blood and pass out and die, and then the game is done. Oh well, too bad."

"And that's going to happen to us," Bruder said.

"Only if you're a pain in the ass. If you just give up and say you're sorry, and all the money is here, it will be much better for you. We'll shoot you and bury you in some field or put you on a burn pile and bury the bones or give the bodies to the pigs. Have you seen that before? Amazing. Maybe the boss chooses that if you put up a fight. Tie you up or cut your joints and toss you in with the pigs. That way the pigs get some free food, so it's win-win."

Claud seemed impressed by this and nodded to himself, then looked up at Bruder.

"So give me my phone. I will make one call and we'll get started."

***

Bruder took the phone out of his pocket and looked at the dead screen.

It was a newer iPhone and certainly had tracking capabilities, allowing others to see where the phone was if it was on and had signal.

But he didn't know if the Romanians used apps that kept track of the last known location, which for this particular phone would be the end of the two-track, right before he turned it off.

Turning it back on to check wasn't an option.

He said, "What happens if you don't call?"

Claud frowned. "I think we've been over that already."

"No, I mean what happens if you don't call, you don't go back, you don't tell anybody about us and where we are."

Now Claud was very confused.

"You're not making sense to me."

"Say, hypothetically, we gave you a stack of the cash to get back in your car and drive away, but not back to town. I'm sure you know the people at all the roadblocks and can get through. You take the cash and keep driving. Someplace warm. Maybe LA, maybe Miami. A guy like you would love Key West."

"A bribe?"

"Call it whatever you want," Bruder said. "What happens then? Do they pivot the hunt for us toward you, thinking you're in on the whole thing? Or are you just some peon and it'll be a week before anybody notices you're gone?"

Claud looked at the other men to see if they were buying it.

"Are you serious?"

"I'm still collecting options."

Claud closed his eyes and shook his head, then rubbed his face with both hands before sliding them over his thinning hair.

"I thought you were a little bit smart, but you must be a fucking moron to ask me that."

He spat on the floor, a white bullet slapping the floor between Bruder's boots.

"I just told you what will happen if you cause more trouble. What do you think they would do to me if I took a payoff? And it wouldn't even matter. You'd still be stuck here and I'd have some of the money. What's the point? What does it get you?"

"More time," Bruder said.

"Time? What does time matter? Today or a week from now, we will come in here and get you if you make us."

"We'll blow the money."

Claud gave a wry smile.

"That's right, you boobytrapped the bags."

"And the woods," Bruder told him.

Claud kept the smile and swept a hand around the trailer, over the food and water stacked against the wall.

"You will run out of supplies. Your heaters will grow cold. You want to have siege warfare, Americans? We fought the Ottomans. We fought the fucking Mongols!"

Connelly said, "How old *are* you?"

Claud thumped his chest.

"It's in the blood, asshole."

"What about an exchange?" Bruder said. "We hand you over with some of the money, then we're on our way out of town."

"Oh, now I'm a hostage? I thought this was a friendly negotiation."

"We can tie you up if it makes you feel better."

"There will be no deal," Claud said. "Get it through your fucking heads. You can stick your bribe up your ass, and trying to use me like a—what is it—a bargaining chip? That will only make things worse for you."

Bruder thought about it for a moment.

"Then I guess we're out of options."

Claud said, "There never were any. I told you from the start."

"I don't suppose you want to tell us anything else about

your operation. Where the boss is right now. That sort of thing."

"From negotiation to hostage situation to interrogation. What's next, torture?"

Bruder shook his head.

"Relax. We aren't the torturing kind."

Claud smiled along his nose again.

"I know."

Bruder took the man's iPhone out again and dropped it on the floor, then used his boot to smash it. He picked up the mess and twisted it in his gloved hands until he got to the SIM card, then snapped it in two.

Claud looked on with growing concern.

Bruder looked at Rison.

"You have your ears in?"

Rison nodded.

Claud looked at Rison with a slight frown, and before he could turn back to Bruder to see what was happening Bruder shot him in the side of the head.

***

They all pulled their balaclavas off, then Bruder's earbud clicked.

From his spot by the road Kershaw said, "Did I just hear something?"

"You did, we're fine," Bruder told him. "Our guest just left."

"You need me back there?"

"Not yet. How loud was it?"

"Barely, but I was listening for it. Or something louder."

He was referring to the explosives nestled in the bags of money.

"We aren't there yet," Bruder said, and let go of the radio button.

Connelly frowned at Claud's body, slumped over the arm

of the camp chair.

"I think I could have worked something out of him."

Bruder shook his head. "He was enjoying it too much, playing with us. He wasn't going to give up anything. Except a trap."

Bruder and Connelly carried Claud's body outside and around the back of the trailer.

They dropped it on the ground, sending out a brief halo of snowflakes, and Bruder looked at Claud's car, thinking.

Connelly interrupted him.

"Should we stash him in there? Maybe we can put him in the trunk and leave the car somewhere. Throw them off the trail."

"What trail? He's the only one who found us."

"Well, like you said, they gotta have more guys out looking. If they're reporting back, it's only a matter of time before this dickhead gets missed. Somebody goes, 'Where was Claud looking? You, Grigore, go look for him.' But if we can drop the body across town, somewhere they'll find it, everybody goes that way and we hoof it out the back door."

Bruder shook his head.

It was a decent idea and would have been worth trying except for one thing.

"How do we get the truck and his car across town with the roadblocks up and all the other Romanians patrolling without catching someone's eye?"

Connelly stared down at Claud and chewed his lip.

"Wait until dark?"

"It'll be worse then. Less traffic, easier to stand out. And I don't think we're going to stay here that long. Come on."

They rolled and shoved the body under the trailer and left it there and went back inside.

Rison was staring at the TV and scanner.

"I think these things are busted."

"They work fine," Bruder said. "There's just nothing on them."

He turned to Connelly.

"You're up."

Connelly closed his eyes.

"Ah, shit."

CHAPTER FIVE

FIVE WEEKS EARLIER

Connelly rode the bus from Omaha into Iowa and eventually into the town, arriving at three o'clock on a brisk, sunny Thursday afternoon.

He wore jeans and a hooded sweatshirt under a barn jacket and had thick silver rings on most of his fingers and both thumbs. He carried a faded army surplus duffel bag full of clothes and a black guitar case covered with random stickers.

The guitar inside was his but the case was used, found in a Vegas pawn shop, and Connelly had spent most of the bus trip coming up with stories about how and where he got each sticker. It passed the time and might be good fodder for small talk.

He was the only one to get off at the town's depot, which was a room with benches on the back side of a drug store, accessed by a narrow lane running one block north of the highway. The road didn't seem to get any direct sunlight, and there were piles of old snow crusted with dirt piled against the cinderblock wall.

Connelly went past the benches and through the drug store, nodding at the old sourpuss behind the cash register, and emerged on the main east-west road through town. He stood there for a moment and got his bearings with his eyes watering from the bright sun and cold air coming down the highway like a wind tunnel.

The four lanes spread to five at the main intersection to include a left-turn lane. Connelly could see where they'd had to encroach upon the sidewalk at some point to add the extra lane, and he could picture what it looked like years ago, just dirt tracks with the two-story buildings on all four corners.

He didn't see anybody who looked like a Romanian thug, but he also didn't know if he would be able to tell the difference between that and a farmer.

So he turned left and headed straight for Len's.

***

The buildings along the north side of the main drag were all two levels, connected to each other by shared walls with no alleys or sidewalks in between.

The facade for Len's was made of faded and warped wooden shingles with a row of short windows running along the top half of the first floor. The second floor had standard double-hung windows. Connelly figured that level was either offices, apartments, or a more formal dining area for people who didn't want the bar experience.

The first floor windows had neon signs in them, but they couldn't compete with the daytime sun and Connelly couldn't tell what they said. The shingles were covered with paper posters advertising the kinds of beer and liquor you could get inside — exotics such as Bud Light and Captain Morgan.

There was also a wind-whipped banner, a physical version

of the image Connelly had seen on the website proclaiming the world-famous Lenburger, as seen on *Dash & Dine*. This banner included a faded photo of the two hosts of the show flanking a short, pudgy man with a red face beneath a blue trucker hat with *Len's Bar & Grill* on the front.

Connelly committed the face to memory, assuming it must belong to Len.

He pulled the heavy steel door open and stepped into what seemed like a pitch-black cave compared to the street. His eyes adjusted and he found himself in a small waiting area enclosed by a paneled half-wall with thick wooden newel posts forming the upper half. Wooden benches ran along the walls, and all of the wood from floor to ceiling was stained dark brown.

The laminate flooring had a pattern of brown and maroon tiles, and the array of six gumball and candy machines had greasy fingerprints on the chrome and glass.

The gap in the wall that led into the bar had a podium next to it with a sign that said, "Please wait to be seated."

Connelly put his stuff down and waited.

Through the gaps between the newels he could see four-top tables spread out in an area between booths along both walls. TVs mounted near the low ceiling showed football and hockey highlights, with one of the sets running some sort of truck drag racing event.

A few of the tables and booths had patrons; a young mother trying to keep her two kids from toppling out of their chairs on purpose, two grizzled men in work clothes and hats perched high on their buzz-cut heads drinking coffee with baskets of burgers and fries, a chubby man wearing a shirt and tie with his sleeves rolled up, talking to a woman in between bites of salad. The woman wore a blazer and skirt and was taking notes on a legal pad.

Past all of them was the actual bar along the back wall.

Two men sat with an empty stool between them, talking

and laughing with a woman behind the bar. She looked to be in her forties, but it was hard to tell with people in the restaurant business.

A short hallway in the back right corner had a sign for the bathrooms and an exit sign.

Another woman who might have been the first woman's twin sister came through a door behind the bar and saw Connelly all the way at the front. After a brief exchange with the bar group, she wove her way through the tables and stopped to check on the mother and kids before getting to the podium.

"Sorry hon, you didn't really have to wait."

She leaned over the podium, giving him an eyeful of breast spilling over the top of her shirt, and flipped the sign over.

Now it said he was free to seat himself.

"Stupid sign, we always forget to change it."

She raised an eyebrow at the duffel bag and guitar case at Connelly's feet.

"You get here on the bus?"

"Nah, my limo's waiting for me outside."

The eyebrow went even higher, though that hadn't seemed possible a moment earlier. She planted a hand flat on the podium and put her other hand on her hip, cocked out to the side.

"Oh, you're gonna be one of those, huh?"

Connelly grinned.

"One of what?"

"Trouble. Not here five minutes yet and you're already giving me grief."

"I wouldn't dare."

"Not if you're smart, buster. Now come on."

She pulled a menu out of a bin and led the way to a booth near the front of the restaurant, away from the other diners and the bar. The mother with kids didn't notice, but the two farmer-types paused to look him over then went back to their late lunch or early dinner. Or supper, if that's what they called it in Iowa.

Connelly dumped the bag on the bench on the left and set the guitar case on top, then slid into the empty side. From there he could see the whole dining area, the bar, and the door off to his left.

The woman said, "I'm Marie, I'll be taking care of you today."

She used a painted fingernail to tap the name tag on her shirt, giving Connelly another reason to glance at her chest. She noticed and didn't seem to mind.

"Where you coming in from?"

"Omaha," Connelly said.

Marie made a face, scrunching her nose up.

Connelly played along with whatever she was conveying.

"Yeah, that's why I left."

She laughed and pointed at the guitar case.

"Can you actually play that thing or is it just to get girls?"

"Marie, can I tell you a secret?"

She leaned forward.

"It's both."

"Bull. I bet you have a bunch of dirty laundry in there, taking it home to your momma. I raised three boys, and not one of them can wash a pair of jeans to save their lives."

"Are you offering to do my laundry?"

"Hell no!"

She winced and looked back over her shoulder to make sure the mother and kids hadn't heard.

"Okay, Springsteen, what do you want to drink?"

"You got anything local on tap? Any microbrews?"

"We got Hawkeye Hops, one of the families makes it in their barn. Some people like it. I think it tastes like a stick."

"I'll give it a shot. You like Springsteen?"

"No. I like country."

"How about Johnny Cash?"

The eyebrow went up again.

"Maybe. If it's done right."

"I wouldn't do it any other way."

"Mm-hmm."

She turned with the eyebrow still raised and went to get the beer.

Connelly watched, and waited, and when she turned back to see if he was watching he knew he was off to a good start.

***

Connelly ended up getting the Lenburger, and it wasn't bad, though he needed ten napkins to get through the mess.

Obviously, Marie would be used to the burger crime scene, but he was still concerned about blowing whatever mystique he'd built up. He made sure she wasn't looking when he licked his fingers.

They chatted and flirted some more, then an early bird crowd came in and things picked up and he had to make his move when she brought him the bill in a black leather folder.

He put cash in with a hefty tip and said, "So, do you do music here on Thursdays?"

"Like, tonight?"

"Sure."

"It's football season," Marie said, like that explained it.

Connelly nodded, but she could tell he wasn't up to speed.

"Thursday Night Football on the TVs," she said. "Plus, the crowd that comes in after the freshmen and JV games. If you tried to strum that thing tonight, you'd get drowned out."

"You don't have any regulars coming in and playing?"

"Not this time of year. They know better."

"What about Fridays?" he asked.

"Varsity football," she said. "But hold on…It's an away game, so it would be a late crowd. Maybe something be-fore? I can check with Len."

"Great," Connelly said, and sat back.

"Oh, he isn't here right now. What's your number?"

Connelly kept from smiling while he gave her the number of the burner he carried. She jotted it down on her pad.

"I'll let you know, hon. Don't get too hopeful, unless all you want to play is the Iowa fight song and the Monday Night Football theme."

"It would be my honor to play any requests. Where's a good place to spend the night?"

The eyebrow moved again but Connelly didn't expect an invitation, not that quickly. If it happened he wasn't sure what he'd say—shacking up with Marie so soon would limit his mobility and options for chatting with other people, and she'd mentioned three sons...if they still lived with Marie he didn't want any part of it.

But she did seem like a wildcat...

She said, "There's the motel, less than a mile down the road we're on."

"What's it called?" Connelly said, like he didn't already know.

"The Sleep Inn. Just keep going east, you can't miss it."

"It's clean?"

She stepped away to wave a new group of four men, farmers in flannel and jeans, to one of the tables.

Then she looked back at him and winked.

"Clean enough for Springsteen."

Connelly grinned and gathered his duffel and guitar case.

He walked past the table of farmers and didn't slow down or look over when he heard them speaking Romanian.

***

The walk in the crisp late-fall air and sunshine was good medicine after the restaurant's darkness and beer, burgers and fries.

The breeze coming from the west nudged him along and he had to keep to the left of the sidewalk to avoid the full brunt of the wind generated by the traffic going into town, mostly big rigs pulling trailers. It was nearly impossible to look cool while getting buffeted around in the vortex, so he kept his head down and wished he'd opted for the motor-cycle instead of the bus.

Bruder and Rison both thought the bike would be over the top—a guitar-wielding stranger rumbling into town would get too much attention—and when Connelly re-vealed he didn't know jack shit about motorcycles, that was the end of it.

He crossed five side streets running north and south into quiet neighborhoods. From what he could see, and what they'd all seen from the satellite map view, the blocks nearest the main intersection had tall Victorian-style homes that took up a quarter or even half of a block. This, according to the town's website, was considered the historical district.

As the grid of streets expanded away from the center of town the houses turned into small post-World War II homes with aluminum siding and square yards.

He walked in front of a large gas station with pump stations coming out of both sides like unbalanced wings, one side for civilian vehicles and the other for big rigs, then crossed the last side street and found the end of the sidewalk.

He had to walk along the shoulder of the four-lane high-way, the jet wash unavoidable, until he came to the crushed rock driveway leading to the motel.

The motel was set about fifty yards back from the road with a horseshoe-shaped driveway sweeping in from both ends of the parking lot. The space in the middle of the horse-shoe had a sign by the road with *The Sleep Inn* outlined in neon with a trail of Zs coming off the end of Inn, like the two Ns were sleeping eyes.

The sign also announced free cable and discounts for multiple nights and Connelly thought the Vacancy neon was lit, but as with the bar signs, it was impossible to tell in the full sun.

The rest of the horseshoe infield had at one time been a miniature golf course. Now it was a series of landscaping bricks and concrete curbs outlining the holes and speed-bump hills and ragged green turf. A central pile of fake rocks looked like it might have included a waterfall at one time and now had a summer's worth of weeds sprouting around it.

Connelly felt regret.

If the course was operational, he would have made it his secondary goal—slightly behind getting his share of the fourteen million dollars—to get Bruder to play a round of miniature golf.

The motel office jutted out from the center of the complex with ten units each on the left and right, set further back with a covered walkway running the length of each wing.

The parking lot looked about half full with cars and trucks parked in front of the units where, Connelly presumed, the tenants were staying. They were spread evenly across both sides of the office.

He went inside and smelled coffee and wood paneling and some mashup of apples and cinnamon and cloves coming from a candle the size of his head burning on the counter.

A bald and slope-shouldered man wearing a pink golf shirt with a toothpaste stain on the chest sat behind the counter staring at an iPad. The device was in a protective case that could be configured to prop the screen up like a TV, and the man watched it for a few extra seconds while Connelly stood there, then he tapped the screen to pause it.

He turned to Connelly with a sheepish grin and confided, "Don't tell my wife."

Connelly played along. The man had a name tag that said Ed, with Owner/Manager underneath.

"I wouldn't dare, Ed. But, uh, what shouldn't I tell her?"

"We're supposed to be watching this show together. But

she always falls asleep and gets mad if I keep watching, so we only get fifteen, twenty minutes a night. So I have a secret account and I've been watching it by myself."

"I hope you have a good divorce lawyer."

Ed found that hilarious.

"Oh lord, she would too! She'd rake me over the coals! What can I do for you?"

"First, don't give me any spoilers. I haven't started watching it yet."

"Oh, you have to. It's so good! I don't want to root for the bad guys, but, you know? The good guys are just as bad! Maybe worse!"

Connelly put his hands over his ears and Ed lifted his arms, relenting.

"Okay, okay, I'll shut up now, I promise. I'm guessing you'd like a room?"

"Indeed, sir. I'm on foot, so as close to town as you can get me. Even a few feet can make a difference at the end of the day."

"Don't I know it. I keep telling Barbara—that's my wife, Barbara—we need to get one of those anti-fatigue mats for behind the counter here. You know what she told me? Just wear thicker socks."

Connelly sensed about thirty years of Barbara resentment simmering under the surface and wouldn't be surprised if the whole thing ended with a murder/suicide over who got to hold the TV remote.

Ed said, "I can't put you all the way at the end, but number two is open. I try to spread folks out with an empty room in between, like a sound buffer, unless we're too full up and can't do it. Not that the walls are thin, mind you, it's just that most people like a little elbow room. So if you don't mind a neighbor…"

"Number two is fine," Connelly said.

"There is an adjoining door between one and two, but it

has two doors and they lock from both sides, so it's completely safe."

"Can you tell me there's a bunch of bathing suit models staying in number one?"

Ed laughed again.

"Oh no, no no. But it's great for families with younger kids, you know; naps. And every year we get some of the high school kids renting a bunch of rooms on prom night and they open all the adjoining doors and have a big sleepover."

He looked up, suddenly alarmed.

"The parents know about it, of course. Sometimes they even chaperone."

"I hope they get laid too," Connelly said.

"Oh! Oh, uh, well…just the one night then?"

Connelly made a show of thinking about it.

"At least two, so let's start with that."

"Wonderful. I just need a credit card to put on file."

"I'm only carrying cash these days, but I'm happy to pay for the first night now."

Ed feigned shock.

"Cash? What is this thing you speak of? Of course, cash it is! And I see you have a guitar there—I hope you aren't planning on busking."

"I stopped in at Len's before here. I might get some mic time there tomorrow."

"Oh, good. It's just, we have some local ordinances about that sort of thing, and some of the folks around town wouldn't really go for it, even if it was allowed."

"No worries," Connelly said, getting a strong feeling Ed was one of those folks.

He got the key to unit two and left Ed to his scandalous show watching and carried his things along the left wing, almost to the end. It was colder there, under the overhang and out of the sun.

The key worked and he opened the door. The carpet was

thin and brown, like the bedspread on the queen-sized bed against the left wall.

And the fabric on the single chair in the corner, next to the big window by the door. The chair had a round table next to it, just big enough for a game of solitaire.

The air smelled like old smoke and air freshener, so Connelly dropped his bag next to the door to keep it propped open.

He walked between the foot of the bed and the low dresser on his right. The dresser had a cheap flat-screen TV on top of it, along with a compact coffee maker and two mugs stuffed with packets of sugar and powdered creamer. A framed print on the wall above the TV showed a small pond with a bunch of cattails and ducks coming in for a landing.

The back wall had a short hallway with a closet along the right wall and a door into the small bathroom on the left.

The bathroom contained a shallow sink, a toilet, and a cramped tub caulked into three walls. The shower curtain was brown with flying geese on it. The tub and toilet and sink all had brown stains and Connelly swiped a finger across the one in the sink. It didn't budge or leave any residue on his skin—iron, possibly from the Iron Age.

The closet had a dozen wire hangers with thin paper wrappers advertising a local laundromat. A light blue cloth bag hung on a hook. Connelly pulled one corner to spread it out and saw the same name printed on the side along with brief instructions—leave your dirty laundry in the bag outside the door and they'd handle it for you and add it to your motel bill.

Connelly thought about it for a moment and decided: If he stayed here long enough to need fresh laundry, things had either gone horribly wrong or shockingly well.

He stepped back into the main room.

The solid metal door between units was next to the bed, in the corner made by the main room and the bathroom.

It was locked, and when opened would hinge toward the bathroom and take up zero real estate.

Connelly went back to the front of the room and lifted his gear, then closed and locked the door.

He put the duffel and guitar case on the bed. They sank about six inches into the mattress, not a good sign for sleeping or any other bed-centered activities he might engage in.

He went back to the adjoining door and unlocked it and pressed it against the wall, where it stayed.

He tapped on the door locked from unit one.

After some snapping and clicking the door opened and Rison was there, looking him up and down.

"You get laid yet?"

***

Rison sat on the edge of the bed and punched the Mute button on the remote, silencing the sports highlight show.

Connelly went into the room, a mirror image of his except for the print above the TV. This one showed a fish jumping out of a lake to catch a wily dragonfly.

Bruder was in the chair by the window. He had a cup of steaming coffee next to his arm on the small round table. He and Rison both wore suits with no ties, looking like road warrior salesmen or reps for a heavy machinery company.

Bruder said, "How'd you do?"

"I hit Len's on the way out here," Connelly said. "I might have something lined up for tomorrow night. I left my number with the waitress, she needs to check with Len about it. If she doesn't call I'll go back tomorrow, but something tells me she's gonna call."

He stuck his hands in the back pockets of his jeans and grinned.

"Let me guess," Rison said. "This waitress's name is Marie."

Connelly's grin fell.

"You guys met her?"

It was Rison's turn to smile.

"Oh, I imagine there isn't a man who passes through this town who doesn't get to meet Marie."

"Son of a bitch," Connelly said.

"Don't let it get you down, sport. She's a nice woman and I'm sure you'll be very happy together."

"Yeah, shove it. And hey, it's still a good lead. If she gets around like that, maybe she's spent time with the Romanians. Who were at Len's when I left, by the way."

Rison looked over at Bruder, who said, "Just now?"

"Twenty minutes ago, maybe? They just sat down when I was walking out."

"How many?"

"Four of them."

Rison looked at Bruder again.

"What do you think?"

While Bruder thought about it, Rison told Connelly, "We went there for lunch yesterday and got the impression it's pretty common for people to come into town just for the Lenburger."

"Told you," Connelly said. "And I got the same feeling. A couple farmers in there looked me over, but they weren't hostile or alarmed or anything. I was just another new face passing through."

"And you're sure these were Romanians?" Bruder said.

"They were speaking Romanian."

Bruder stood up.

"I want to get a look at them."

"Both of us?" Rison said.

"Yeah. It'll be familiar to the staff. Marie was still working when you left?"

Connelly nodded.

"The dinner rush was picking up and she was hustling around."

Bruder grabbed a set of keys off the dresser and walked out the front door.

Rison followed, and before he got outside Connelly said, "What am I supposed to do?"

Rison shrugged and gave him a wolfish grin.

"Take a shower. Rest up. Marie's gonna need a foot rub tonight."

"Fuck you, buddy."

CHAPTER SIX

Bruder and Rison took the rental car down the road and backed into a spot in the dirt lot behind Len's.

The car was rented under Bruder's false set of identification and credit cards, which he'd also used for the motel. They walked in through the back door and started to wade through the tables to get to the front, where they could officially wait to be seated, but Marie cruised past them with a tray full of food and told them to sit wherever they liked.

Bruder picked the last booth along the wall, closest to the back exit, and sat facing the room. Rison sat across from him and could watch the back door and bar.

The place was already half full, and a blast of orange evening sunlight came through the front door when it opened and a group of six walked in. The conversation was loud and the speakers hung near the ceiling played classic rock about two steps too loud for the space.

Marie hustled past, going the other way.

"Be with you in a minute boys!"

They nodded at her, and Bruder scanned the room without lingering on anyone in particular.

"See them?" Rison asked.

Bruder nodded and looked down at his menu.

"Four of them, like Connelly said. They're close to the front, first table you get to coming out of the corral up there."

"Should I look?"

"No need. They're all big with thick necks. I can see at least one tattoo coming up out of a collar, some kind of snake or serpent."

One of the Romanians raised his voice, telling what seemed like the punchline to a joke or story, and the rest of the table burst into laughter.

Rison squinted.

"That's them?"

"Yeah."

"Man, I hate loudmouths. If I sit down at a table in Vegas and some asshole sounds like that, putting on a display, I'm moving on. It's not worth the headache. The guy making the others laugh—he's in charge?"

Bruder looked up at one of the TVs and risked another glance at the table of Romanians. The four-top was a cluttered landscape of empty burger baskets and wax paper and wadded napkins and beer bottles.

"Hard to tell. None of them look like upper management. I'd say they're muscle. But that guy might be in charge of them, or at least the alpha. He's the largest."

He checked the tables around the Romanians, looking mostly at the food like he was trying to decide what to get, but scanning faces and posture as well.

"Nobody appreciates the show they're putting on."

"Anybody look scared?"

Bruder went back to his menu.

"There's a family right next to them and nobody is looking over, even though one of the Romanians is pushed back and practically bumping into their table. An older couple, at your nine o'clock, you can see the man's jaw muscles working while he stares down at his beer. Go ahead."

Rison turned, casual, just looking around.

"Oh yeah. That guy's seething about something. But his wife's playing a game on her phone while they're at dinner, so that might be it."

Bruder didn't see any benefit in further speculation.

Marie slapped a palm on their table and shooed Rison toward the wall.

"Slide over, I gotta sit for a minute."

She bumped in next to him and blew a strand of hair out of her face.

"How are my drug dealers doing this evening?"

Bruder gave her a smile of acknowledgment and Rison barked a laugh.

"Drug dealers, that's good. I tell you what—we'd make a helluva lot more money, that's for sure."

At lunch the day before they'd told Marie they were in the pharmaceutical business, and when she broke the news that they were too ugly to be drug reps they had to come clean and admit they were on the packaging side, selling boring stuff for the production lines like fillers and cappers and torquers and shrink wrappers.

They'd flown from New Jersey to Omaha for a site installation and the equipment was delayed, so they were driving around the heartland for a few days, seeing the sights, and couldn't resist trying the Lenburger.

Now Marie said, "You guys doing the Len again?"

Bruder nodded. "With a beer, please."

"Same kind?"

"Sure."

She nudged Rison in the ribs.

"What about you?"

Rison made a turtle face at the menu.

"How's the New York strip?"

"Better than anything you'll get in New Jersey."

"That's outrageous. Now I have to try it."

"Rare? And any other answer is wrong, by the way."

Rison gave Bruder a look of fear.

"Rare it is, then. With whatever beer you think goes best with it."

Marie approved the trust.

"It comes with broccoli and the loaded baked potato. I'll put extra bacon on it for you."

"I'm in love," Rison said.

She laughed and pulled herself out of the booth.

"I'm impressed, by the way. Most folks who try the Lenburger are too scared to try anything else."

She shot a judging look at Bruder and said, "But when you come all the way from New Jersey, you gotta try the steak. See what you're missing."

Bruder suspected they weren't just talking about steak anymore, but he said, "What's the furthest anyone's come for the burger?"

Marie looked at a blank spot on the wall.

"I had a couple from Australia once. They were cycling across the country and had us marked on their map as one of the spots to try. Some folks from China, but I think they were living in the U.S. already. And I'm not sure what's farther, China or Australia…"

"And they all just stop in for the burger and head back home? Or wherever they were going?"

"Pretty much," Marie said with a smile, but her eyes had lost the mischief of flirting with Rison.

Bruder was trying to get her to mention something about the Romanians, and he figured that was the closest he was going to get without pushing too far.

"I'll be right back with those beers."

She turned and left, and Rison said, "She's scared."

Bruder nodded.

He checked the room again and saw the table of Romanians looking back at him, all four men, each of them with the sort of flat eyes that wouldn't change whether they were tickling or stabbing you.

Bruder didn't let his gaze linger, but he didn't rush his eyes away either.

He didn't want to challenge them with a stare-down.

It could be equally troublesome, though, to seem like an easy mark, somebody they could brace and shake down.

He looked at Rison and said, "They're scoping me, so let's talk about work or sports or something."

Rison caught on right away and started droning about conveyor belts and barcode scanners and whatever else he'd learned in his research about pharmaceutical packaging equipment.

Bruder nodded along and commented here and there and kept tabs on the Romanians in his periphery.

The four of them finished their beers and turned to look at the booth a few times, possibly discussing plans about who was going to do what when the time came.

Then the loudest one, the one Bruder thought might be the alpha, reached into a pocket and pulled out a cell phone and looked at the screen. He stood up and the others followed suit, then trailed him out the front door without looking back.

A family of four waiting near the pedestal clustered into the corner by the gumball machines to get out of their way.

"They're out," Bruder said.

"We gonna have any trouble when we leave?"

"It looked like they got summoned via text. But who knows. A couple of them might think it would be fun to have a chat with us."

Marie and another server hurried over and cleared the mess on the four-top, putting everything in brown plastic bins. Bruder could see the thin line of Marie's mouth, and when the other woman said something to her Marie just shook her head.

A skinny kid wearing an apron carried the bins into the back while Marie wiped the table down and reset the condiments, then waved the family of four over.

"They didn't pay," Bruder said.

Rison risked a glance over his left shoulder.

"The Romanians?"

"Yeah."

"So maybe they left in a hurry because of that? The good ol' dine and dash. Hey, like the show, but flipped."

"No. It looks like the staff here is used to it."

Rison took a drink from his beer.

"So people are scared. And pissed."

Bruder nodded.

"The question is, who's ready to do something about it?"

***

They ate and chatted with Marie, who never got back into her rhythm after the Romanians left.

Rison agreed the steak was better than anything he'd had in Jersey, and he did a good job not mentioning the ones he'd had in Vegas and Rio and Monte Carlo.

They paid in cash with a tip big enough to put them solidly in Marie's corner—but not big enough to let on they knew she'd been stiffed—then walked into the back hallway and stopped at the door.

Bruder adjusted the FN 509 Compact 9mm just to the right of his belt buckle. It was in an inside-the-waistband holster with just the grip peeking out above his belt, ideal for concealment.

Rison carried the same handgun over his right kidney, preferring that placement for comfort, and that's how he practiced drawing and firing.

"If any of them are out here," Bruder said, "don't shoot them unless it's absolutely necessary."

Rison grinned at him.

"Ain't no bullet worth fourteen million dollars."

***

The sky was dark and pressing down on the single sodium light buzzing over the dirt lot.

The parking lot was full of cars and trucks, but it was quiet and still, all the noise and movement trapped inside Len's.

Bruder checked between the vehicles as they passed and listened for footsteps and vehicle doors popping open. When they got to their car, he slid into the passenger seat and checked the windows and mirrors for anyone coming to brace them in the car, sitting ducks, but then Rison had them moving in a tight turn out of the spot and into the narrow road behind the restaurant.

Other vehicles moved on the streets and looking left at the first intersection they could see a steady flow of traffic on the four lanes running through town, but nobody pulled out behind them or followed them through a series of turns and cutbacks.

"My sense of self-importance is taking a hit," Rison said. "I don't think those Romanians give two shits about us."

"That's their problem," Bruder said.

He pulled a small notepad out of his jacket pocket with notes and sketches that would only make sense to him.

"Let's take another tour around the outskirts. I want to check these places at night, see if they have any lights showing through the trees."

"Want me to swing by and grab Connelly?"

Bruder shook his head.

"I've had enough racket for one night."

***

They got back to the motel just before nine o'clock. Connelly was waiting for them in the connecting doorway, wearing shorts and a t-shirt.

"What, did you guys get the seven-course meal or something? I've been waiting here all goddam night."

Rison locked the room door behind him.

"We got a look at some local spots, for afterward. In case we have to lay low."

Connelly waited for a moment, then said, "And?"

"We found some good candidates, but ideally we scoot right out of town before anybody knows what happened."

Bruder was watching Connelly.

He asked him, "Can you handle sitting still for a few days if you have to?"

"Me? Sure, of course. Why?"

"Because you seem to have trouble with it right now, and you've got a hot shower and cable TV here. The places we looked at don't even have electricity."

Connelly put his hands up.

"Don't worry about me, man. I'm just riled up because this is all coming together around me, and I'm here with my thumb up my ass, looking for something to do. After a job, I'm all about chilling out."

Rison put his jacket on a hanger and left it in the closet, then set his gun on the nightstand.

"You want something to do? Marie might need some cheering up."

Connelly looked back and forth between them, suddenly betrayed.

"What did you guys do?"

Rison said, "Us? Nothing."

Connelly frowned, then, "The Romanians? They were still there?"

Rison filled him in with Bruder adding details when necessary, since he'd had the best vantage point.

When they were done Connelly said, "So you guys think Marie can be our inside source?"

"She knows things," Rison said. "Whether they'll be helpful, or if she'll be willing to talk about them...she seemed pretty shaken up after that crew left."

Connelly crossed his arms and leaned against the doorframe. He frowned at the floor, working through something.

"What is it?" Bruder said.

"It's just...I don't know anymore. Marie's a nice lady. If she talks to us, and we do our thing, and it somehow comes back on her..."

"It won't," Bruder said.

"But if it does."

The look he gave Bruder was full of dire consequences for Marie.

Bruder shrugged.

"Then she deals with it, or she doesn't. She can move. She can start a revolt. But she won't know who we are, or how to find us, so whatever happens stops at her."

"That's cold, man."

Bruder said, "We don't even know if she's worth talking to yet and you're already working out a plan to save her. You going back there tomorrow is a mistake."

"No, no, it's fine," Connelly said. "I'm fine. I just don't like the idea of our actions bringing shit down on other people's heads."

"Except the Romanians," Rison said.

"Well, yeah, fuck those guys."

Bruder said, "Then be a professional. Be careful. Talk to Marie, or whoever, but don't tip her off you're pumping for information. Whoever we talk to, it should never cross their mind we might be connected to what happens five weeks from now."

Connelly nodded.

"Yeah. Of course. I don't know why I got off track like that, guys. I'm good to go."

He rolled around the door frame and went into his room,

where the shifting light of the TV was the only illumination.

Bruder looked at Rison, who knew what the look meant.

"He's good," Rison said, quiet enough to almost be talking to himself. "He'll do fine."

***

Bruder had his things in unit number three. Connelly's room had originally been the empty buffer the motel manager included in his pitch, and Rison had let him know to request a room as close to the end as possible to get the adjoining door.

Bruder used his key and hung up his suit and shirt in the bathroom while he took a hot shower, letting the steam work into the fabric. He ended the shower with a minute of cold water and shut it off.

He put the pistol under the bed on the side away from the door. If somebody came in during the night, he'd roll that way and put the bed between them while he reached for the gun.

He stretched out and thought about how likely something like that was.

If the Romanians were into everything in town and everyone was either scared of them or under their so-called protection, the motel manager—Ed was his name, Bruder recalled—would give up the room numbers and extra keys of the two guys from Len's.

And Marie would fill them in on the rest.

To the Romanians, Bruder and Rison were just two straight civilians killing time on a business trip, staying in rooms one and three at the motel.

And two guys like that, if the thugs from Len's wanted to have some fun with them—smack them around and take whatever they had—those kind of guys would call the police if they survived the ordeal.

And if talking to the local police didn't do any good because the cops were just like everybody else, scared or paid off, those kind of guys would call the state police.

In short, they wouldn't be smart enough to keep their mouths shut.

They'd make noise.

So it would be stupid for the Romanians to come in and shake them down for pocket change, or just for a laugh, when they had such a sweet deal going with the farm subsidies.

In Bruder's experience, most people were mostly stupid when it came to most things.

The Romanians at Len's hadn't changed his mind so far.

So he kept to the edge of the bed away from the door and thought about the spots he and Rison had scouted, and Connelly and his misplaced morals, and eventually he fell asleep waiting for the Romanians to do something dumb.

CHAPTER SEVEN

FIVE WEEKS EARLIER—FRIDAY

When Rison knocked on his door at 8:30 Bruder was already showered and dressed.

"I got coffee and rolls in my room," Rison said, and Bruder followed him.

He scanned the parking lot and didn't see any new vehicles or anyone parked along the horseshoe driveway, or stopped on the highway out there past the abandoned miniature golf course.

Connelly's door and curtains were closed, but he was standing in Rison's room using the remote to flip through the channels.

Bruder asked him, "Did you have any coffee yet?"

"No, but I'm dying for some."

"Wait. Go down to the motel office and ask them where you can get breakfast. Then go back to your room and come in here for the coffee. Or go to wherever they suggest."

Connelly frowned at him, then got it.

"Yeah, okay."

He tossed the remote onto the bed and went through the adjoining door. A few seconds later Bruder heard the door to unit two open and close, and Connelly went down to the office to provide more proof he was here on his own, just some guy with a guitar drifting around.

Bruder took one of the mugs from the motel's coffee maker set and filled it from a massive styrofoam cup full of hot coffee.

Rison said, "The gas station didn't have any to-go carafes, can you believe that?"

"Yes."

There were three more of the cups, also full, nestled in a carrier on the dresser. A white cardboard box full of cinnamon rolls and donuts and mystery lumps wrapped in waxed paper was next to the carrier.

"Those little things are breakfast sandwiches," Rison said. "Not bad for a gas station. They had a little setup in there, some tables and a row of stools by a counter along the back windows. It looks like it's for truck drivers, but there were a few old guys in there who seemed like regulars. Drinking coffee and talking about how bad this winter is supposed to be."

"Farmers?"

Rison shrugged. "Everybody around here looks like a farmer to me."

"I've been thinking about it," Bruder said. "Unless we see somebody holding a sign with 'Fuck the Romanians' on it, we can't approach them. It's too risky. The people we've seen so far are more scared than pissed."

"Marie seemed pretty pissed last night."

Bruder shook his head. "Connelly's right about her."

Rison was surprised.

Bruder said, "Not the guilty part. She's rooted, she has three boys around here somewhere. She's pissed, but she's also too smart to run her mouth about it. She has too much to lose."

"Yeah, maybe."

Rison froze with his mug halfway to his face.

"Oh, hold on. What if...Hold on, I'm trying to decide if this idea is terrible or brilliant..."

Bruder waited.

Rison said, "Ah, fuck it. What if we're undercover? What if we confide in her, or whoever, that we're on some organized crime task force and we're here to take the Romanians down? That way, they'll figure the gang's done for, they'll go all-in on helping us out."

Bruder chewed and drank coffee and thought it over.

Finally, he shook his head again.

"It could work. It could. But it's too overt. Too loud. If we go that route, everyone will know it was us who pulled the job off when it's done. The town, and the Romanians. Better to leave everybody guessing, if we can."

"Yeah," Rison said. "Not a bad option to keep in our back pockets though, just in case."

"Not bad," Bruder agreed.

They stood there thinking about it, then Rison said, "Are we sure we still need somebody local? I mean, we found some good spots to hunker down if necessary, we know the route they're going to take out of town, thanks to Tug. The only thing we don't know for sure is when they're going to make the rounds. If we come back when I was supposed to meet up with him, and we keep our eyes open..."

Bruder said, "We won't know when they're going to make the collections until they start, and even then we could miss it. We have an idea of where they're coming from once they have all the cash, and where they're going, but not when. We'll either be too early or too late. If we're going to do it, we need more information."

"I know, dammit. It's just...people screw everything up, you know?"

Bruder knew but didn't need to say anything about it.

They heard the door to unit two open and close, then Connelly cruised through the opening and went straight for the spread and drank from the open styrofoam cup.

"Poor Ed. Barbara's on duty in the office, and man, I totally get why he's cheating on her with that TV show. She's a real piece of work."

Bruder looked at Rison to see if it made any sense to him. Rison shrugged.

Bruder said, "We're going to drive around, maybe browse some of the shops along the main drag and see if anyone catches our eye. Then we'll hit Len's one more time for lunch, and that's it for us. We stay here any longer and we'll draw more attention."

"Aw, you're gonna miss my show tonight," Connelly said.

Rison asked him, "You got a setlist?"

"I'm getting a strong John Cougar Mellencamp vibe. Maybe pre-Mellencamp, so just John Cougar."

Rison made a face.

"Hey," Connelly said, "this is the heartland. These are his people. Is Kershaw coming in today?"

"Saturday," Bruder said.

"I'll have the whole town singing the chorus to *Jack and Diane* by then."

"Have some goddam dignity," Rison said.

Connelly started singing with his mouth full of chocolate glazed donut, so Bruder grabbed the car keys and left the room.

***

Bruder and Rison drove around town watching the traffic flow.

They spent some time going north and south from the main intersection, and while there were some cars and trucks and rigs, the east-west roads were much busier. Whenever they cut around on side streets the smaller roads seemed deserted in comparison.

They stopped at the gas station and Bruder went inside to check out the seating area Rison had noticed. He found two white-haired men in battered trucker hats, sitting apart but watching the same cable news show on a TV mounted in the corner.

There was a small section in the gas station dedicated to cheap souvenirs—toy trucks and combines and water pistols—and Bruder saw a rack of pamphlets with information about the train depot and some handmade flyers advertising a local cider mill with hay rides and, starting after Thanksgiving, hot chocolate and sleigh rides.

He took a copy of everything and got two more cups of coffee, since they'd left the first batch in the motel room with Connelly.

He had a story ready about a nephew who loved trains, possibly an opener to feel out the cashier for any information about the Romanians. But she didn't look up from her phone or notice or care about the stack of literature he'd amassed, so Bruder wrote her off and didn't say anything and paid and left.

Rison took the highway west, their rental car getting knocked around by the wind and passing of big rigs on their way to wherever.

A few miles out of town they made the right turn onto the two lanes shooting straight northwest. The street sign said Pine, but Bruder didn't see any pine trees.

It was their third time checking the road, and after a minute or so of nothing but corn stubs and the occasional distant tractor sitting idle, Bruder said, "You're sure this is it?"

It was the third time he'd asked it, once on every trip, and Rison tried to sound confident for the third time.

"It has to be, right?"

"Go through it again."

Rison sighed.

"The way Tug told it, they make their rounds, collect the cash, and meet up at the family compound, some farm out here they bought legally. Then they count it all and pack it up in the armored car and drive it through town like a one-truck Romanian pride parade."

Bruder looked out his window at the lunar landscape. There was nowhere to hide out there, no corners to duck around or doorways to slip into. Not even a pine tree to stand behind.

"And he told you it was northwest of town?"

Rison nodded.

"He said it was a road like a runway, nothing but crops all around, and the armored car would rumble down it to the highway. So if they were coming toward us from their farm out here, they'd be going down, like southeast, right?"

"Is that how Romanians talk about directions? Up is north, down is south?"

"How the hell should I know?"

Rison was getting snappy, tired of the questions he didn't have straight answers for.

A shape appeared in the road ahead. It turned into a flashing stop sign, and beyond that was the berm and railroad overpass with the one-lane passage beneath.

Rison stopped at the sign and made a show of looking left, right, behind, and ahead. Nothing else was moving except a gaggle of geese hunkered out in the corn stumps.

Rison pulled forward, and right before they slipped into the mouth of the tunnel Bruder said, "Stop."

He looked at the concrete retaining walls and the overpass and the way it all funneled into a man-made chokepoint. He got out and took some photos of it with a small digital camera, then took a short video, turning a full 360 degrees.

He walked through the tunnel taking more photos, then did the same routine on the northwest side of the tracks.

Rison idled behind him, watching for any inbound traffic,

and when Bruder got back into the car Rison said, "You like this spot?"

"It has potential."

Rison nodded, happy about anything that looked remotely like progress, and picked up speed as they moved away from the overpass.

Bruder watched the scene shrink in his side mirror.

If Rison was right, and this was the road the Romanians used...

"We're going to need some explosives."

Rison glanced over, alarmed.

"You want to blow the bridge?"

"Not quite."

***

The endless fields of harvested corn and soybeans were eventually broken by a dirt road angling off to the west.

The sign called it 64th Street, not even important enough to get a real name.

Bruder could see a tree line down that way, and beyond it the tops of what looked to be silos with grain elevators.

Rison coasted to a stop but didn't turn. He looked off to the left toward the silos.

"Might be the Romanian compound."

Bruder checked straight ahead, then looked to the right.

Nothing but more fields and tree lines off in the distance. The field outside his window had been left to grow wild and was ragged with tall grass and fading yellow wildflowers.

Rison hit the left turn signal, then looked at Bruder with raised eyebrows.

Bruder shook his head.

"Look around. If it is them, we'd be the only car to drive past all day. And if any of the muscle from Len's is standing around outside, and they recognize us, we're blown. Let's see what's further down this road."

Rison killed the blinker and pushed the car forward.

"I'm gonna take a wild guess and say corn."

***

They drove for five more miles and saw one other farm, sitting right on the stretch of two-lane road they were on.

It had a tall white square of a house surrounded by a few mature trees. Massive barns sheathed in ribbed sheet metal loomed behind the house, in the middle of an immaculate lake of crushed concrete.

Three men stood outside one of the barns next to a machine that looked to Bruder like it belonged on the surface of Mars. It dwarfed the men, who turned from looking up at the cockpit and studied the lone car going by.

"That's a sprayer," Rison said.

The three men stared, and Bruder raised a hand to the window.

The three men waved back, an automatic response, but they seemed unsure about who they were waving at.

"That's not the Romanians," Bruder said.

"No beards?"

"That yard and the equipment are pristine. The Romanians aren't here to farm, they're here to steal and intimidate. I bet they don't even mow their lawn."

He looked through the windshield and saw more fields. There weren't even any power lines along the side of the road.

"Go another mile or so, then turn around. Let's head back to town."

"If those farmers are still out there they'll see us go by. Might be weird. Even more weird than you waving at them."

Bruder shrugged.

"We're two packaging equipment guys from Jersey who got lost driving around while waiting for lunch time."

"Oh, it's lunch time?"

"It will be by the time we get back."

"More like dinner time," Rison said, grousing. "I need to look at this road on a map, see where it goes."

"Northwest."

"No, I mean how far. Because if it goes all the way to South Dakota, or Minnesota maybe, we could use it to get away after the job. Straight shot, right outta Dodge."

He chopped the air with a hand and left his fingers pointing through the windshield to demonstrate.

Bruder said, "I don't like it."

"Why not? If this is the right road, and the Romanians are back there somewhere and they try to take their damn armored car through town, we hit them before they get there and take their back trail all the way here and keep going."

"What if they have a chase car?"

Rison frowned.

"Tug didn't say anything about other vehicles behind the armored car."

"What if they catch on somehow, the guys with the cash get a distress call out? Even if we make it past the Romanian compound, wherever that is, we're stuck on this one road. Unless you see us on snowmobiles or ATVs."

Rison seemed to be considering that, so Bruder said, "No. If this is the right road, we hit them and go the other way. Into town. More options."

Rison found a spot on the shoulder with a little more gravel and used it to swing the car around. The scenery going southeast was exactly the same, but now they had the sun in their eyes.

They went past the immaculate farm and the three men were still out there, now looking even more concerned about the same car going by, but they waved again when Rison gave them a thumbs-up.

After another mile he said, "Okay, so where do we hit them?"

"Let's see how that tunnel looks coming from this way."

***

The tunnel looked good.

Bruder took a few more photos and some video, and jotted down some cryptic notes, then Rison drove them back into town where they parked behind Len's and went inside.

It was close to noon and the lunch crowd was picking up.

Bruder scanned the tables for any Romanians—especially the same crew from the previous day—but didn't see anyone who tripped the alarm. A young woman in a smart gray suit was at the bar with a bowl of soup and an open laptop, talking on the phone while she poked at the keys and trackpad.

Bruder and Rison didn't bother going to the front podium and corral. They just slid into the same booth they'd used the night before and Marie spotted them right away.

"Too early for beers?"

"Never," Rison said, "but we're hitting the road after this, and it's probably not a good idea to show up in Omaha smelling like craft beer. So I'll take an iced tea."

Marie pushed her lower lip out.

"Aw, you guys are leaving?"

"Yeah, and we're flying back to Jersey from Omaha. But we'll be back."

"I hope so."

She looked at Bruder.

"I'm gonna miss the conversation with Chatty Cathy here."

Rison snorted, and Bruder played along and gave her a put-upon face.

She said, "Iced tea for you too?"

"Great."

Marie winked at Rison. "See what I mean?"

"Yeah, he won't shut up."

"I'll be right back with those drinks."

She walked away and Bruder said, "You see the bar?"

Rison nodded behind his menu.

"I do. Lawyer?"

"Maybe. She doesn't seem local. If she is, maybe she knows something about what our friends are up to."

"Maybe she's in on it," Rison said.

Bruder acknowledged the possibility, and also accepted the possibility she was no one of any use or interest to them. But she was an anomaly in the restaurant, and that required some attention.

Marie brought the iced teas and they both ordered the Lenburger.

"No steak?" she said.

"Ah," Rison said, "gotta have the famous burger one more time before I go."

He glanced past her toward the bar.

"Do we have another first-time burger tourist?"

Marie turned to see what he was talking about, then came back and put her hands on her hips.

"Are you cheating on me?"

Rison covered his heart with both palms.

"I would never dream of it."

"You better not, buster. But no, that's Nora. She was a few years behind me in school. And by a few, I mean plenty."

"Hm," Bruder said.

"Hm what?"

"She doesn't look that much younger than you."

"Now I know why you don't say much. You're too full of shit."

Rison laughed again and said, "Is she the mayor or something?"

"Oh, no, she lives in Minneapolis. Her folks have a big spread south of town. Well, *had* a big spread, I guess. They moved away and Nora's been coming down every weekend to handle the estate sale, what to do with the land, all of that."

Rison shared a quick look with Bruder.

Bruder said, "Her folks get tired of the winters?"

Marie paused, just long enough for that thin line to reappear on her mouth.

"I guess so. I'll get those burgers cooking for you guys, be right out."

When she was gone Rison looked at Nora, the woman at the bar, then at Bruder.

Bruder said, "Call Connelly. Tell him to get his ass down here. She's almost done with her soup."

CHAPTER EIGHT

Connelly came in the front door of Len's with the guitar case. The air inside was heavy and warm, almost too hot after the fast walk from the motel, even with the cold wind blowing in his face the whole way.

The corral was empty and he stood next to the podium, the only person standing up besides the servers, and some of the people at the tables gave him and the case speculative looks. None of the people were Romanian, like Rison had said, so he wasn't worried about it.

He spotted Marie at one of the booths with her back to him, then the woman at the bar Rison told him about, and two empty stools between her and a man slumped over whatever was in front of him. Connelly recognized his jacket and hat from the previous day, one of the regulars.

He navigated between the four-tops and nudged Marie on his way past.

"I don't want to take up a whole table. I'll use the bar."

"Of course! And I talked to Len about tonight, calling you was on my list. I'll be over there in a sec."

Connelly went past Bruder and Rison in their booth without looking at them and leaned the guitar against the bar between the two empty stools, then stood behind it like he was shielding it from the rest of the room.

The man with the beer was on his right, worrying over some scratch tickets, and the woman in the gray suit was on his left. She had shoulder-length auburn hair with subtle blonde highlights. The hair on the left side of her face hung free, the right side tucked behind a small un-pierced ear. She wore very little makeup, if any, and her skin and facial structure had the look of someone who takes pleasure in running long distances regardless of weather.

She was focused on her laptop and didn't glance over at him, then her phone vibrated and she picked it up and started stitching at it with her thumbs.

There wasn't a bartender that Connelly could see, but Marie swept around the end and started scooping ice into thick plastic cups for one of her tables.

"So Len said you're welcome to give it a shot tonight, but if people want to hear the TV, we'll have to turn it up."

"My dear," Connelly said, "after a few strums on this beauty here, and the first honey-laden notes from me, your lucky patrons will forget television ever existed."

"I'm gonna barf," Marie said. Then, to the woman in the suit: "Don't listen to a word he says. I think he might be the devil."

The woman finally looked up and considered Connelly, and he noticed her green eyes with slashes of gold.

Then shook her head and went back to her phone.

"The devil's taller."

Marie's mouth fell open, and Connelly fell in love.

***

Marie filled the cups with iced tea and told Connelly, "You probably need some cheering up after that burn. And good news: When you're playing here you get half off, starting now. You doing the burger again?"

Connelly leaned toward the half-empty bowl next to the laptop.

"How's the soup?"

He didn't ask anyone specific but wanted the woman in the gray suit to answer.

"Sufficient," she said. "I only got it because I can eat it with one hand while I work."

"Must be important work."

She made a face, dismissing the notion.

"Some people seem to think so."

Marie said, "I'll come back."

She gave Connelly a look, knowing exactly what he was up to—or the surface version of it, anyway—and carried the drinks away.

"You work around here?" Connelly asked.

She didn't look away from her laptop.

"Minneapolis."

"Oh, so you're in town for the big debut."

That landed flat for a moment, then she frowned and broke away from the screen.

"Debut?"

He nudged the guitar case with his knee.

"Oh," she said. "For sure. Because everybody in the Twin Cities knows about...uh...you."

"Adam."

It was close enough to Aiden to turn his head when someone called it out.

"Right," she said.

He stuck his hand out and she glanced at the laptop again, then finally accepted the fact that she wasn't going to get any more work done while he was standing there. She turned on her stool and shook his hand.

"Nora."

"Hello Nora. I'm Adam."

"You already said that."

"I know. You passing through?"

"I'm from here."

"Oh, born and raised? Then moved to the big city to... what? No wait, let me guess."

He narrowed his eyes and leaned back, giving her and the laptop and phone and soup a full appraisal.

She raised an eyebrow and waited, fighting a smile.

In Connelly's experience, most people wanted to know how others saw them, usually to measure how it compared to their own self-image, the one they tried to project into the world. It could be tricky—if he wanted his guess to be accurate, he risked creating discord by naming the thing they didn't want to be but were all day, to the core, no matter how they tried to hide it.

It was usually safer to be wildly inaccurate and go from there.

"Submarine captain," he said.

It caught her off guard and she laughed, a loud, short sound that she cut off immediately.

"Russian spy?"

"Okay," she said. "You caught me. Now what about you? We seem about the same age."

"That's rude."

"I mean I don't remember you from school. You're not from here."

"I'm a drifter, Nora. A bard."

"A bard."

"That's right. I travel from kingdom to kingdom, entertaining the royal courts and the plebeians alike. In return they offer me hamburgers. And soup, when it's sufficient."

"Not to be rude—again—but aren't you a little old to be playing rock star?"

"I'm actually ahead of schedule."

She blinked.

"Explain."

"I already did the corporate thing and the house thing and the long-term relationship thing, and now I'm having my midlife crisis about thirty years ahead of schedule."

This was mostly bullshit.

Nora studied him again, trying to figure it out.

"You used to be corporate?"

"Why does that surprise you?"

She just looked at him and waited for him to stop screwing around.

Connelly grinned. "Yeah, up in Seattle. Marketing, for almost ten years."

Which was true, except it was closer to ten weeks.

In his early twenties he'd made what he considered to be a half-assed attempt to go legitimate in a field that utilized his gifts and interests and gotten fired for pitching what amounted to an illegal gambling ring to one of the clients.

The firm had found this unacceptable, especially coming from someone working in the copywriting bullpen and pitching the client in the bathroom.

It had only taken Connelly one week to realize everyone in the company was either secretly or overtly miserable, and now he was trying that angle with Nora; the notion of freedom and escape to someone who felt trapped in a gray suit and shackled by a laptop.

He gave it a fifty-fifty shot.

Maybe she loved her work and felt as comfortable in the suit as other people do in pajamas.

She said, "Ten years, then you got out. And now you do this."

"And I've never been happier."

She thought about that, then said, "Huh."

"What do you mean, huh? You thinking about getting out?"

"No, oh no. I love my job."

"Because I could use a bongo player."

"Good lord, no. I love my apartment, I love the city... the idea of wandering around with no agenda gives me the hives."

"Yeah, I get it," Connelly said, with a tiny bit of pity but not enough to be condescending.

Just enough to make her want to prove something to him.

He said, "So you just go back and forth between Minneapolis and here for what, the soup? Your folks?"

"Ah, it's a whole mess," she said.

And Connelly settled in, getting down to it.

***

"I come back every weekend to handle the sale of my parents' farm," Nora said.

Connelly winced.

"Oh, man. Are they still around?"

"Arizona. Retired, I guess, but they seem busier now than they ever did here. Mostly golf and pickle ball."

"Sounds nice."

Nora moved her spoon around in the soup but didn't bring any out of the bowl.

"Yes and no. I don't think they want to be retired. I think they're trying to stay busy so they don't have to think about it."

"The farm?"

She pushed the bowl away, apparently done with it.

"Yeah, and how things ended. And how I'm not taking over the homestead like they'd hoped. And, of course, how things might be different if they'd had a boy along with me. Or instead of me."

"Whoa," Connelly said, legitimately surprised by her candor. "That's a whole other layer of drama."

"Like I said. A mess."

"You said 'how things ended'. Not to get too personal,

but was it a bank thing? Foreclosure?"

Nora shook her head.

"Nothing like that. Although the bank is being a pain in my ass right now. They won't give anybody a loan to buy it because the appraisal keeps coming back lower than the asking price. But that's a whole other thing. For my folks, some things changed around here in the past few years and they decided it was time to get out of the business altogether. Out of Iowa, even."

"What, like the government wanted them to start growing weed?"

She laughed again, softer this time, and let it run its course instead of cutting it short.

"That would actually be nice compared to reality."

"So...it's pretty bad?"

Nora ran a finger around the edge of her laptop, not touching any keys, just clearing some bits of dust and smudges.

"When you were working in Seattle, did you ever see a corporate takeover?"

"Like, hostile takeovers?"

"Sure."

Connelly pursed his lips.

"I commandeered the catered omelet bar once. That got pretty ugly."

Her mouth smiled but her eyes were focused on the middle distance, looking at something only she could see. Whatever it was, it made her sad.

Connelly said, "Let me try another guess. This time I'll get it, you watch...Okay, some corporation came in and tried to buy the farm from your folks, and they were all, Hell no, Nora's taking it over. Then you were like, I'm doing what now? Uh, no, hard pass. And they got pissed and moved to Arizona."

"Not quite," Nora said. "But it's closer than submarine captain."

"So lay it out for me. Maybe I can help."

"Do you want to buy my family farm?"

"How much?"

Connelly reached into his pocket for his wallet and came out with the key to his motel room.

He made sure she saw it, just a peek, then stuffed it back in.

"If it's more than forty bucks I probably can't afford it. But hey, I could write a song about it. Spread the word about your plight. A ballad, something about how the collapse of the nuclear family is causing fallout across the heartland."

Nora was slightly horrified.

"That's terrible. I mean, not a terrible song idea. But the idea of it is terrible."

"Such is the burden of the bard, sweet Nora. Just ask John Cougar."

"Who?"

Connelly caught movement and turned to see Rison and Bruder walking out, empty baskets and a small pile of cash on their table. They didn't look over at him.

He turned back to Nora.

"Tell me more about the farm. I want to be able to picture it."

***

Nora told him a little bit about the spread, southwest of town with enough acreage around it you couldn't really see any of the neighbors, who were also farmers.

She seemed eager to tell a stranger about it, like she could create the version she wanted and not have to worry about any cracks or stains.

"My dad dug a pond in the front yard with a backhoe and put a fountain in it, and I used to run around it and count the frogs jumping in. And there's this huge pine tree next to the house, and we'd use a bucket truck to put Christmas lights on it every year. You could see it for miles. It was obnoxious."

Connelly said, "Are you sure you want to sell this place? I mean, it sounds like a Norman Rockwell painting."

"God, yes. I'd go crazy out there by myself. And even if I leased the farmland, like I did this year, there's a ton of upkeep. My dad loved puttering around on his tractors all day but I'd get bored in about ten minutes."

Connelly ordered food and they talked more, bouncing around on topics like the live music scene in Minneapolis to how her folks liked the weather in Arizona but missed the fall colors to Ford vs. Chevy, which turned playfully contentious.

Nora kept one eye on her phone and dismissed a few incoming calls, a good sign for Connelly.

Marie was behind the bar clearing his basket and silverware, grinning at the two of them, then she glanced over Nora's shoulder at the front door and the smile vanished.

"You might want to go, sweetie."

Nora and Connelly both turned, and Connelly saw two of the same Romanians from the previous day walk past the podium and take a table near the front of the restaurant.

There was a third man with them Connelly didn't recognize, and he was absolutely certain he would have remembered him.

The man was at least six and a half feet tall, ducking his way out of the corral, and so thin Connelly could see the angles of his skull. His cheeks were hollow triangles and his eye sockets looked sucked into his head, and when he looked around at the other tables Connelly noticed the bright, burning blue eyes of someone who, at one point in time, knew real hunger.

The eyes landed on Nora and the man smiled, his lips sliding over large teeth, a few capped with silver.

Nora turned and put the laptop and phone into the messenger bag at her feet.

She told Marie, "I need to pay. Now."

"Don't worry about it. I'll get you next time."

Nora gave her a look of gratitude.

Connelly pretended to be ignorant of all of it.

"You can't stay for the show?"

"No, sorry. Maybe next time."

"Tomorrow night?"

Connelly looked at Marie for confirmation that was a possibility.

She shrugged.

"College football's on, starting at noon. Before that, even, with the pre-game stuff."

"I'll come in anyway, just in case."

He looked at Nora, who had her bag slung and was moving toward the back door.

"I'll see you then?" Connelly said.

"Maybe. Sorry, I have to go. I'm...sorry."

She went down the hallway next to the bar and the light in there changed, then went back to normal when the door closed.

Connelly asked Marie, "Was it something I said?"

"Not you, hon."

She looked past him toward the Romanians and her mouth slashed into the grim line again.

Connelly didn't turn, playing oblivious.

"She seemed scared about something."

"Yeah. She's...she's just dealing with a lot right now."

"In case I don't see her tomorrow, will you give her my number? You still have it, right?"

The smile threatened to come back, tugging at Marie's lips in a sly way.

"I do. You got a little crush on her?"

"Naw, I just wanted to ask her some more questions about Minneapolis. I might head that way from here."

"Mm-hm."

"Seriously."

She cocked an eyebrow at him, then took a deep breath and visibly steeled herself before walking around the end of the bar toward the table of Romanians.

Connelly stayed facing the bar.

He could feel the blue eyes on his back.

***

Connelly texted Bruder's current burner phone about the Romanians in Len's without mentioning Romanians or Len's.

Bruder and Rison were already at the motel, packing up, and Connelly figured it would be odd for them to come back to the restaurant just to get a look.

And sure enough, Bruder texted back: "No drama."

Meaning, don't bring any attention to yourself.

So Connelly stashed his guitar in the storage room off the kitchen and walked around town for a while, hoping to catch sight of Nora again, then watched a movie in his motel room before returning to Len's just before the dinner rush to get set up.

He had a decent set, nothing anyone would video and post online, and made a few lifetime fans when he sang Happy Birthday to a couple of twins turning six.

No Romanians came in that he noticed, and neither did Nora.

He spent the rest of the evening watching college football and chatting with patrons and staff—Marie's shift ended halfway through his set and she departed with an enthusiastic double thumbs-up—and carried his guitar back to the motel at eleven, the cold country air a nice slap in the face after the thick odors of fried food and beer.

He fell asleep wondering if he could find Nora's farm from what she'd told him so far.

He believed he could—but would she be happy if he did?

***

When Kershaw went into room one at the motel at ten o'clock on Saturday morning, the first thing he did was unlock the adjoining door.

Connelly was there, leaning on a palm against the doorframe like he'd been standing there for an hour.

"How'd you get this room?" Connelly said.

"I told the guy my lucky number is one, and I'm hoping to get a job interview on Monday. He said I could have his job if I wanted it."

"So you talked to Ed."

"That's him."

Kershaw started moving clothes from his bag into the dresser.

"Any more luck with the woman? Nora?"

"Not yet. I'm playing Len's again tonight, hopefully she'll show up."

"And the Romanians haven't flagged you?"

"Just the usual stink-eye for somebody new. One of them really leaned into it yesterday, but I think it's because I was chatting Nora up."

Kershaw paused with a stack of folded t-shirts in his hands.

"Jealousy?"

"Not the vibe I got. More like she was terrified of him, and he didn't want anybody messing with that dynamic."

"Huh."

Kershaw finished with the clothes and dropped a small leather bag next to the bathroom sink.

"You think you can sneak out to the car and get into the back seat without anybody seeing?"

"Sure. We got a mission?"

"Bruder wants me to check out some railroad overpass and bring you if I can. I looked at the satellite view, it's outside of town, nobody around. So once we're clear of here you should be able to sit up and look around."

"I wish you weren't so ashamed of our friendship."

"Get used to it," Kershaw said with a grin. "And I haven't even heard you sing yet."

CHAPTER NINE

Once they made the turn off the four-lane highway onto Pine they didn't see another person or vehicle.

They found the overpass up on the berm and the tunnel beneath—impossible to miss them—and Kershaw took some photos and videos of his own, and some requested by Connelly, things they wanted to be able to reference as the guys who'd design the explosives.

They wore Department of Transportation hard hats and Kershaw had a clipboard in case anyone asked what the hell they were doing, but nobody even drove past.

Connelly kicked along the sides of the tunnel and frowned up at the concrete ceiling, apparently strong enough to support the passage of freight trains. He crouched down and looked at the middle of the road beneath the tunnel, seeing how the charges would work.

They chucked the hard hats into the trunk and got back into the car.

Connelly said, "What do you think?"

"If this is the road, it'll work."

"I agree," Connelly said. "Especially the 'if' part."

"I have a bet with Rison. One hundred American dollars, I'll find out before you do."

Connelly was amused.

"You? You just got here. I'm practically already sleeping with two women in town."

"You and I have a vastly different definition of 'practically'."

"How are you gonna find out?"

Kershaw pulled a tight u-turn and got them pointed back toward town.

"It doesn't matter. What matters is it gets done. And that I get a hundred bucks from Rison when I get it done before you."

"You're on, buddy. Wait a minute, I'm not even in on the bet. How come I don't get any of this cash?"

"Because you're already getting all those tips from your rock shows. But man...John Cougar?"

"Ah, fuck all you guys."

**

Connelly played that night with Kershaw in the dinner audience.

Kershaw only acknowledged him once, when he broke into *Little Pink Houses*, and Kershaw looked up from his burger and fries to shake his head.

He didn't see Nora again and no Romanians showed up.

Connelly was disappointed about Nora and Kershaw was disappointed about the Romanians—he wanted to get a look at them.

Connelly coordinated with the staff at Len's to come back the following Friday and run the same schedule. He checked out of the motel on Sunday morning and took the two-hour bus ride to Sioux City, where he walked around for a while until he was absolutely sure no one was following him from the bus, then he took a cab to the Sioux Gateway airport and used the ticket Kershaw gave him to fly to Vegas.

Rison picked him up and took him to the suite, where Connelly and Bruder each had their own rooms.

After a long steam shower Connelly emerged into the common area of the suite where Rison and Bruder were going through the online property deeds for the farmland around the Iowa town.

They were focusing on the plots northwest of town, in particular the spot they'd seen through the tree line with the silos and grain elevators but were also giving attention to every public record they could find in case something caught their eye.

Connelly said, "You know, I could get used to this. Most jobs, I'm holed up in some shitty motel the whole time or sleeping in a van."

Bruder said, "Will sleeping in a van help you actually do your job?"

Connelly stopped halfway to the open balcony doors.

"Hey, I'm working on it. We got time."

"First we find out when it's happening. Then we'll know if we have time."

Connelly went onto the balcony and looked down at the Strip for a few minutes, then came back inside.

"You want me to go to Minneapolis?"

Bruder didn't look up from the laptop he and Rison were using.

"Will that make Nora happy? Or will she think you're a stalker?"

Rison did turn and look at Connelly, waiting for an answer.

Connelly said, "It would be weird. She'd shut me out."

"Then don't go," Bruder said.

"Make up your mind, man. Should I wait and go back on Friday, or should I get out of here and do something? Do we have time or not?"

Bruder sat back and explained it to him.

"If what you're doing isn't working, don't just do it faster. Change your angle. You're sure she's coming back to town on Friday?"

Connelly nodded.

"Every weekend. She's been doing it for months now. No reason to stop."

"And when the Romanians came in, she spooked."

"Big time. There was one guy, I hadn't seen him before, and he seemed to be the reason. He was bird dogging her pretty bad, staring at her with these blue eyes like butane torches. Tall dude, real skinny. As in, prison camp skinny. You guys see him when you were there?"

Bruder and Rison exchanged a look, then both shook their heads.

Bruder said, "Can you be the white knight? Without actually fighting anybody?"

"Yeah...maybe. I don't know if she needs one, though. She got freaked out, but she's tough. She has this undercurrent of farm girl, like if she had to, she'd kick her heels off and use a shotgun to put a wounded animal out of its misery."

Bruder said, "Everybody out in that world needs a white knight. Somebody to come along and wipe their biggest problem right off the board."

Connelly chewed his lip.

"She's too proud to ask for help."

"Then don't make her ask," Rison said.

"Okay. Yeah, okay. I might have to lay into somebody, but yeah, it could work."

"Try to not to do it in front of the whole restaurant," Bruder said.

"Of course. I'll also try not to get shot or stabbed."

"That's up to you," Bruder said.

***

They agreed Connelly should have a vehicle in case he needed to extract himself—and possibly Nora—in a hurry, so Bruder worked with a man he knew in Denver to get a fifteen-year-old Honda Civic with clean numbers, registered under the name of a non-existent friend Connelly was supposed to be borrowing the car from.

Connelly spent most of Thursday driving it into the northwest corner of Iowa, then chatted with Ed for a bit when he checked into room number one at the motel and slept in late on Friday.

He parked behind Len's and carried his guitar inside, where Marie actually gave him a hug and got him set up at the bar with coffee. She was an excellent hugger, pressing her whole body into it instead of just her shoulders.

Connelly took his jacket off, keeping the hooded sweatshirt he had on underneath zipped up, and spent a moment lamenting the likelihood they'd never get a chance to explore anything beyond the hug, then Marie said, "Did Nora ever call you?"

"No. You gave her my number?"

"You asked me to."

"I was kind of joking," Connelly said, acting half-embarrassed. "But she took it?"

"She laughed about it, but she took it."

"What else did she say?"

Marie put a hand on her hip.

"Are we back in middle school? If you want to know if she likes you, if she thinks you're *totally rad*, ask her yourself."

Connelly looked around the restaurant. A few farmers were at a table and some older people who looked like they'd just left church were in a booth, but that was it.

"Is she coming back today?"

Marie gave him a sly smile.

"Just like every Friday. But she also gave me this and asked me to give it to you."

She held up a business card.

"Did she now?"

Connelly reached for it and Marie pulled it away.

"What are you going to do with it?"

Connelly frowned.

"I'll probably call her."

"Probably?"

"Okay, definitely."

"And then what?"

"Marie, are you vetting me to date Nora?"

"So you want to date her? Go steady? Or just screw her?"

Connelly feigned shock.

"Marie!"

"I'm serious, buster. She is in no condition to be played around with."

"Then it's a perfect match, because I am not a player."

"That's the biggest pile of bullshit you've dropped so far. Now, I'm gonna give you this card because she asked me to. But if you mess with her—if you cause her any sort of trouble—you're done here. No more shows. No more John Cougar. Mellencamp or otherwise."

Connelly placed his left palm on the bar and raised his right.

"I assure you, my dear. My intentions are pure."

Marie raised an eyebrow and shook her head, and Connelly felt sorry for her. A woman who'd heard every line and lie and excuse possible from the sad, simple minds of men, yet knew she'd always be willing to at least listen.

She gave him the card and said, "Just make sure you invite me to the wedding."

***

When Marie walked away Connelly sent a text to the cell number from the card.

"It's Adam, the rock star from Len's. You in town?"

He drank his coffee and waited.

A few minutes later she called.

"Returning a text with a call? I'm flattered."

Nora said, "Yeah, well, I'm driving, so calm yourself. I'm about forty minutes away, you want to meet for lunch?"

"Sure. You want me to get some soup going for you?"

"No, I'm starving. It's a burger day."

"Then a burger shall be waiting for you."

"My hero. See you soon."

He put the phone down and couldn't help grinning like an idiot. The fact that someone liked him—no matter who he was pretending to be—made him feel good.

The inevitable fallout was for another day.

Ten minutes later the lunch crowd started flowing in, so he relocated to the booth Rison and Bruder had used and let Marie know about the burger baskets he'd need in another fifteen minutes. He had a hunch Nora picked up speed after their call and he wanted the food waiting when she arrived.

And if she was late, and the food was cold, she might feel bad and want to make it up to him.

When she slid into the booth it was exactly thirty-three minutes after the call.

"You made good time," Connelly said.

She smiled at him, then down at the food.

"No offense, but I'm going to talk with my mouth full."

"Do your thing."

They ate and talked a little about her job—which was in the logistics department of a massive office supply company, not a submarine captain or Russian spy—and the drive, and what kind of car she drove: a leased Lexus paid for by the company, and he eventually turned the conversation to the farm.

"So how long do you plan on making this trip every weekend? Is the end in sight?"

"God, I hope so. I mean, I love this place and the people,

the ones from here, but the drive is killing me. And just the stress of it, you know? It's like this thing hanging over my shoulder, and sometimes I'll get caught up in work or a run, or whatever, and forget about it. Then I'll go, wait a minute, what was I supposed to be worrying about? Oh yeah, that's right. And boom, it all comes back down on me."

He said, "What do you mean, 'the ones from here'? You're not a fan of wandering musicians?"

"Hm?"

"You said you love the people from here. Like there are other people, not from here, who don't deserve your adoration."

"Oh. I did?"

Connelly nodded and squinted at her.

"Nora, are you a xenophobe?"

"Oh, please. No. Stop squinting at me. No!"

She took a handful of his fries, and it worked. His suspicion became outrage.

Nora said, "I'm not a xenophobe. But I don't like assholes, no matter where they're from."

"What's that got to do with the farm?"

"It doesn't matter. Forget I said anything."

She pointed at his guitar case.

"You're playing tonight?"

"I am. Did you bring your bongos?"

She smiled, and Connelly was thinking about how to guide her back to the farm talk when the front door opened and three men came in, laughing and speaking Romanian.

***

Connelly recognized them but couldn't recall from which group.

None of them were the tall bony one with the torch eyes.

All three had wide shoulders and thick necks and big hands. They wore insulated flannel jackets and knit caps, and with the beards and neck and hand tattoos they almost looked like gym hipsters, but one look at their flat eyes—not a shred of irony or mirth in them—shattered that suspicion.

Nora followed Connelly's gaze.

Her body stiffened and her knuckles turned white around the napkin clutched in her hand.

The men saw her and did a terrible job of acting surprised. They waved and smiled, eyebrows cocked like the four of them were in on a secret, then their eyes slid to Connelly and they went back to looking like sharks.

Connelly made a mental note that somebody at Len's—and he really hoped it wasn't Marie—was telling the Romanians when Nora arrived.

He leaned forward and touched her hand.

"You okay?"

"Yeah."

She turned and looked down at her food and got busy moving things around. The ketchup bottle got nudged a few inches, then her glass of water slid where the bottle had been.

Connelly said, "Those guys friends of yours?"

"No."

"This is gonna sound like a crazy jealous guy thing, but… ex-boyfriend?"

She reared back.

"Oh, *hell* no. You think I'd…no. Ug."

She shuddered and poked more things around, taking her anxiety out on the salt and pepper shakers.

The men took a table near the front of the restaurant and sat so all three of them could watch the booth.

Connelly didn't know if they were the advance team, checking things out before more showed up—possibly the tall one, to terrorize Nora—or if these three were just there to make her jumpy.

Either way…why?

Nora had something they wanted, or knew something they didn't want her to know, and they were making a concerted effort to keep her uncomfortable.

Maybe it had something to do with the farms and the money, maybe not.

Regardless, Connelly decided to make something happen before the place got more crowded with Romanians or otherwise.

***

Connelly said, "I'm gonna hit the bathroom. You need anything?"

"From the bathroom?"

She was distracted now, thinking about something else and working hard to keep from looking over her shoulder at the three men.

She didn't want him to leave the table but didn't want to say so either.

He said, "Yeah, you want some soap? Toilet paper?"

"No. Thanks."

Connelly stood up and unzipped his sweatshirt and tossed it onto the bench, then turned and walked toward the back hallway.

After two steps he heard one of the Romanians yell, "Ey!"

Then a chair scraped back on the floor.

Connelly kept walking but looked back, naturally curious about the racket, and saw one of the men standing and pointing at him.

The other two were looking but still sitting.

The one on his feet said, "You! You Hungary?"

Connelly stopped and frowned, then looked at Nora, who was just as confused but on the verge of alarm.

Connelly said, "Me?"

"Yuh, you."

"Am I hungry?"

"The shirt, man. You like Hungary?"

Connelly looked down at the shirt he was wearing. It was dark red with some stripes on the shoulders and was made of thin, sweat-wicking jersey material. It had a brand logo on the right side of the chest and a golden crest on the left.

He looked back at the man.

"I don't get it. What's wrong with my shirt?"

He actually knew exactly what was wrong with it.

Back in Vegas, when they were brainstorming how to pick a fight with the Romanians without actually picking a fight, Rison had come up with the jersey idea. Being a professional gambler—some, including Bruder and Connelly, would call it compulsive—he'd placed bets on just about every sport at one time or another and recalled the Romanians having a soccer rivalry with somebody...

A quick internet search turned up Hungary, and it was even better than Rison remembered. The two teams and their fans shared a mutual hatred, getting into brawls with each other, cops, the military, pretty much anyone within reach of a punch or kick or thrown chair or burning shoe. Some of the games had even been played in empty stadiums in a failed attempt to curb the violence.

So when Connelly stood up and waved the Hungarian flag in front of the Romanians, he may as well have spit in their faces.

The man took a few steps toward Connelly and jabbed a finger toward him.

"You like the *Magyarok*?"

"The what? Look man, this isn't even my shirt. I mean, I got it at a Goodwill, I just like the color."

He looked down and touched the crest on the left side, the traditional Hungarian coat of arms.

"I don't even know what it means."

"It means fuck you, man."

Nora said, "Hey! Knock it off!"

The man ignored her and took another step forward.

Connelly put his hands out, open and appeasing.

"Whoa, easy buddy."

The other two men stood up and spread out behind the first, closing in and pressing Connelly toward the back hallway.

The other people in the restaurant were silent, either unable to look away from the incident or staring down at their tables.

Connelly glanced behind the bar, where Marie stood frozen with empty burger baskets in each hand.

She yelled, "He's supposed to play here tonight, Grigore!"

The Romanian in the middle—Grigore, apparently—scoffed.

Marie gave Connelly a helpless look and mouthed, "Run."

He looked at Nora, perched on the edge of the booth, looking like she was going to step out in front of the man coming up on Connelly's left flank.

"Guys! I said knock it off!"

The three men didn't even glance at her.

Connelly told Grigore, "Bro, take it easy."

What he needed was for one of them to say something to her, or make a move toward her, before he shifted from confused and easygoing to aggressive, possibly ballistic.

But they just swept right past her, closing in on him, and now he was stuck with defending himself instead of both of them, or just Nora.

It would have to do.

***

Grigore had a crooked nose, a mangled ear, and scars running through his eyebrows.

He was also smiling.

This told Connelly the man had been in fights, had gotten hurt, and he still enjoyed it.

He was going to be a handful.

As for the other two...if they were around to keep him from squirting away while he and Grigore squared off, great.

If they were around to stomp him once he was on the ground, there was a good chance he wasn't going to walk away from this without some damage.

On the bright side: Maybe Nora would feel sorry for him.

Grigore was almost within kicking range, so Connelly brought his hands up to keep Grigore's eyes high.

That part worked, but Grigore showed another sign this wasn't his first go-round when he turned his hips sideways and covered his balls with his left hand.

There went Connelly's Plan A.

The other mitt reached out toward him like a scrapyard claw, grabbing for shirt or hair or flesh.

Connelly backed up until he hit the wall just inside the hallway. The corner leading to the bar was on his right, and Grigore shuffled that way to cut off any escape.

The only way was back, out the rear exit, and if Connelly went for that he'd have more room to work in the parking lot, but so would Grigore and his comrades.

Better to get it done here—whatever *it* turned out to be—where Nora had a good view.

He pushed off the wall, straight into Grigore's outstretched hand, and let it grab the front of his shirt. Grigore responded the way Connelly wanted.

He shoved the hand forward, pushing Connelly back, and cocked his right hand back for a punch.

Connelly reversed and twisted, using the momentum to pull Grigore off balance. He also smacked his right ear with a hard open left palm and kept that hand going, driving Grigore's face into the corner of the wall.

When the face bounced back Connelly slammed the heel of his right hand into it—had to keep those guitar fingers safe—then kicked him in the balls, wide open and exposed now.

Grigore stumbled back but didn't fall. He blinked through the blood coming from his forehead and snorted more blood out of his nose, then shook his head and grinned, showing Connelly red teeth.

Fuck, Connelly thought.

Grigore brought his hands up and stepped in again, and this time the other two came with him.

***

When Nora racked the slide on the compact pistol, everybody froze.

Grigore frowned at Connelly and turned his head, and Connelly peered over his shoulder at Nora, standing there with the gun aimed at the floor somewhere in the middle of the triangle formed by the Romanians.

"I told you idiots to knock it off."

She spoke through bared teeth, her eyes slashing from Grigore to his two pals and back.

"Now turn around and get out of here."

Grigore chuckled and looked at Connelly.

"This woman, she is something."

"You heard her," Connelly said, with no idea how he should be acting right then.

The man to his right, furthest from Nora, said, "Grigore."

Grigore looked at him and the man lifted his shirt, showing the butt of a pistol stuck in his belt.

Grigore shook his head, then turned and put a row of tables between himself and Nora while he strolled toward the front of the restaurant, watching her the whole time.

"Who give you gun?"

"Shut up and keep walking."

Grigore tsked.

"Guns, very dangerous. You need to be careful."

The other two backed up to their table but didn't move

any closer to the front door.

Grigore joined them and sat down, still watching Nora.

"I told you to get out of here," she said.

"I'm hungry," Grigore said. "Not bullshit Hungary, like your friend. Hey, friend."

Connelly waited.

"I'm going to bury you in that shirt."

Nora said, "Adam, get your things."

She kept her eyes on the Romanians and the gun pointed at the floor while Connelly got his guitar case and sweatshirt and coat. He carried all of that with his left and used his right hand to dump Nora's food into his basket, which had his half-finished burger and most of his fries.

He backed toward the hallway again and told Marie, "I'll bring the basket back tonight."

She was still standing there with the two empty baskets, her eyes wide and blinking like hummingbird wings.

Connelly went along the back hallway with Nora right behind him, both of them watching their trail and listening for chairs scraping on the floor.

Connelly used his butt to open the door and they pushed out into bright sunshine and a shock of cold air.

"My car," Nora said.

Connelly followed her to the Lexus. She used her fob to pop the trunk and Connelly dumped his stuff in but kept the burger basket and carried it to the passenger seat.

Nora left ruts in the dirt when she pulled out of the spot, then another set when she turned onto the road and accelerated away from Len's.

Nothing was happening in the rear-view mirrors.

Connelly glanced down at the pistol, which was resting barrel-first in the middle console cup holder.

He looked over at her, and she looked back at him with wide eyes and pursed lips.

He said, "Holy shit, Nora."

Then he burst out laughing and she joined right in, releasing stress like air shooting out of a balloon, the adrenaline coursing and letting them know they were still alive.

CHAPTER TEN

Nora drove them out of town in the passing lane of the southbound road, whipping past other cars and big rigs until Connelly reached over and touched her hand on the steering wheel.

"I think we made our getaway."

She glanced down at the speedometer.

"Oh, shit."

She let the Lexus coast until it was at the speed limit, then set the cruise control.

"Where are we going?" Connelly said.

"I don't know. I'm just driving."

"Burger?"

He held the basket up, and she seemed to notice it for the first time.

"Oh, no. I think I might throw up, actually."

She pressed shaking fingers to her lips.

He could have told her about the blood sugar drop that came after an adrenaline dump, and how when that passed her body might want to feast on food and drink and pleasure.

But Adam the wandering bard wouldn't know all of that, so he stayed quiet and put the food between his feet.

"Take some deep breaths. If we see a gas station, let's stop and get you something to drink."

She moved her hand back to the steering wheel.

"I think I'm okay."

"Then can you please put the gun away? I think it's still loaded."

"God, yes, you're right. Here, steer for a sec."

Connelly put a hand on the wheel while Nora ejected the magazine and worked the slide to eject the round in the chamber. She pressed the round back into the top of the magazine and slid it home, then put the pistol in her bag.

"Uh, okay, Annie Oakley," Connelly said.

Nora shrugged.

"You grow up around here, you learn to shoot."

"I kinda figured that, but like…shotguns and deer rifles. What is that thing?"

"It's a Sig Sauer P365."

"Sure. Of course. Look, Nora, I know this is all happening fast and we don't know each other very well, but…"

She glanced over at him.

"Will you be my bodyguard?"

She laughed, relieved he didn't ask her to let him out of the car.

"Sorry buddy, that was a one-time deal. You didn't know what you were getting into back there, I did."

"What was I getting into?"

"They were going to hurt you. Badly."

She stared out at the road and Connelly assumed she was replaying the incident and her role in it, the decisions she'd made, what she could and should have done differently, if anything. It was keeping her from focusing on what he had done—namely splitting Grigore's face open—and that was good.

He said, "Just because of this stupid shirt?"

She nodded.

"Yeah, that stupid shirt. Well, and because of me."

"You? Why?"

She took a deep breath and told him.

***

Nora said, "You know how I asked you about corporate takeovers last weekend? And you took a guess about how that's what happened with my folks?"

"Sure. I remember everything we talked about."

She indulged him for a moment, letting him know with a look she knew what he was doing, then moved on.

"Well, that's pretty much what happened, except it wasn't a corporation. It was—still is, actually—a group of people."

"Like a co-op?"

"No. More like a gang."

Connelly leaned toward the door to get a better look at her.

"A gang? In Iowa?"

"It's…How can I explain this without sounding racist? Or maybe nationalist."

"Just go ahead. I'll assume you aren't a racist or a nationalist, and if you convince me otherwise I'll let you know."

"Okay. Fine. So when we were at Len's and you caught me talking about people from around here—God, that seems like it was days ago—and I said I'm not a xenophobe, I just don't like assholes."

"Right."

"This gang, they're Romanians. But really, they're just assholes who happen to be Romanian."

Connelly said, "So those guys back there were in the gang?"

"Yep."

"And they…what? Just go around harassing farmers and

people in Hungarian soccer jerseys?"

Nora shook her head.

"They came here five years ago and started making trouble, scaring and intimidating people, and they have a whole thing going on where they're defrauding the government but nobody wants to make it worse, so they just go along and keep their heads down."

Connelly put on an even more confused face.

"Defrauding the government? How?"

"It's this whole thing with farm subsidies. It's not worth explaining, just know they're using the people here to steal a lot of money."

"So...they're like Romanian mafia?"

"Pretty much, yes. And my parents were some of the people they scared. My dad almost shot one of them once, when they came to look around and wouldn't get off the property. They came back with more men and told my dad if he did that again, they'd set the house on fire and shoot anyone who tried to run out."

"Holy shit," Connelly said.

"I know. And that's when my folks decided to move to Arizona. Since then I've been trying to sell the farm, but nobody from around here wants to buy it and add to their troubles. The Romanians don't want anyone from outside this little kingdom they've created buying it, because that person might not understand the gravity of the situation and do something stupid, like go to the police."

"That was going to be my next question. I mean, why—"

"Why hasn't anyone reported them? Other than the whole burn-your-house-down-and-shoot-you part? Well, the local cops are in on it, more or less. They're on the payroll. I guess we could go to the state police, or the FBI, but people would still get hurt. One of the Romanians, the one in charge, he's made it clear that even if they all get arrested, there are more of them who will come here and make us all pay for it."

"Who's the one in charge?"

"He came into Len's last weekend, when we were there. That's why I had to leave."

"Wait, the skinny guy?"

Nora's mouth twisted in disgust.

"That's him. Razvan."

"He looked like Skeletor."

"He's a monster. He wants to buy the farm, in cash, and I won't let him."

"But...won't that solve it for you? Sell the farm to him, you're free and clear."

Nora shook her head.

"I already broke my parents' hearts by not taking over the farm myself. If I sold it to Razvan and his crew...I think it would kill them."

They both stared through the windshield for a while, then Connelly said, "Nora, are you even trying to sell the farm?"

She shrugged but wouldn't look at him.

"It's technically for sale. And I already told you I'm leasing the fields out in the meantime, but that's mostly because I have to pay Razvan when the time comes."

"And when is that?"

"Soon," she said, and Connelly didn't push it.

He said, "What are these Romanians going to do to you, if you don't sell your home to them?"

"Keep making threats. Keep harassing me."

"And then what?"

She shrugged again.

He said, "Is that why you're carrying the gun?"

She nodded.

***

They found a gas station a few miles later and Connelly got her a ginger ale while she filled the tank, then she got into the northbound lanes and headed back toward the town.

Connelly said, "I don't want to sound too concerned, but do you think those guys are still at Len's?"

"We aren't going there."

"We aren't?"

"No. You want to see the farm?"

"Oh, sure. Yeah. If you want to show me."

"I want you to understand why I can't just sell it to them."

"You don't have to explain yourself to me."

"I appreciate that, thank you. But I also kind of want a second opinion. Maybe I should just cave in and sell it. Maybe I'm being stubborn and stupid and ridiculous."

"You can be all of those things," Connelly said, "and still be right."

***

They had to drive all the way into town before Nora could turn left, west, then left again to work her way in a general southwest direction.

When she slowed along a straight road with fields on both sides Connelly looked at the house coming up on the right.

It was was tall and white with black shutters and a wrap-around porch with an actual porch swing hanging next to the front door.

The crushed stone driveway led past the manmade pond in the large front yard, up a gentle hill to the right side of the house and under a canopy of mature trees.

Off to the right of the driveway and about even with the house was a large weathered barn that had been painted red at one point and now looked like driftwood with red veins.

Past the trees, the driveway spread into a wide gravel lot where you could curve left behind the house or go straight.

Left led to an attached three-car garage that had been added on at some point and made to look like part of the original construction.

Straight took you into the gravel lot with two larger, newer barns made of metal along the left. The huge sliding doors along the fronts were closed.

Nora stopped the Lexus between the house and the wooden barn, under a canopy of leafless branches.

Connelly got out and looked around and pointed at a tire hanging by a rope from one of the trees.

"A porch swing *and* a tire swing? You were spoiled."

"Every time I pull in, I tell myself to cut that down so it doesn't hurt the tree. Then I take my stuff inside and forget all about it."

Connelly studied the tire.

"I'd offer to help, but that seems like a private moment."

Nora shrugged.

"I'm trying to think of everything here as assets, rather than memories."

"So forget the swing. Let the buyer decide what to do with it."

She seemed to like that idea.

"Come on. I'll show you the inside."

Connelly got the feeling she was trying to maintain the demeanor she carried in Minneapolis, but it was hard to do here at her childhood home. Her shoulders were more relaxed, her hair bounced a little more when she walked to the set of stairs leading to a side door.

He followed her up the steps and waited while she unlocked the door.

"So...I heard your parents are out of town."

She smiled.

"They are."

***

Two weeks after that, when Connelly came into the Vegas suite and said, "I know when it's happening," Bruder and Rison and Kershaw all looked up from the catalog of surveying equipment.

Connelly had been spending the weekends with Nora and getting some decent results, background and such, but nothing solid to act or plan on.

So Bruder was skeptical when he said, "When?"

"Two weeks from Wednesday."

"How do you know?"

"Nora told me she's going to be in town early, Wednesday instead of Friday, and wondered if I could meet her. I asked why, and she said the subsidy checks come on that Monday, she'll cash hers, and the Romanians will come on Wednesday morning to collect."

Bruder said, "Just hers, or everyone's?"

"She said it they make the rounds that morning."

"So everyone," Rison said. "That's the day."

Bruder looked down at the catalog.

He and Rison and Kershaw had spent their time gathering the gear—the truck, weapons, disguises, surveying tools—and he wanted a few more things to complete the facade.

If Connelly was right, they had time.

He asked, "What did you tell her?"

"Nothing yet. I just got the message when I landed."

Bruder said, "Tell her you'll be there Wednesday night."

"I think she wants me there for the pickup, in the morning. When the Romanians come to her house."

"You're going to be busy in the morning."

"Yeah. Yeah, you're right."

Bruder looked at him.

"You can keep things going with her until then?"

Connelly shrugged.

"Sure."

"And it won't be a problem when you don't show up on Wednesday night."

"What do you mean?"

Bruder glanced at Rison, then told Connelly, "After the job on Wednesday morning we're gone. You can't see or speak to her again."

"Right, I know that."

He wanted to say more, so Bruder waited.

Connelly said, "But I was thinking, if I don't show up, or call, or anything, she's going to put two and two together and realize I had something to do with the heist."

Rison said, "So? She doesn't know your real name. She knows your face, but if you stay out of the town, and maybe Minneapolis, you're fine."

"Yeah," Connelly said, like he still thought it was an option.

Bruder said, "I don't care what you do or where you go after the job, but you can't go back to her. You do that, you're putting all of us on the line. And her."

"She'll already be on the line, man. After the job the Romanians will be on the warpath. If they hear anything about me going missing, they'll ask her some hard questions. No doubt in my mind. They might do it no matter what, to her and everybody else in town."

"She has a gun," Bruder said. "And so does everybody else in town, probably. And I'm not just talking about the Romanians."

Connelly stared at him, then looked at Rison and Kershaw, who both just looked back at him.

"What the hell does that mean?"

"She's already close to being a loose end," Bruder said. "If you go back to her after the job, you make a direct connection from her to us. The Romanians or the cops get a hold of her, and then you, it makes trouble for us."

"You can't just kill her," Connelly said.

"Yes I can," Bruder said, "but I won't. If you go back to her, she becomes your problem to deal with."

"You want *me* to kill her?"

"I want you to decide, right now, that you aren't going to do something stupid that will force you to."

"Okay, fine. Just...give me a minute to process everything."

"You knew going in this was the deal," Rison said.

"Yeah, I get it. I'm just still in character, you know? I'll be fine. You don't have to worry about her."

Bruder didn't bother telling him that if it came down to it, if they gave him reason to worry, he'd clip both of them off.

Rison broke the tension by clapping his hands once.

"My boy came through."

He looked at Kershaw.

"You owe me a hundred bucks, amigo."

PART 2

CHAPTER ELEVEN

Inside the hunting trailer, Bruder pulled a can of compressed air from Kershaw's tools and used it to freeze the blood and brains Claud had left on the wall.

He looked over at Connelly, who seemed to be taking his sweet time looking for the phone he'd been using with the Nora woman.

Bruder went back to the blood and brains and thought about what to do with Claud's car. Someone would find the body, eventually, but if the Romanians came around he didn't want any obvious signs they were a man down.

Better to keep them guessing.

He used his knife to scrape the frozen bits off the wall, then the edge of his boot to shove it down the ragged drain hole in the floor.

Done with that, he said, "What's taking so long?"

"I didn't think I'd need it again," Connelly said without turning around.

It was a feeble dig, implicating Bruder and his demand that Connelly act like a professional and sever all communications with Nora.

Then Connelly straightened up with the old phone and SIM card and battery, separated but in the same plastic bag.

Bruder looked at it like it was radioactive. It went against every rule he had to still have the phone around, but Connelly and the other two convinced him it might be necessary.

Bruder had said, "If we need you to call her again for some reason, just use a clean phone."

"Oh," Connelly said, "so right after we pull the job and shit goes sideways—because I'm guessing that's the only way you'll grant me permission to call her—and I call her from a strange number. That won't seem odd?"

"Will it matter at that point?"

"It might."

"No reason to tip our hand any more than necessary," Rison had said, and Kershaw agreed.

So they'd kept the damn phone, and now Connelly reassembled the pieces and fired it up.

Rison was still in his camp chair listening to the police scanner and news, but his eyes slid back and forth between Bruder and Connelly, waiting for something to happen.

The phone made some noises.

Connelly looked at the screen and shook his head.

"Five messages. Seventeen missed calls. All of them from Nora."

"So she's still alive," Bruder said.

"Or the Romanians have her, and the messages are her screaming for help."

"We don't have time to listen to all of them. Just call and see what happens."

Connelly walked toward Bruder and the door.

"Where are you going?" Bruder said.

"I'm going outside to make the call. Is that okay?"

"I want to hear what she says. Put it on speaker."

Connelly looked at him.

"You know, you can be a real prick bastard sometimes."

Bruder just waited for him to make the call.

Rison said, "Sometimes?"

***

Connelly held the phone like a waiter holding a tray, with the speaker aimed toward the ceiling.

Nora answered after the second ring.

"Adam, where are you?"

She sounded like she'd been running.

Connelly said, "Hey, is everything okay?"

"No, I mean...I don't know. Are you coming today? Where are you? Why aren't you answering your phone?"

Bruder frowned at the phone, then nodded.

Connelly said, "Yeah, I'm on my way now. My phone was dead and I lost my charger, it's a whole thing. Why, what's up?"

"Something happened with the...you know. The rounds."

"They didn't show up this morning?"

"Oh yes, they did. They took it all. And I talked to some neighbors, they all got a visit. But now everybody is freaking out, the whole town is on lockdown."

Connelly said, "Police? Did they finally get busted?"

They heard footsteps through the speaker and more breathing.

Connelly mouthed: *She's on the porch.*

He could picture her pacing back and forth, doing laps and watching the road.

Nora said, "No, I don't think so. Nobody I talked to has seen any police. It's all the, you know. The group."

Connelly smiled. He'd told her she needed to be careful about what she said on the phone, but she was taking it to the extreme.

"The Romanians," he said.

"Shh, yes. They aren't letting anyone out of town without getting checked. They have the four roads completely blocked."

"So what happened?"

"I don't know. But you might not be able to get here."

Connelly looked at Bruder, who nodded again.

"I'm still gonna try."

"Adam, I don't know. I think something happened to the truck. The one with the money. That's the only thing that would cause this kind of trouble."

"Are they letting people into town?"

"I don't know. Shit, I just don't know. But they already don't like you, and you're from out of town. I don't know if you're safe here right now."

"I'll check it out. If it looks sketchy, I'll turn around and call you back."

"Okay. How far out are you?"

"Twenty minutes, maybe? But probably longer if I have to go through some stupid-ass Romanian checkpoint."

"Please, please be careful. And don't cause any trouble."

"Me?"

"Yes, you. And if you get too close and then turn around, they might think you're hiding something and chase you down. So if you're going to turn around, do it before they see you."

"You got it, babe."

"Okay. I love you."

Connelly looked at Bruder, whose expression didn't change.

"I love you too."

He ended the call and Bruder took the phone out of his hand before he could put it away.

"Don't smash it," Connelly said.

Bruder put the phone in his jacket pocket.

If they had to carry a live grenade around, he wanted to be the one holding the spoon down.

"Get the truck loaded," he said. "Let's go see Nora."

***

While Connelly was inside the trailer pouting and repacking his bag, Bruder opened the back of the white truck, then stopped and walked around to stare at Claud's Honda.

Rison followed, looked between him and the Honda a few times, then said, "What?"

"I'm figuring out how much of the money we can put in there and still have room for us."

Rison squinted at the Honda.

"Not all of it."

"No. But if it's enough to make us happy, we might be able to use the car to get close enough to one of the checkpoints without raising an alarm. Everybody but the driver ducks down. The Romanians see the car and wave it forward. By the time they see it's me at the wheel, it's too late. We go loud with the guns and floor it out of town."

Rison said, "Yeah, but how many guys are at this checkpoint? Do they have chase vehicles set up? We blast our way through one level but end up in a high-speed chase in this piece of shit. Does it stall out? Does it only go up to fifty?"

Bruder thought about it.

Rison said, "What if you're in this car and we're behind you in the truck? You get us close, maybe even through, then jump in the truck and we're off to the races. We won't set any records, but at least we know what the truck can do."

Bruder shook his head.

"We have to assume the truck is burned. The guys from the armored car saw it from behind, maybe even spotted the DOT logo on the side. If we roll up to a checkpoint in that thing we're in a shootout."

"Shit," Rison said. "Then let's just peel the logos off."

"I thought about that. The Romanians will still be looking for a white truck full of men. If they see us, it won't matter what's on the doors. But if we run into any locals, the DOT charade might still be helpful."

"Yeah...I can see that, I guess. So what are we gonna do with the car?"

"I don't know yet. I'll think about it while we work."

***

They put the money into the truck bed first, consolidating it into the minimal number of duffels and stacking them against the front of the bed like sandbags.

Rison said, "Fourteen million?"

Like he wanted to believe it but wasn't convinced.

"Feels like less," Connelly said.

"How would you know?"

"It just seems like fourteen million dollars would take up more space."

They looked at Bruder, who shrugged.

"Whatever it is, it won't change just because we count it."

That was unsatisfying to them, but they got back to work anyway.

The hard case with the explosives went in next, all three charges toggled on in the event they had to use the cash as a bargaining chip, and Connelly put the remotes in the middle console cupholders.

Then they started on everything from the trailer.

If any of the Romanians came after they were gone it would be obvious someone had been there, even if they swept every track and wiped every surface, but as with the Honda and blood and brains from Claud, the more questions they could leave unanswered the better.

They moved the gear out of the trailer like a bucket brigade, with Rison inside handing bags and boxes and gear to Connelly on the stairs, who carried it all to Bruder at the truck.

Connelly was standing in the doorway, waiting for the next

load, when he said, "How are we gonna get to her place?"

"Carefully," Bruder said.

"We have to cross the main road going east-west."

That didn't require any sort of response, so Bruder just waited by the truck.

Connelly said, "If we get spotted, they'll come after us. I heard you guys talking about the truck being burned."

He still hadn't said anything new, but he seemed to require some sort of confirmation.

Bruder shrugged.

"You want me to go back in time and kill the guys at the bridge?"

"That's not what I'm talking about. If they come after us, we can't go to Nora's. We can't lead them to her."

"Why not?"

"Because they can't know she has anything to do with this."

"She doesn't."

"You know what I mean."

Rison appeared in the doorway with a stack of three cardboard flats full of soup.

He said, "Yeah, we know," and handed the soup to Connelly.

Connelly carried the load down the steps and handed it to Bruder, who slid the flats into the covered bed and followed them in to find the best spot.

Connelly stood at the tailgate. "Well?"

"Well what?"

"What are we gonna do if they spot us?"

"Whatever we have to."

"That's not an answer."

Bruder climbed out of the bed and looked at Connelly.

"Yes it is. What are you really asking?"

Connelly frowned.

"I'm asking what the goddam plan is."

"But it's not what you want to ask."

They looked at each other, then Rison showed up in the doorway with another stack of flats in his arms.

"Hey."

Nobody looked at him, so he dropped the stack at the top of the stairs and went back for another load.

Connelly finally asked Bruder, "Do we have to go to Nora's place?"

"That's it," Bruder said. "And the answer is yes."

"Why?"

"She said why on the call. She's in the loop. She can give us real-time information about what's going on in the town."

"So you're going to talk to her?"

"No. You are."

Connelly trudged over to the steps, slid the flats out of the doorway and carried them to Bruder.

"And what, you guys are just gonna wait in the truck?"

"You said the barn has some space in it."

"The barn? The old one?"

"You said they'd moved all the equipment into the new ones years ago. We're going to put the truck in the barn and stay there while you talk to Nora. Find out how we can get out of town."

"I can do that over the phone."

"No."

Connelly waited, then said, "No? That's it?"

Bruder shrugged.

Connelly said, "I'm gonna need more than that, man. I know you're in charge and all, but if there's any sort of method to this madness, even if it's half-assed, I need to know."

"We can't stay here, so we're going there."

"Why can't we stay here? Wasn't that the whole point of setting this trailer up? So we can lay low for as long as we have to, let everything settle down?"

"That was assuming the trouble would eventually settle

down. That was stupid on our part. We should have known better after seeing how the Romanians operate. The longer they go without finding the money, the worse it's going to get around here. We have to move."

Connelly pointed under the trailer in the general vicinity of Claud's corpse.

"That asshole's dead, and nobody knows where he is. If anybody else comes looking, Kershaw will let us know. I'll call Nora and tell her I can't get into town, and she can keep me updated on what's happening, thinking it's to help me get to her. But we'll use the info to get out of town instead."

He spread his hands out: *Viola!*

"No," Bruder said.

Connelly waited, clenching his jaw.

"Come on, dude."

Bruder said, "What if the next people who come looking have ten vehicles with six guys in each one, with rifles and grenades? Where do we go? Into the woods, leaving the money here?"

"There's always more money, man."

"Not if we're dead. I'm telling you, if we stay here, we're trapped. We'll lose the money and get killed. And if your face is still recognizable, guess who they'll go see next?"

Connelly didn't say anything, but he knew the truth.

"We have to move," Bruder said again.

"And it has to be Nora's?"

"I already answered that," Bruder said. "Go get the soup."

CHAPTER TWELVE

Bruder keyed his radio and told Kershaw, "We're coming to you."

Rison led the way with the truck, Connelly in the passenger seat. The truck bed was packed and had the surveying gear closest to the tailgate, good enough for any cursory examination, but they all knew if it came to that, the guns were probably coming out.

Bruder followed in Claud's car with the windows down, choosing the cold air over the stale smoke and fast food smells. He had the AR barrel-down in the passenger footwell, ready to lift up and point through the passenger window or windshield if need be.

The vehicles stopped before the last curve and Bruder used the radio to ask Kershaw, "Clear?"

"Clear."

The truck rolled around the curve and Bruder followed.

He saw Kershaw standing by the post with the chain in his hand, watching the road.

The vehicles turned right on the road and braked, exhaust coughing and drifting into the cold ditch.

Kershaw reconnected the chain and swept the tire tracks with another branch, then walked backwards to the road while erasing his own tracks and tossed the branch into the woods.

He stopped at Bruder's window and peeled off the camouflage parka, eyeballing the Honda.

"What are we doing with this thing?"

"Looking for a lake to drop it in."

"Not around here, pal."

"Then we'll find something else," Bruder said. "If we see any Romanians, let me pull around front."

Kershaw was skeptical, but said, "Okay."

He got in the back seat of the truck and they moved out.

***

They drove the mile south and turned left, eastbound, without seeing anyone on the road or otherwise.

Everyone was either at work or hunkered down or in town, probably just as confused as Nora had sounded on the phone.

A quarter of a mile after the turn Bruder's radio clicked.

Rison said, "Incoming. Truck, I think."

Bruder eased across the centerline and saw it, just a boxy shape between the fields so far.

He said, "I'm coming around."

"No, wait there," Rison said. "It's one truck, one guy. Connelly just checked him through the optics. If he's a farmer, we'll just cruise past. If he's not, we'll nail him before he can call anybody."

"He might be calling somebody right now," Bruder said.

That made the truck pull ahead, and Bruder pushed the Honda to keep up.

Rison said, "Ah, shit. He's flashing his lights."

Bruder saw it, then an arm came out the driver's window and patted the air, wanting the truck to slow down.

"What's the call?" Rison said.

"Stop the truck. Let him come to us. We can't let him get behind us without knowing who he is."

Connelly said, "I'm gonna lock my radio open so you can hear."

"Good. If I need to go loud, turn on the right blinker."

"Yep," Rison said.

The brake lights flared and Bruder angled to the right, keeping the car somewhat hidden behind the DOT truck. If whoever was in the other truck hadn't seen him so far, there was a chance he could stay in the blind spot, get out, and come around the truck with the AR before anything else happened.

Rison stopped the truck in the eastbound lane, leaving plenty of room for Bruder to pull onto the shoulder and tuck in near the back right fender while the other truck coasted to a stop.

Bruder left the Honda running, got out with the AR and stood next to the truck's rear passenger tire and listened.

A man said, "Morning!"

Bruder could hear the voice coming around the truck and through the radio. It was hard to tell from one word and without seeing him, but he sounded local and middle-aged.

"Morning," Rison said.

"You boys lost?"

"Well, maybe. We got a little mixed up out here, we're trying to get to 75 but hit some traffic around town, some kind of accident or something?"

"Ha! Yeah, something like that."

He sounded antsy, a little too loud.

Rison said, "We tried to loop around town, but all these roads seem to bring us right back in."

"Yep. That's the way they are. We figure whoever made these roads back in the day had one leg shorter than the other, kept walking around in circles."

Everyone in the truck laughed.

The man said, "You can get through town, eventually, you just need to be patient. But, ah, I don't want to get into anybody else's business, and to tell you the truth I'm nervous as hell right now."

Rison said, "Nervous? Why?"

"Well, word has it the fellas causing the traffic jam are looking for a white truck with some other fellas in it. And I see that Honda back there behind you—I haven't heard anything about that, but again, I don't want to get into anybody's business."

He was talking fast now, trying to get the words out before something bad happened to him.

"But if I was to come across that truck, I'd tell the boys inside to be careful. I don't have any respect for those men in town, and I'd like to see them get what's coming. But there's a reward out for anybody in town who sees the truck and calls it in, and some people might be willing to make that call."

"Is that right?" Rison said.

"But I'm not one of them, sir, and I haven't seen anything."

There was a moment of tense silence.

Bruder watched the right blinker, still dark.

So far.

He checked the road.

No other traffic.

So far.

Then Connelly said, "Out of curiosity, what's the reward?"

"One thousand dollars."

Connelly scoffed.

Rison said, "If you did happen to see this truck, how would you recommend it get out of town?"

"You can't. I mean, it can't. I wish I had a better answer for you bud, but it's a no-go. They got the four main roads blocked. They even got some of the cops helping, which nobody likes. Our tax dollars at work, right? But everything else, like you said, it just winds around and ends up back in town somewhere."

"Huh," Rison said. "Well, if we see that truck we'll let them know."

"Okay, yeah. Okay then."

"Hey, just to be safe, why don't you hand over your phone."

"My phone?"

"Just in case you change your mind once we're out of sight."

Rison wasn't bothering with the facade anymore.

"That won't happen, sir. I guarantee it."

"Still. It would make me and the other guys feel better. Relaxed. We don't want to cause you folks any more trouble than you've already seen."

"Yeah, okay. It's just…I got a lot of important stuff on here."

"Tell you what," Connelly said. "The next intersection we come too, I'll put it on the side of the road, in the grass. You come by in a couple hours and grab it."

Bruder didn't like the compromise, but he understood it.

The alternatives were to destroy the phone and piss off the farmer and possibly push him into making the call from somewhere else or kill him and leave even more of a trail.

They already had to get rid of the Honda.

Another truck and body would just add to the hassle.

The farmer said, "Which ditch?"

"Right outside my window," Connelly said. "So, let's see…the southwest ditch at the intersection."

The farmer thought about it and Bruder's finger crept toward the trigger.

It didn't matter how much of a hassle another body would be, they were taking too much time sitting out here in the open.

If the Romanians came now, a hassle would be welcome.

Then the farmer said, "Okay, that seems fair."

After a moment Connelly's arm came out of the passenger window with the phone in his hand. He gave a thumbs-up.

Bruder stepped back to the Honda and got in.

Rison said, "You got a CB radio in there or anything?"

"No sir, you can tell by my antennas. I just got the radio, the music one. That's it."

"Okay. Hey, thanks for the heads-up about what's happening in town."

"You're very welcome. Like I said, I got no respect for that group. Nobody knows what got them all stirred up, but we all know it's collection day, so I'm guessing it has something to do with that."

Nobody in the truck said anything.

"Okay then," the farmer said with a nervous laugh. "Best of luck to you."

He pulled forward and glanced over at Bruder in the Honda. They locked eyes, then the farmer immediately looked away and stared straight ahead, as if to let Bruder know he hadn't seen him and was too busy minding his own business to do anything else.

The white truck pulled forward and Bruder followed it, watching the farmer in his mirrors.

***

After another quarter mile Bruder hit the radio.

"Stop."

They pulled onto the shoulder and Bruder got out and went to talk to them without the radio.

"We can't do that again. Too risky being separated like that. We need to dump this car."

"Just leave it here," Connelly said. "We're far enough from the trailer, aren't we?"

"Maybe," Bruder said, looking around.

Kershaw said, "What if we torch it? Get a nice plume of smoke going, bring the Romanians to it."

Bruder shook his head.

"If they act fast, we'll get trapped between them and the fire. Run right into them."

He pointed east along the road, to a field full of something tan on the north side.

"Is that corn?"

Kershaw leaned out the window and used the optics on his AR to check.

"Looks like it. Feed corn that hasn't been harvested."

"Why not?"

Nobody said anything, then Rison said, "I bet that farmer knows."

Bruder said, "Let's go."

He took the lead and pushed the Honda as fast as it would go for the half mile to the field, then coasted while he scanned the side of the road. There was a drainage ditch running parallel to the asphalt, shallow but deep enough to bottom-out the Honda.

Then he saw it.

An access point from the road to the field, just a narrow strip of dirt and gravel and scrubby grass with a culvert running underneath it to keep water flowing in the ditch.

He took the Honda across, then turned left and drove parallel to the road back the way they'd come, bumping over tractor tread ruts and clumps of dirt toward the corner of the field.

Out his passenger window the corn was higher than the car's roof. Dry, tan leaves as big as his arm occasionally slapped the windshield and rustled along the side.

Rison kept pace on the road in reverse, a small, amused smile on his face from watching Bruder jounce around in the car.

When he got to the corner of the field Bruder turned right, willing the car to keep going when the grass got taller. No one had bothered to mow here, which was good for hiding but bad for foreign cars with no ground clearance.

The car was working hard though, and Bruder kept it going until he knew he was pushing his luck. Then he cranked the wheel hard to the right and pressed the accelerator, bulling his way into the feed corn.

Stalks scraped along the doors and undercarriage and cobs thumped against the hood, like he was driving through an automatic carwash made of corn, and after ten seconds Rison came through the radio.

"You're good, we can't see a thing."

Bruder stopped and killed the engine, waiting to see if anything pressed against the exhaust under the car was going to catch fire right away.

He didn't smell any smoke or hear anything crackling, so he grabbed the AR and followed his path of destruction to the edge of the field and looked at the road, then at the hole he'd made.

The angle wasn't great.

Anyone coming eastbound would be able to see the path into the corn, but maybe it was a common thing. Kids messing around, farmers checking on...whatever they checked on.

It didn't matter now, because the car was staying there.

Bruder walked to the road and got into the back seat of the truck with Kershaw.

They had three ARs in the back—Rison's along with Bruder's and Kershaw's—Connelly had his in his lap again now that the farmer was gone, and Rison had a Glock 19 stuck in the inside handle of the door.

Bruder reached into the front seat and pulled the three remotes for the remaining explosives out of the middle console.

"The charges are armed?"

Connelly nodded.

"Charges are armed, remotes are off. Let's keep it that way, huh?"

Bruder handed him one of the remotes, gave the second to Kershaw, and tucked the last one into his coat pocket.

Rison got the truck rolling and said, "You know, I don't think I've ever heard of a crew using the money as a hostage. But hell, if we get in a standoff with these guys, it might be the only play we got."

"Unless they want to kill us more than they want the cash," Connelly said.

"Fourteen million dollars? You're not that big of an asshole."

Kershaw said, "You didn't hear him play *Little Pink Houses*."

Bruder let the chatter go.

He preferred silence in moments like this, when everything could go to hell in a heartbeat, but some guys needed to keep talking, using it like a reminder they were still alive.

He ignored the banter and watched the road, front and back, with his finger relaxed on the trigger guard.

***

The road dead-ended into another going north and south, and when they stopped Connelly got out and set the farmer's phone in a nest of grass and covered it enough so it wouldn't stand out, but wouldn't be impossible to find either.

He got back into the truck and Rison turned south onto the road that would take them three miles before ending in a T intersection just west of the main crossroads in town.

Connelly said, "When you get to the road, turn right if you can."

"I know," Rison said.

"That's the fastest way to Nora's from here."

"Okay."

"Unless we can see a checkpoint off that way, to the west. If that happens, turn left. Then a quick right, the first road you see. That's gonna be Dolan Street."

"Yep."

Rison's knuckles were white on the steering wheel.

Connelly was talking around what everyone knew: If things turned bad, it was likely to happen while they tried to get across the main east-west road.

Four lanes, totally exposed, with backed-up traffic and flat lines of sight for miles.

They'd all agreed, if the Romanians had a block set up to the west, they probably wouldn't have another one until the crossroads in the middle of town.

Rison's job was to get across the highway as quickly as possible, whether that meant going right or left before diving south again and getting off the four-lane shooting gallery.

No other vehicles were on their road, which Bruder found good and bad.

Good, because they didn't have to worry about more farmers or Romanian patrols.

Bad, because the only moving vehicle would attract more attention.

Especially if the Romanians had mandated some sort of no-fly zone or curfew, and everyone else in town was hunkered down.

The three miles went by fast, and they all watched the main road pull closer.

The houses and blocks on both sides of their road blocked the east-west corridor except for a narrow window, straight ahead, and nothing moved across the gap.

Then, when they were a quarter-mile away, a big rig pulling a livestock trailer idled left to right.

"Okay," Connelly said. "He just came from the crossroads, and he's in no hurry. So they got something set up to the west, right?"

"Makes sense," Rison said. He braced an elbow on the console and pushed himself up, then dropped back down, getting set for whatever he needed to do.

"So plan on going left."

"I know, I know."

Bruder watched the road ahead.

When they got to the residential blocks, he checked driveways and garages out the passenger side and Kershaw did the same on the drivers.

If the Romanians had a blocking team staged out here, watching and ready to close off the road behind the truck, that team would be the ones first to die.

"Another truck," Rison said.

Bruder glanced through the windshield and saw another rig creeping left to right.

Then a car drove right to left, in the far lanes, going a little faster than the truck but still looking like it was in no hurry, prepared to stop once it got to the crossroads.

"Left then right," Connelly said. "Left then right. Dolan."

Rison said, "Shut up, I got it."

They came to the road and stopped.

Bruder saw the western checkpoint off to the right, maybe a half-mile away.

It looked like a pickup truck and a police car parked nose-to-nose, blocking both lanes. Then the police car backed up to let a vehicle through before closing the lane off again.

Rison said, "Oh, shit."

Bruder glanced at him, then followed his attention toward the crossroads, four blocks to the east.

The van they'd watched pull into the intersection was still there. They could see at least two men walking around, checking the vehicles as they approached and stopped.

Rison said, "Check the rooftops."

They all bent down to look up and saw two more men standing on top of the buildings at opposite corners.

"I see long guns," Kershaw said. "And binoculars."

"Shit," Rison repeated.

Connelly said, "They must be turning people away further

out of town. There should be a lot more incoming traffic backed up."

"Just the rigs," Bruder said. "They're just letting the rigs through. Any cars or trucks we see, they must be local."

"We can't sit here any longer," Rison said. "They're gonna spot us."

Connelly pointed on a diagonal to the left.

"Left then right," Connelly said. "Scoot across and make that first turn. Dolan, right there."

"Right, I'll just scoot across...no big deal. You guys ready?"

"Go," Bruder said, "but easy. Don't let the truck off its leash yet. Windows down."

They got the windows down and Rison blew out a slow breath as he pulled onto the four lanes and turned toward the crossroads.

He recited to himself, "Easy. Easy. Easy."

Another big rig passed on their left.

It would have been nice to have one right in front of them, a lead blocker, but there wasn't.

Rison feathered the gas along the block and drifted into the far right lane.

Bruder could hear men shouting, but it sounded like communication and orders given in a semi-loud environment, not alarms.

"Okay," Rison said. "Okay, here we go."

He eased the wheel to the right, rolling into the turn to get them onto Dolan and off the runway.

Halfway through the turn one of the shouts got louder, more urgent, then something thumped into the driver's side of the truck.

The rifle crack followed a split second later.

"Go," Bruder said, and Rison floored it.

PART 3

PART B

CHAPTER THIRTEEN

When the explosives knocked the wheels off the armored truck, Razvan was a few miles away at the compound eating sausage and toast.

The place was actually a farm, foreclosed and purchased in cash five years prior, but Razvan refused to call it that and wouldn't allow anyone else in his crew to utter the word.

He'd grown up on a damn farm in Lehliu Gară and nearly starved to death when their land got flooded because some committee decided to build a dam in a place he'd never heard of, across the border in Bulgaria, so what was the point of busting his ass to come to this country and work his way up in Chicago, then find and leverage this little corner of Iowa, just to live on another farm?

So, no.

It was a compound.

He was starting in on his third piece of sausage when the cellphone rang.

He took his time wiping his hands and face before reaching for it.

His family and close friends called him the Groapă, which

meant pit, hollow, and sometimes grave. His metabolism had never recovered from the time back home when he'd almost died, and since then he could eat all day and not feel full or gain a pound.

It was like dumping food into a pit, a groapă.

He checked the screen and saw it was Benj calling.

"Yes."

"Raz, there is a problem."

***

Benj said, "I haven't seen the truck yet."

Razvan checked his watch.

The truck should have passed Benj's spot four minutes ago.

"Did you call Pavel?"

"Yes, no answer."

"Go look for him. Call me back."

Razvan ended the call.

Benj was on the side of the highway where Pine ran into the four lanes, waiting for the money truck. When it arrived, he and some of the other vehicles staged further along the route would follow it out of town and keep an eye on things until the crew from Chicago took over the babysitting duties in Dubuque.

But apparently the truck hadn't arrived yet.

Four minutes...

Pavel and Costel knew to call if there was any trouble or delay, even it was just thumping into a deer and they had to get out to wipe the truck off.

So four minutes was too long.

Razvan wasn't worried about any of the farmers or other locals when it came to the money.

They knew better than to mess with it, which would mean messing with him and his men.

Not possible.

When he'd first arrived in the town it had taken some work—first the bribes for the right officials, then a few burned barns and houses, a few vanished people, some others left where they could be found—before the locals realized the new reality.

And when they did, the chance of them causing any trouble had dropped to zero.

But the old Italians in Kansas City weren't too happy about Razvan being in Iowa, and they'd made some quiet threats about going north to do some hunting.

They didn't know anything about the farming subsidies scam Razvan had going—they thought it was just a group of Romanian thugs picking on some hillbillies—and Razvan knew it was only a matter of time before someone somewhere said the wrong thing, and the Italians would come looking for a cut.

Was that time now?

He shook his head and thumped bony knuckles into his temple, a mild punishment for getting too comfortable.

Five years he'd been pulling this off without a problem, and that success should have made him more wary instead of less.

He should have had Benj follow the truck from the compound rather than sit and watch the intersection for any trouble.

Luca and Claudiu were at the main crossroads—he should have brought them up to Benj's spot.

But he only had so many men, and the stretch of Pine between the compound's road and the highway was a ghost town. Any sort of ambush or attack would be visible for at least a mile.

Had Pavel and Costel done something stupid?

No.

Also not possible.

Their families were all from the same village, they were

basically brothers.

And Pavel and Costel knew what would happen to their families back home if they stole from Razvan.

He thumped his head again.

The first two years he'd been inside the money truck all the way to Chicago with his men spread in front and behind like a parade, but nothing happened and it was a waste of time and manpower, so now he used the phones and waypoints and sent the rest of the men around town to make sure the locals weren't too upset about the whole thing.

This sometimes, meant gifts, or extra muscle to help move some bales of this or that, or extra muscle to hold someone's head underwater until they stopped being upset.

He picked the phone up and started calling them to tell them to get their asses into town.

If this was a false alarm, no problem.

They could just go back to whatever they'd been doing.

But if it wasn't—if something happened to his money—his killers would go to work.

***

When Benj called two minutes later Razvan was already in his truck, speeding down the compound road toward the right turn onto Pine, northwest of the railroad tunnel.

Benj yelled, "Pavel and Costel, they're tied up! The truck is destroyed, the wheels are gone. Well, they're here, but not on the truck anymore."

"The money," Razvan said, bringing Benj around to the only thing that mattered.

"Gone. It's all gone. I passed a white truck on my way here, the only vehicle on the road. It must have been them."

"White truck?"

"Yes, full of men."

Razvan hung up on him and called Luca.

"Raz, what's going on? Is the truck delayed?"

"It's been robbed."

"What!"

"Listen: Have you seen a white truck go through town?"

"A white truck? I don't...hold on."

Razvan heard him talking to Claudiu in the background.

"We don't think so. I mean, maybe, but not one that stood out. Is that who took the money? Are Pavel and Costel okay?"

"I don't know. Shut the roads down. Check everyone who comes through. If it's a white truck full of men, show them guns and get them out of the truck."

"Okay, sure. You'll tell the police it's okay?"

"Don't worry about the police."

***

Razvan stopped on the northwest side of the tunnel and slashed his way through the tarp.

It was dark in the tunnel, nearly pitch black, but Benj had a flashlight on the ground next to his feet. He was crouched in front of Pavel and Costel, sitting with their backs against the concrete wall.

Razvan snatched the flashlight up and pointed it into the back of the truck.

Empty, like Benj had said.

He looked at the doors and saw the shear marks from the explosives, then stabbed the beam at Pavel and Costel.

They blinked in the light and held their hands up, but Razvan could still see their faces, a mixture of anger, embarrassment, and shame.

They hadn't done this.

"Meet me on the other side," Razvan said.

He threw the flashlight at Benj and went back out to his truck, a Ford F-250, and drove it up the slope on the right side of the tunnel. He bumped over the train tracks and went down the other side, keeping the truck straight so it wouldn't roll, and stopped next to Benj's Tacoma.

The three men were standing there, waiting.

Pavel and Costel looked dazed and grimy from whatever they'd been through, but that was their problem.

Razvan said, "Pavel, get in with me. Tell me what happened. Costel, ride with Benj and tell him."

Everyone started moving, and Razvan watched the two men for any glances of anxiety or agreement.

He'd grill Benj about it later, and if the stories didn't match up, he'd have to revisit his decision about their involvement. Maybe with a blowtorch.

But they didn't seem concerned about being split up, and Pavel told the story while Razvan pushed the truck to its top speed all the way to the main crossroads, slowing down once, just enough to make the turn from Pine.

White truck.

Four men.

And if Luca and Claudiu were right, these men were still here, somewhere.

***

Razvan parked in the middle of the crossroads and ignored the cars and trucks backed up in all four directions while he got out and walked to Luca and Claudiu.

Luca was big-boned with dark hair all over his head and face and small black eyes.

Claudiu looked like a slob, but his stooped shoulders and bored expression hid the brute strength and tenacity of a true sadist.

Razvan towered over the two men like a sentinel pine—albeit a narrow one—next to two shrubs. He wanted the people in the vehicles to see him so they would know things were being sorted out and dealt with, and so they wouldn't open their mouths to complain.

Luca said, "We've been talking, and the white truck has

not passed through here. Everyone we've seen since the money left the compound has been someone we recognize, or a rig."

Now Razvan scanned the windshields while he listened. Local, familiar faces were on the other side of most of them, and none of those eyes met his.

They knew the drill.

Some of the big rigs had strangers at the wheel, but those men pulled loads of livestock and grain and manure, and they showed the patience of veteran haulers, accustomed to stopping for no apparent reason.

No one touched a horn.

Claudiu glanced at Razvan's truck with Pavel inside, then Benj's truck with Costel in the passenger seat.

"No one got hurt, eh?"

"I don't think they did this," Razvan said, quelling any ideas Claudiu might have about interrogations.

"But did they put up a fight?"

"Pavel said it happened too fast. The thieves disabled the truck. Pavel and Costel had to decide: Stay in the truck with the money and wait for reinforcements or get out and try to fight with pistols against automatic rifles."

Luca said, "Four men with machine guns?"

Razvan nodded.

"That's what they tell me. While they were deciding what to do, the thieves blew the back doors open. The details are limited after that. But they remember the white truck, and Benj passed it on his way to the tunnel. He saw it turn toward town."

"It didn't come through here," Luca said again.

Razvan turned to look west along the four lanes.

"So they are over there, somewhere. North or south of the highway. Driving around or hiding."

He told Claudiu, "Get your car, take the north side. Make calls, check with our contacts. Someone has seen them.

And these men, they've scouted us. So they know the area, but not as well as us. Check the dead spots first, where they think no one will go."

Claudiu didn't seem thrilled about it, like this errand was taking him out of the action. He spat on the pavement on the way to his car and didn't say anything to Pavel when he passed Razvan's truck.

Razvan waved Benj over and told him, "Put Costel in my truck, then check the south quadrant."

He gave him the same directives as Claudiu, but Benj accepted the mission with enthusiasm and made sure Pavel and Costel both had bottles of water before he sped off and turned south into the side streets.

Then Razvan called Grigore and Mihail, who were stuck out on the highway east of town in separate vehicles, where they'd been waiting for the money truck to pass. They knew the situation and were slowly working to get past all the backed-up vehicles.

Razvan told Grigore, "Come through the northeastern quadrant, just to be sure. They may have slipped through the neighborhoods."

"If they are there, we'll find them," Grigore said, and hung up.

Razvan was dialing a number in Chicago when Luca said, "Police."

Razvan put the phone away and watched Sheriff Wern's truck coming from the south, driving in the middle of the empty south-bound lanes with his flashers on but no siren.

The sheriff, who was reasonably tall but soft and fat around the waist, stopped next to Razvan and stayed in his truck, like he didn't want to be seen standing next to the Romanian.

Razvan stepped close to the door, forcing the Sheriff to duck down and twist his head up.

"Good morning, Sheriff."

"Razvan."

He pronounced it with no grace: *Razz-Van*.

"Mind telling me what's going on here?"

"We're looking for something."

Wern nodded.

"I kinda figured that. Your armored truck is blocking the road under the tracks."

"Nobody needs that road but us."

Wern grimaced and looked past Razvan at nothing in particular.

"Well, that's not necessarily true."

"It is today," Razvan said.

"You can't just stop the traffic like this."

"There's been an accident. Or road work. Or a high school car wash. Traffic will adjust. And you need to tell the people in town to stay at home. Or at work, wherever they are. Stay put."

Wern looked up at him again. The angle made the fat rolls around his neck gleam in the morning sunshine.

"What, like a curfew?"

Razvan shrugged.

"If that means they stay where they are. No cars moving on the side streets, they'll only get in the way."

Wern shook his head and sighed while he looked at the mess piling up around him.

Razvan didn't care. If you accept the money, you have to earn it at some point.

Wern said, "Are you going to let anyone through here?"

"Eventually, yes. Luca here is going to check the drivers. When others arrive, they will help. Tell your men to do the same."

Wern shook his head.

"Not everybody—"

"The ones I pay. For the rest of them, whether I pay them or not, tell them if they locate the white truck I'm looking for, and the men inside it, I will reward them."

"White truck," Wern said.

Razvan nodded.

"And the men inside it."

"Do you know these men?" Wern asked.

"Not yet," Razvan said.

***

When the Sheriff drove away Razvan took his phone back out and called Chicago.

The number rang inside a blank brick building on Halstead Street and was picked up on the second ring.

An ancient male voice spoke in Romanian.

"Yes?"

Razvan also used Romanian, since the man on the other end was bad with English and the translation created one more step for anyone else who might be listening.

"It's me. The truck is down. The delivery was stolen."

The phone was silent.

Then: "By who?"

"I'm working on that part."

"This is a large delivery, my friend."

"Yes, I know."

The old man said, "Many people are expecting it. Here, and back home."

"Yes."

"You will get it back."

"As I said. I'm working on it."

"I'm sending more men."

Razvan had expected this.

"It's not necessary, I have enough."

Which wasn't true—he needed more men—but the men from Chicago would have two jobs: Help Razvan and his crew find out who stole the money and how; and if that didn't work, find out if Razvan and his crew had anything to do with it before executing them and burying them in a cornfield, then taking over the work in Iowa.

"It's done," the old man said. "It won't be the babysitters expecting you in Dubuque. They'll drive, so expect them in seven or eight hours. If you resolve this before then, if you get the delivery back, just sit tight and wait for them. They will have some questions. Then they will bring the delivery to me."

"And if I find the people responsible?"

The old man chuckled, which turned into a wet cough.

Razvan waited until it was done.

The old man said, "As I told you, the men from here will have some questions. Who they ask...now, that is up to you."

***

The sun stayed closer to the Iowa horizon this time of year, and Razvan watched it creep near its apex at about the same speed as the traffic going through the crossroads.

The cars going north and west got waved through at a faster clip—there was almost zero chance the men in the white truck had somehow gotten south or east of town, and absolutely no chance they would come back through the crossroads if they had another option.

Razvan checked his watch again.

Two hours.

Two hours of him and Benj and Luca and Costel checking cars and trucks at the intersection, with Claudiu, Grigore, Pavel and Mihail scouring the neighborhoods and homesteads and fields and two-tracks.

There were some false alarms—apparently there was more than one white truck in the world—but so far the only real result was a snarl of traffic around town and a group of savages from Chicago getting two hours closer.

Yes, Razvan needed more men, but not those men.

He seethed when he sent the update to his crew via text, knowing they would see the message and look at each other, maybe even wonder out loud if he couldn't handle what was happening.

Of course he could handle it.

But first...just what the hell was happening?

He needed to know within six hours.

It was almost eleven o'clock, time for the next round of twenty-minute check-ins.

He called Grigore first and got the same answer he'd been getting all morning: "Nothing yet."

Grigore and Pavel were now in the southwestern quadrant, having swept the northeastern part of town with no results.

Razvan said, "How is Pavel?"

"Angry."

"Good."

"But his eyes are still glassy from the explosion. He needs to lay down for a while, I think. Drink some tea."

"He can sleep in the truck."

Razvan hung up and called Mihail, who'd set up a checkpoint west of town, out on the four-lane highway past Pine. He was working with one of the sheriff's men to check the vehicles coming from town. The white truck might try to slip out that way from the side streets, but Razvan doubted it.

He figured the thieves had found a place to hide and were waiting for things to die down.

They might even be getting updates from someone local, which irked Razvan.

Not the betrayal aspect—just the idea of someone not being afraid of what he would do when he found out.

Mihail answered.

"No sign of them."

"Be ready. They might not wait in line. They might just try to smash their way through along the shoulder or median."

"Right. We're ready."

Razvan knew Mihail had an M249 light machine gun in the passenger seat of his truck.

"What does the cop have?"

Mihail said something away from the phone, then came back.

"He says he has a shotgun and a semi-automatic rifle. I'm guessing it's an AR-15. He—hold on. Hah?"

Razvan heard someone else talking in the background.

Mihail said, "He also has his sidearm. Which, you know… big deal. And he was in Iraq, and he shot enough people over there and he's not going to shoot anyone here. This one has a lot to say."

Razvan said, "So it's up to you. If you have to shoot, leave at least one of them alive."

"Yes, you told me."

"And if you spot them, call and we'll come in from behind. So don't shoot us."

"Yes, Raz. I got it."

Razvan ended the call and dialed Claudiu's phone.

Claudiu was searching the northwest quadrant, which had the fewest places to hide.

Ideally Claudiu should have another man with him and a second or third vehicle in the area, but Razvan couldn't move anyone from what they were already doing.

He took solace in the fact that if the thieves were there, they were trapped.

All Claudiu had to do was spot them—or anything close to something looking like them—and call it in.

The man was excited by the idea of interrogating the thieves, and Razvan had made a promise: If he found them, Claudiu could do whatever he wanted to them as long as they didn't die.

As long as he got his answers, the ones expected by the man in Chicago, Razvan didn't care about anything else.

But one thing was starting to edge to the forefront of his concerns.

Claudiu's phone was still ringing, and he wasn't answering.

***

Razvan called Mihail back.

"Have you seen Claudiu?"

"No, not since this morning at the compound, before all of this happened. Why?"

"He's somewhere out by you, north of the highway. He's not answering his phone."

Mihail said, "Is he pouting?"

"I don't give a shit if he's pouting, screaming, or being stabbed. When I call, he answers."

Razvan took the phone away from his ear and fought the urge to hurl it at the side of the building.

Why would Mihail even ask that question?

What, now it was okay for Claudiu to do his job based on how he was *feeling*?

And everyone knew it?

"Fuck!"

The outburst startled a woman sitting in her car in the northbound lanes with her window cracked. She had two children in the back seat who gaped out at Razvan and glanced at their mother to see what she was going to do.

She looked away from him, this tower of a man with skin stretched taut across his face like rubber over a skull and put the window up.

Razvan told Mihail, "Just watch for him. If you see him, tell him to call me."

"Sure, Raz. You got it."

Razvan killed the call and stalked toward the car, alarming the woman and children inside, and turned left to walk toward the crossroads only when he felt satisfied by their level of terror.

***

Another twenty minutes, then thirty, then close to forty minutes.

Nearly two cycles of missed check-ins, with a dozen unanswered calls in the meantime.

Razvan's anger grew.

His main concern was Claudiu had found the thieves and was already going to work on them, sneaking in some personal time with them before he reported back.

What Claudiu never seemed to understand was that people will tell you anything if you hurt them too much, too quickly.

Razvan needed truths, not just confessions.

If—when Claudiu finally called back—if he summoned Razvan to a slaughterhouse, with these men from the white truck spread out all over the walls and floor and begging for death, Razvan decided he might just add Claudiu to the pile.

It was clear his men needed a prompt, a reminder, about who Razvan from Lehliu Gară was.

He was thinking about this when Benj shouted something from up on the roof of the building on the northwest corner.

Razvan looked up at him, then shielded his eyes to look down the four lanes stretching to the west, where Benj was pointing.

And he saw it.

A flash of white, a large crew-cab truck with a cap over the bed, coming toward the crossroads and turning right down one of the side streets, the first one, Dolan.

"Shoot them!" Razvan screamed.

Benj fired his rifle once, being too careful about the other cars.

"Keep shooting, you idiot!"

But the truck was gone, around the corner and out of sight.

Razvan ran to his truck, an awkward lope as he tried to call Grigore at the same time.

"Yeah?"

"They're coming your way, they just turned on Dolan from the highway."

"You saw them?"

"Yes! We'll block them from coming back this way. Where are you?"

Grigore said, "Out in the farms, I'm turning around now."

Razvan heard the other truck's engine open up.

"There aren't many roads they can take, find an intersection and wait there. You'll spot them. Hold them and call me back."

"Okay, right."

He called Mihail next, who said, "We heard a shot."

"Come into town, I need you to block the neighborhood streets going south off the highway."

"You found them?"

"Yes, move your ass!"

Razvan got into his truck and started it, then Luca was at the window.

"What about this?"

He swept a hand across the lanes of backed-up traffic.

"Let them all go through. We block just the southwest quadrant, nobody in or out. I don't care about the highways anymore."

"Thank Christ," Luca said.

"Now move! I have to go!"

Luca jogged away, waving at Benj and Costel, yelling at them to come down from the rooftops.

Razvan pulled his truck through a tight U-turn and raced south on the highway, peering west down the side streets, waiting for another glimpse of the truck.

Praying to see it coming toward him, the thieves trying to slip out of town and get south.

He didn't see them and knew they hadn't turned around to go north again.

So they were in this corner, somewhere, heading toward Grigore, or Mihail, or himself.

Razvan could not wait.

CHAPTER FOURTEEN

When Bruder said, "Go," Rison went, and the modifications to the truck worked.

The Vegas garage Rison had used was discreet, cash only, and kept no memory or records about the vehicles they worked on. Bruder, Rison and Kershaw had tested the mods out in the desert before driving to Iowa, and everyone agreed: They'd be able to outrun anything except a radio.

When Rison hit the gas the truck jumped forward, all four wheels digging into the asphalt, and fans and blowers and belts kicked in beneath the hood to make a spinning-up sound like they were about to take flight.

Rison took the first right, then the first left with everyone inside tilting to counter the vehicle's sway.

Kershaw gripped the handle above the door with his left hand and kept the AR in his right and asked Rison, "How's it feel?"

"Heavy. We should have tested it with a full bed."

He took another right, another left, and continued that pattern to stair-step away from their last known position.

Bruder looked through Kershaw's window and watched

for any Romanians roaring down Spruce, which was now
four blocks to the east, then out his own window when Rison
came to an intersection and turned left.

The northbound road out there didn't go all the way to
the highway, so anyone following them would have to start
from the same entry point, or close to it.

Rison said, "Keep going or find a place to hole up?"

"Keep going until we can't," Bruder said.

Connelly said, "You think they're calling everybody in?
If the checkpoints get sucked in to trap us, we can loop
around and get the hell out of here."

Bruder shook his head.

"Not if they're smart. They know where we are now, still
inside their bubble. It's just a matter of time before they see
us again. How do we get to Nora's from here?"

"Uhh..."

"Don't bullshit."

"I'm not, I'm trying to figure it out!"

Connelly looked around.

"She's southwest of here, I know that...Turn left there,
right there, and keep going south, I think...yeah, this road
gets us out of the neighborhoods."

Bruder said, "Does it intersect with anything coming from
the north-south highway?"

He was thinking about Romanians coming from that direction and cutting them off.

"No, uh...No. Once we get out of these blocks, there's
nothing that connects to the highways. It's all just the crazy
farm road loops."

"Is this the only road that gets us out of downtown?"

Connelly was quiet for a moment.

"I don't know, man. Shit. Sorry."

Bruder was also thinking about their back trail. If this
was the only road out of the neighborhoods, the Romanians
would know for sure they'd used it.

Everyone else in the truck was thinking the same thing.

Rison got onto the straightway and pushed the truck past one hundred miles an hour. A woman standing in her driveway holding a folded newspaper watched them blow past with her mouth hanging open.

"At least one eyewitness," Kershaw said.

They cleared the residential blocks and got into farmland, which still had some of the larger, newer houses and of course the farm spreads, and Bruder saw one of the loops coming in from the west.

Rison jammed the brakes and the truck responded with rubber squawking on the asphalt.

"What are you doing?" Bruder said, pushing against the back of Connelly's seat.

"Leaving some false footprints."

Rison glanced at his side mirror and grinned, then stomped the gas again and whipped past the road on the right.

Bruder stuck his head out the window and saw the black marks in the road behind them, looking like they'd braked in order to make the turn.

Rison shrugged at him in the rear-view.

"Might help, can't hurt."

He was right, so Bruder just nodded and watched the road. No other vehicles in front or behind.

The Romanians were either very slow to respond after the single shot they'd taken, or they knew there wasn't any reason to hurry.

They knew the white truck was in the southwest quadrant somewhere, and it wasn't getting out without somehow getting back onto the west- or southbound highways.

So why hurry?

Then Rison said, "Ah, fuck me."

They all looked through the windshield and spotted the vehicle coming at them.

***

The vehicle was still a mile away, but there were no other intersecting roads within view.

No turnoffs or two-tracks, nothing except the flat fields stretching off to the left and right.

"Another farmer?" Connelly said.

Rison shook his head.

"They're coming on fast. And look, they're straddling the centerline."

"Must have gotten a call from town," Kershaw said.

He moved the bundled camouflage parka away from his feet so he could turn sideways and get ready to lean out the window with the AR.

"Wait," Bruder said.

There wasn't a lot of leg room in the back row, but he managed to slump down in the corner between the seat and door, below his open window, angled so he was looking past Rison and out the driver's door.

"You do the same," he told Kershaw.

Kershaw did, and ended up looking past Connelly and out the front passenger window.

Bruder set the AR on his knees and lifted them so the barrel followed his line of sight.

"Half a mile," Rison said. "It's a pickup truck, lifted for off-road."

He glanced into the back seat and looked straight down Bruder's rifle.

"Shit!"

"Just keep your chin tucked in," Bruder said.

Then, to Kershaw: "You good?"

Kershaw peered through the holographic sight, past Connelly and out his window.

"As long as Connelly doesn't stick his tongue out."

"I don't like this one bit," Connelly said.

Bruder said, "If either one of you has to move, keep it close to your body."

Connelly moved his pistol to his left hand and set it in his lap.

"What's the point of hiding? They have to know this is the right truck."

"They're looking for four guys," Bruder said. "Anything that causes hesitation, or doubt—even for a few seconds—is good for us."

Rison said, "Quarter mile. Looks like two guys in the cab. They're waving. I can stop now, we all jump out and put a magazine into the cab. Problem solved."

Bruder sat up long enough to take a look.

"Are you sure they're even Romanians?"

Rison paused.

"No."

"Then we do it this way until we know."

He grabbed the camouflage poncho and spread it over himself and Kershaw like a tarp. He wedged himself back into the corner and adjusted the poncho, so the only gap was at the end of their rifles.

He told Rison, "Go around them if you can."

"I can't. They're taking up the whole road."

"Anybody coming behind?"

"Nothing so far."

"Then stop. Whatever this is, let's get it over with."

***

Bruder's view through the slit was of Rison, the window, and blue sky beyond, so it was hard to tell exactly how fast they were going.

But he felt the truck slow down and heard the engine noise drop.

When the truck rocked back and settled, he could hear the other truck getting closer.

A man yelled, "Turn the truck off! Show me the keys!"

Romanians?

Rison said, "What? Why?"

"Do it, motherfucker!"

Romanians.

Rison pulled the keys out and showed them.

The man said, "Throw them on the ground!"

"What's going on, man?"

"Throw them out or we shoot you!"

Rison tossed them out the window.

Connelly kept a narration going, his voice low and tight. To Bruder it sounded like he was trying not to move his lips.

"Two guys, I think. Truck angled in front of us, windshield glare. Driver has pistol on us."

The man in the truck said, "Keep your hands up! Show me hands!"

Rison lifted his hands and spread the fingers out.

The man in the truck said, "Where are the other two?"

Rison said, "Huh?"

"There are four of you!"

"What?"

The man in the truck said, "Where are the rest of you? In the back?"

"Buddy, take a minute and tell me what's going on, please. Are you guys cops, or what?"

Bruder heard the man talking but couldn't make out any words.

Connelly said, "Passenger door open. He's getting out. Driver still in, gun on Rison. Shit. Shit. shit."

Bruder waited, then whispered, "What?"

"I know the passenger. Grigore. The one from Len's, busted his nose. Coming this way, has a shotgun on me."

Bruder stared through the slit, waiting for something to enter the blue sky outside Rison's window.

He heard footsteps outside his door, someone coming

closer along the shoulder.

Then, closer than he'd expected a man barked a laugh.

"Hey, it's the singer boy! The Hungarian!"

The driver asked something in Romanian and Grigore answered him, then said, "Hey boy, where is your girlfriend? You going to her place? Was it her idea to steal our money?"

Connelly stayed quiet.

Grigore yelled to the truck in Romanian.

Rison said, "Who are you calling?"

Letting Bruder and Kershaw know the man had his phone out.

Grigore said, "Shut your mouth. Singer boy, I'm going to open your door. Then you get out here and keep your hands up and kneel in the grass. If you do anything other than that, I'll blow your guts out and let you die slow. Got it?"

"Got it," Connelly said.

Bruder heard boots scraping on asphalt.

"Ah, is that our money in the back—"

Kershaw's shot was deafening inside the truck, even with the suppressor.

Bruder yanked the poncho back and sat up in the same motion, pushing the AR into the front seat and searching for his target.

The man was behind the wheel of the pickup, which sat a little higher than the DOT truck because of its off-road package.

His pickup idled at an angle across the road with the front bumper near Rison's door and the bed pointed away at the two o'clock position.

The driver had a pistol in his right hand, pointed at Rison, and a phone in his left.

He was using his thumb to swipe the screen.

His mouth was open, and his eyes were wide from the sudden gunshot, and Bruder fired just above the steering wheel, through the windshield. The bullet went into the man's open mouth and scattered the back of his head inside the truck.

Rison scrambled out the driver's door and kept his Glock aimed at the pickup until he got close enough to peek inside, then he stuck the gun in his belt and clamped both hands over his ears.

"Fuck! I'm deaf!"

Bruder opened his door and looked down at Grigore. His eyes were open and dull. He had a hole next to his nose and his head was misshapen.

Bruder walked around the front of the truck and met Kershaw next to the pickup.

After a glance inside he opened the door and found the phone on the seat near the driver's left leg.

The screen showed a list of recent calls, which the driver had been scrolling through when Bruder shot him.

"No call," Bruder said.

He opened the message app and saw the most recent conversation was a group text with eight people, all of them represented by one or two letters.

B

Cl

G

P

R

Like that.

The messages were in a foreign language.

He showed the screen to Kershaw and said, "Romanian?"

Kershaw peered at the phone.

"If it isn't, we're in a bigger mess than we thought. Here, let me see."

He took it and scrolled through the conversation while Bruder looked in the truck for anything useful.

Kershaw said, "Apparently the Romanian word for *Chicago* is *Chicago*."

Bruder stood up, suddenly wary.

"When was this? They talking about the delivery schedule?"

"No, it was...an hour ago. So after we made the grab."

Now Bruder was concerned.

"What else about Chicago?"

"Hold on."

He fiddled around until Bruder said, "What are you doing?"

"Copying and pasting into a translator site. It won't be conversational, but we'll get the gist. And there are some numbers, which is good. Don't need to translate those."

He looked around at the flat fields.

"They get really good service out here."

Every second they stayed with the truck and phone made Bruder feel tighter, but he let Kershaw work.

Kershaw said, "Okay, something like, 'Chicago sending package, arrive 5-6."

"Who wrote that?"

Kershaw went back to the messages.

"R."

"Razvan," Bruder said. "A package from Chicago."

"Arriving between five and six. O'clock, I assume."

Bruder checked his watch. It was getting close to one in the afternoon.

He pointed at the phone.

"Toss that."

It would be helpful to keep track of the conversation, but it would also pinpoint the location of whoever held it.

Kershaw tossed it back into the cab and shut the door.

Bruder went back to Grigore's body.

Connelly had a finger in his left ear and was opening and closing his jaw.

Bruder asked him, "Can you hear?"

"Barely. Scared the shit out of me."

Bruder raised his voice and addressed everyone.

"Listen up. The Romanians have reinforcements coming from Chicago. Arrival time between five and six, tonight. We need to be gone before then."

Then he told Connelly, "Get out here and give me a hand. He's going in the truck bed."

Connelly got out and they carried Grigore's body to the pickup.

The bed had no tailgate, just an open end, and they swung the body in and shoved it toward the cab.

Bruder reached in the driver's window and shifted the truck into Drive. It rolled forward and off the asphalt into the scrub grass before bumping into the field, which had some freshly turned furrows but those weren't enough to stop the pickup's knobby tires and high idle.

Rison scooped his keys off the asphalt and everyone got back into the DOT truck. The windshield was spiderwebbed around the bullet hole but still usable.

"Still Nora's?" Rison said.

Bruder tapped Connelly.

"You've been there. How's it look for a standoff?"

"Uh, not great."

Bruder shrugged.

"It's all we got. Let's go."

They drove away, leaving the pickup to trundle away across the field until it came across something to make it stop, or not.

***

They pulled into Nora's driveway and everyone saw her pacing on the wraparound porch. She wore a thick maroon and cream sweater jacket and had her arms wrapped across her ribs.

When she saw the strange truck turning in she stopped and stared.

"Ah, man," Connelly said. "Ah shit."

"This could be a good thing," Rison said.

Connelly looked at him, waiting for the revelation.

Rison said, "Well, right now she thinks you're a former marketing asshole who scrapes up gas money by playing shitty songs in dinky town bars. When she finds out you're actually a criminal asshole who makes millions of dollars through strong arm robbery...it might be an upgrade."

"You're a big help," Connelly said.

Bruder looked out his window at the road they'd come down.

So far, no other vehicles were in sight.

The other side of the road was a harvested field of something that hadn't been corn—soybeans, maybe—and he could see a tree line way off in the distance and, beyond that, hints of barns and silos and smaller structures that were probably houses.

The sight lines out here were troublesome.

If he could see those buildings, they could see Nora's house.

And the white truck pulling in.

He told Rison, "Go around the house, to the metal barns back there."

"Let me out by the porch," Connelly said.

"No," Bruder said.

"I need to talk to her. Smooth this out."

"Sure. We'll help."

Connelly didn't say anything, but it was clear he didn't want the assistance.

Rison drove between the house and the old barn with remnants of red.

Nora was at the top of the stairs now, waiting for the truck to stop. When it kept going, she leaned down to peer through the windows and spotted Connelly in the passenger seat.

She unwrapped her arms and held them out to her sides:

What the hell?

Connelly waved and Rison held up a finger to let her know they'd be a minute.

As they approached the metal barns Bruder said, "Is there room in there for the truck?"

"No," Connelly said, with attitude. "They're jammed with big-ass machines. Combines and hopper trailers and tractors. And everything you need to keep them running. Plus the doors are locked."

Rison snorted a laugh at that, locked doors being the least of their concerns at the moment.

He took the truck around the corner of the barn and reached for the keys.

"Hold on," Bruder said.

He got out and looked around.

Nothing but fields and trees off in the distance.

He still didn't like the wide open view, but at least no one would spot the truck from the road or across it. The metal barns were like a set of medium-sized warehouses.

He told Rison, "Okay."

They all got out and Bruder pulled his balaclava up over his nose and mouth, hiding everything except a small slit for his eyes.

Kershaw and Rison did the same.

Connelly watched them, then looked at the ARs slung across the chests of Bruder and Kershaw.

Rison still had his pistol out.

Connelly said, "Is all of…this…necessary?"

"She's already seen our faces once," Bruder said. "We don't need her making any connections."

"Then just stay here with the truck."

Bruder shook his head.

"We all need to have a chat."

He turned and walked around the corner to meet Nora.

***

Nora was halfway across the crushed concrete in front of the barns.

When Bruder walked around the corner she stopped, her eyes wide and moving to the others around him.

Three large men in black masks and heavy boots and thick outdoor work clothes, long guns slung across their chests and pistols sticking out. As a group, they looked like they should have been assaulting a hostage situation or protecting the ambassador to Serbia while he crossed a tarmac.

It was probably an alarming sight.

Then Connelly came around the corner with no mask and no gun and Nora saw him and blinked.

"Hey," he said.

Nora's eyes got wider for a moment, then narrowed.

She asked Connelly, "What the hell have you done?"

"I'm pretty sure you can figure it out."

"Did you...did you take their money?"

"It's not theirs," Bruder said. "It's ours."

Nora frowned at him.

"Who are you?"

Bruder tilted his head toward Connelly.

"A friend of his."

"Did you mess with their armored truck? Are you guys the reason we're all being terrorized right now?"

"To be fair," Connelly said, "you were all being terrorized before. It was just, you know. Low-grade."

Nora's eyes were bright with furious tears.

"Do you know they stuck a gun in Helen's face? In front of her husband?"

Kershaw looked at Connelly and asked, "Who's Helen?"

Connelly shrugged, helpless.

"They have the entire town locked *down*," Nora said.

"And here I was, worried about what they might do to you because you were trying to come see me. To help me."

"I am trying to help you," Connelly said.

Nora just shook her head.

"You have no idea what you've done. You've committed suicide, Adam."

She looked around at the barns and fields and open sky, coming to conclusions.

"And I think, because you came here...I think you've killed me too."

***

Bruder waited for Connelly to say something, to calm her down, but he was stuck.

Speechless, for once.

Bruder said, "Let's go inside and talk this through. You're cold."

"I'm fine," Nora said, "and you're not stepping foot inside my house. Get back in the truck and leave."

"That's not happening."

Bruder glanced at the massive steel barns with their billboard-sized doors, closed and locked. Then he looked at the older barn near the house.

"We'll go in there. Out of sight, but I bet we can see through some cracks. Watch the road and listen for vehicles while we talk."

"No," Nora said. "And talk about what?"

"What happens next."

"I know what happens next. You get back in the truck and go away."

"We already talked about that," Bruder said. "Where's your gun?"

She twitched a hand toward the right pocket of her sweater, where Bruder had already spotted something heavy pulling the fabric down.

"You're not getting my gun," she said.

"I don't want it. I just want to know where it is. Leave it in there unless one of us says it's okay to take it out."

She glared at him and seemed like she might pull the Sig out just to prove a point.

"I wouldn't," Bruder said. "Brandishing is illegal in Iowa." He stepped past her toward the old barn.

CHAPTER FIFTEEN

The barn smelled like a fire waiting to happen—straw and dry wood and dust.

The early afternoon sun splayed through cracks in and between the planks, highlighting the motes drifting around.

There was a large open area on the ground floor. The only thing taking up space was a rusty contraption about the size of a car with a metal seat and discs and tines that looked like it used to get dragged behind a horse.

Above, an empty loft wrapped the four walls with a rectangular hole in the middle for moving things up and down. A rough wooden ladder that was part of the structure led to the loft, and while the high ground was attractive, the few remaining planks looked ready to break from a heavy sigh.

They checked the cracks along the front wall and the gap in the big hinged doors being held in place with a length of scratchy rope and could see the road just fine.

Kershaw took the northeast corner, watching for anything coming from the town.

Rison had the southeast, in case any Romanians were further out than Grigore and his buddy had been.

Bruder peered through the gap between the doors and said, "Who can you call to find out what's happening in town?"

Nora didn't respond, so Bruder turned from the doors and looked at her.

Connelly was by her side, standing between her and Bruder like a mediator. He had his rifle now, slung across his chest, and she kept frowning at it and him like they wouldn't fit together in her mind.

He told her, "Come on. Help us out."

"Help you *out*? Are you kidding me? How much of what you've told me is actually true?"

Connelly opened his mouth, ready to get into it, but Bruder cut him off.

"That doesn't matter now. Sort it out later. Or don't, nobody cares. What matters right now is what the Romanians are doing. Are they still holding the crossroads? Are they flooding this area with men and trucks? Who can you get that information from?"

Nora still didn't answer.

"Do you know how many men there are? We know of eight."

Kershaw said, "Well, five now."

Bruder nodded.

"Right. Nora, who can you call?"

She just stared at him.

Connelly said, "What about Helen?"

She gave him a look like it was too soon to mention that name, and he might never be allowed to say it.

"Call Marie," Bruder said.

Nora squinted at him.

"From Len's?"

"Yes."

"No, I...she and I aren't friends like that. I don't even know her number."

"*Adam* does," Rison said from his spot in the corner,

providing zero help.

Before that could change the subject Bruder said, "Call somebody. Trust me, you'll want to know if they're coming this way."

"Trust you…" Nora said.

But she took her phone out and started tapping.

Bruder told Connelly, "Watch the screen."

Connelly leaned closer and Nora let the arm holding the phone drop.

"Watch the screen for what?"

Bruder said, "To make sure you aren't calling any Romanians. Or cops."

"Oh, right, let me scroll through my contacts. Here's Razvan, a fucking murderer who almost killed my parents and threatened to burn their house down. I'll just hit him up real quick and let him know you're here. Please."

Connelly said, "See? We're all on the same side."

Nora whirled on him.

"No. No we are not. The people around here—me included—are just trying to live their lives without any trouble from Razvan and his men. You, you assholes come in and steal from them, and now you want my help to get away. Well what happens if you do get away? When you disappear? Guess who pays the price for what you've done?"

"I'm not going to disappear," Connelly said, and everyone looked at him.

Nora said, "What?"

"I'm not going to disappear. I have money. From before, other jobs, and now this, of course. I'll buy this place from your folks so you don't have to worry about it anymore. You'll be free and clear to stay in Minneapolis or go wherever you want."

"With you?"

Connelly shuffled his feet and glanced at Bruder and the others.

"I hope so, yes. And if you want to stay here, that's fine too. I'll stay with you and keep an eye on the...the fallout from our little endeavor."

Kershaw said, "You against the Romanians?"

Connelly just shrugged.

Kershaw and Rison both looked at Bruder.

The sensible thing would be to shoot both of them, right then, and find another way to get status updates about the town.

But Bruder didn't want to make that sort of decision without talking to the others first, in case they had a good reason not to do it, one he didn't see yet.

He told Connelly, "Watch the road."

Then, to Kershaw and Rison: "Let's talk in the back."

***

They left Connelly and Nora at the front of the barn and walked around the rusted cultivator and stood in the opposite corner under a part of the loft draped with cobwebs.

Kershaw kept his voice low when he said, "We can't kill them."

"Convince me," Bruder said.

Rison looked back and forth between them. His eyes were wide in the hole of his balaclava.

"Holy shit guys, that's where we're starting? Killing them?"

Bruder said, "This little lover's quarrel or whatever it is can get us all killed. Better to cut it off now. It was bad enough before, now we got a crew coming in from Chicago. We don't have time for this."

"No, no, listen."

Rison glanced over at Connelly, who stood close to Nora so they could have their own private chat.

"He's good to go. Even if he does stay here with her, or wherever they go, he's a stand-up guy. He won't ever speak our names. To anyone."

"He will if the Romanians start playing that card game with him. Or her."

"They don't know he's in on this," Rison said. "Everybody who's seen him with us is dead."

"They don't have to know. They just have to wonder. That's how it starts."

Rison looked at Kershaw.

"You said we can't kill them. Can you jump in on this, please?"

Kershaw told Bruder, "All the dead bodies so far are Romanian. When their crew finds them, my guess is they'll go in a pit or a burn pile and nobody outside that group will know about it. If we start dropping other bodies—civilians—it'll bring attention."

"We can make bodies disappear as easily as the Romanians can," Bruder said. "And even if they do get found, we make it so the finger gets pointed at Razvan."

Kershaw thought about it.

Rison said, "So this is what we do now? We don't like how somebody acts, so we put a bullet in him?"

Bruder nodded.

"When how they act puts the rest of us at risk. He's making himself a loose end. I warned him not to do this."

"You didn't warn her."

"That's on him, not us."

Rison looked down, shaking his head.

"What happens if I don't go along with it?"

"I don't need your help," Bruder said.

"No, I mean what happens if I don't allow it? You gonna shoot me too?"

He looked up at Bruder, then Kershaw.

It wasn't quite a standoff, but it was heading in that direction.

"You feel that strongly about it?" Kershaw said.

"I do. It'd be one thing if he fucked up, like he didn't set the charges right or ran his mouth before the job and got us jammed up. But he did everything right. Hell, he's the reason we know all we do. Him and Nora. I just can't get on board with punishing him for...well, let's call it what it is: Falling in love."

He pulled a bottle of water out of his jacket and turned away from Nora's direction, then tugged his mask down and took an aggressive drink. He didn't look at Bruder or Kershaw, and Bruder had the sense he was embarrassed, talking about love.

After a moment Kershaw told Bruder, "I see his point. I'm not sold on Connelly being a liability yet. I don't like what he's doing, but he doesn't have blinders on. He knows what we're talking about right now. And he's still willing to try to make it work. My opinion, it's not worth a bullet."

"By the time your opinion changes, it'll be too late," Bruder said. "But I'll let it play out. For now."

***

While the three men talked in the back of the barn Connelly watched the road and, out of the corner of his eye, Nora, to gauge her level of anger.

He was a little worried about the gun in her pocket.

"So, what do you think?" he said.

She didn't answer for a while.

Then: "About what?"

"Me sticking around. With you, wherever that is."

"I think it's pretty goddam presumptuous."

He glanced over to see if she was smiling when she said it. She was not.

He couldn't think of anything to say, so he said, "It's a lot to process."

"Not really. You lied. Why go any further than that?"

"I lied out of necessity."

She turned to him.

"Oh, necessity? You *needed* to steal Razvan's money? You *needed* to put my life in danger, and everyone who lives here?"

"Well, no. But once the job was a go, certain things had to happen. Lying to you was one of them, to keep you safe."

"No," she said. "Don't even. Don't try to make yourself feel better by framing this as some bullshit white knight scenario. If you wanted to keep me safe, you never would have talked to me. But you did, on purpose, because why? I'm starting to see it all, right now—you got me to tell you all about them. About the town."

She shook her head, bewildered.

"And just now, when that man said your name. '*Adam* does.' The way he said it. That's not even your name, is it?"

Connelly dreaded this, knowing it wasn't going to make anything better, but lying again would only make it worse.

"No."

"You piece of shit. What's your real name?"

He winced.

"I'll tell you when this is all over."

Her mouth fell open.

"*What*? You're not going to tell me?"

"Nora, I'm serious, it's for your own safety. If you don't know my real name, or how the other guys look, their faces, you're better off."

She crossed her arms and said, "In case of what?"

"I think you know."

"I want you to say it."

Connelly couldn't help wishing she wouldn't give him such a hard time, even though he knew he had it coming.

He said, "In case the cops come asking. Or the Romanians."

"Ah. There it is. And from what you've seen—oh wait, and from what I've *told* you—do you think they'll be nice to me when they ask? When I tell them, I don't know your name, or how ugly the rest of your team is, do you think they'll just say, okay, sorry to bother you, have a nice day?"

Connelly stared out at the road through the gap in the barn doors.

He wanted her to keep her voice down but couldn't say so, not then.

Not if he didn't want to get shot by that pocket gun.

He knew what the other three were talking about, back there in the corner. If they looked over and saw him and Nora going at it, possibly a sign of what was to come, it might tip their decision a bad way.

"You're right," he said. "It's mostly in case of cops."

"And what about Razvan and his men? Should I just start packing now for Arizona so I don't get tortured to death?"

Something caught in her voice and Connelly looked over and saw tears in her eyes.

Outraged, frustrated, terrified tears.

He told her, "You don't have to worry about Razvan. Or his men."

"No? These are the people who have the entire town locked down right now. Putting guns in people's faces, and no one is stopping them. And no one stopped them when they threatened to kill my parents. I don't have to worry about that?"

"No."

"Because?"

"Because if they come here, we'll kill them."

She blinked.

"We?"

Connelly nodded toward the back corner, where Rison was fired up about something.

"We. And you, with that dinky peashooter, if you feel like getting off your ass."

She finally smiled, a small flash that lasted less than a heartbeat, but it was there, breaking the tension and maybe, just maybe, putting them back on the same team.

She cuffed at her eyes with the sleeve of her sweater and glanced at the men in the back.

"One of them...I can't tell which one anymore, maybe the one with glasses...he said five."

"Five?"

"Yes, when the bigger one was taking about numbers, how many men Razvan has. He said, eight, and the other one said, 'Well, five.'"

"Yeah?"

"What does that mean?"

"Oh. Huh. It means they started with eight, we think, and now they have five. We think."

"What happened to the other three?"

He squinted out at the road.

"Remember, way back in the day, when I said you shouldn't know things for your own safety?"

Nora shook her head.

"Don't start with that bullshit again. My safety is up to me, and I need to know what's going on."

Connelly couldn't argue with her.

He'd demand the same.

"They're dead," he said.

She absorbed that for a moment.

"How? Did you kill them?"

"I can't say any more than they're dead."

"Oh, I get it. Some kind of code?"

He wasn't a fan of the tone, like he and the others were just playing a jackass game of cops and robbers, but he couldn't expect her to jump on board with all of it right away.

"That," he said, "and knowing I deserve the same fate if I run my mouth about the details."

"Oh," she said, pulled down a bit by the gravity of the truth.

They both watched the road for a bit, then she said, "They're talking about what to do about us back there, aren't they?"

"Yep."

"I think I'm more concerned about them than Razvan. The big one, anyway. He seems mean."

Connelly shook his head.

"He's not mean. Just very serious. I think they invented the term *Zero Fucks Given* for him. If negative fucks were possible, he'd give negative fucks."

He was jabbering, making noise because he sensed they were wrapping things up back there in the corner, and made himself stop.

Nora said, "What are they going to do?"

Connelly heard footsteps and turned to see the three of them coming back to the front of the barn.

Bruder and Rison still had the long guns slung across their chests, but nobody had a hand on the grip. Rison's pistol was tucked away somewhere.

"Let's find out," Connelly said, and kept his finger near the trigger.

***

Bruder noticed the trigger finger and watched Connelly's eyes twitching between the three of them.

He said, "You—"And stopped when Nora's phone started ringing.

She pulled it out and looked at the screen.

"It's Donna."

Everyone waited for more information.

"She lives north of here, in the neighborhood southwest of town. You probably drove past her house to get here."

"Put her on speaker," Bruder said.

Nora hit the button.

"Donna?"

"Nora, sweetie, are you okay?"

Nora glanced at the four men looming around her.

"Yes, why? What's happening?"

"They opened up the crossroads, so that's good, but this whole part of town is still locked down. I just talked to Yvette, you know Yvette, from church?"

"Um, sure."

"I just talked to her, and the tall one came to her house with another one of them, and they opened her barn and looked in her garage, then her house! Can you believe that? Her house!"

Nora's face grew tight.

"What are they looking for?"

"I don't know, hon. Yvette said they had another vehicle parked at the end of her driveway, with another man there, and she saw a gun. They left her place a mess and drove down the road to her neighbors', the Judsen place."

Nora said, "So they're coming this way?"

"Yes, that's why I'm calling. We're all making calls, letting folks know. Not that you have anything to worry about, but just so you know and don't get a nasty shock when they show up. They're coming to search your property. Just let them do it and they'll go away."

"Thank you so much, Donna. I really appreciate it."

"Of course, sweetie. You be careful. I need to make some more calls, but I'll check in with you later."

"Okay, bye."

She ended the call and looked around.

Bruder said, "We need to get rid of the truck."

***

Kershaw stayed in the barn to watch the road.

Everyone else started moving.

Fast, purposeful steps but no rushing.

On the way to the huge metal barns Bruder asked Nora, "How far away are they? If they just hit...who was it?"

"The Judsens," Connelly said.

"Them."

Nora said, "Ten minutes if they're driving straight here. But if they have to stop and check every property along the way, I mean...an hour? It depends on how long they stay at each place."

Bruder grunted.

However long it was, it wasn't long enough.

He pointed out to the south and west.

"What comes after these fields? More fields?"

"Mostly. You can see the tree line out there to the west, and there's a drainage ditch in there too."

"Can the truck get through?"

"No. The ditch is probably fifteen feet deep, deeper mud at the bottom. With steep sides. Deer get stuck in there sometimes."

"No bridges?" Connelly said.

"Not that we can get to. It's a property line for as far as you can see. Last I knew there was one to the south, but that's on the other side of the southern property line, which is another drainage ditch."

"So you got yourself a moat," Rison said.

Nora blinked.

"I suppose so."

Bruder had already looked to the east, across the road where another tree line waited.

Maybe they could swing back north through the fields and slide around the neighborhoods and hit the highway.

Maybe there wouldn't be any checkpoints still up.

And maybe no one would call Razvan and tell him about the white truck bouncing around in the fields behind their house.

He looked north and saw a dark line right below the horizon.

"Another ditch?"

Nora nodded.

"'With a fence. They keep horses."

He looked at the barns.

"I know these are full. If we pull something out, is there anywhere inside we can hide the truck?"

She chewed her lip.

"They're just big open spaces, like hangars. So...no?"

"Show me."

She made a face but pulled out a set of keys and unlocked the sliding door.

Bruder pushed it—much easier than he'd expected—just far enough to look inside.

It was a hangar full of huge machinery, like a tomb for alien crafts.

Rison looked past Bruder's arm.

"We can hide the money in there. If the Romanians don't have any reason to go digging, they'll stick their heads in, look for a white truck, and call it good."

"Find a good spot," Bruder said.

And to Connelly, "Keep the charges with the bags."

Connelly nodded.

They started pulling the surveying equipment and camping gear and food and water out and tossing it on the ground to get to the duffel bags.

Nora helped, and when she saw the wall of bags said, "How much did you take?"

Connelly grinned.

"All of it."

"Yeah, but..."

"We don't know yet," Bruder said, killing the conversation.

They got the bags out and Connelly and Rison followed Nora into the nearest shed to find a good spot.

Bruder stayed outside, looking around, and it crossed his mind that Connelly and Rison might decide, in there in the shed, they'd rather split the money two ways instead of four.

It sometimes happened when part of a crew got alone with the money and started thinking too much.

It also sometimes happened when a woman was involved.

He didn't find it likely from those two, or Nora, but he'd thought of it now and wouldn't be surprised if it happened.

He'd be ready.

And though he didn't appreciate irony, it was ironic how the Romanians might be the main factor in stopping any sort of double-cross—everyone was too preoccupied with not getting stabbed in the front by Razvan and his crew to come up with a backstab plan.

The three of them came back out empty-handed.

"Where?" Bruder said.

He followed Rison inside, where they had to squeeze between the door and the front of something huge and green with a cab floating above Bruder's head.

"Combine," Rison said, like he was proud of the wisdom.

They got around the front and Rison led them down a narrow alley between the combine and a tractor with dual back wheels and a hopper wagon behind it.

"Up there," Rison said.

Bruder stepped up onto the wagon and found a ladder built into the side.

He climbed up two steps and looked over the top.

The bags were there, in the bottom, among some loose corn kernels.

Rison said, "We toss some more bags, then the charges, then the rest of the bags. Then cover all of it with a tarp, from over there past the back of the hopper. But me and Connelly thought of something."

Bruder turned and looked down, ready if Rison went for his gun.

"What if we have one or two of us in here, hidden away, and we lure Razvan and whoever he has with him inside? We take them out, then the guy out by the road, if they run the same setup the lady on the phone talked about. That's three more down. Which leaves two, if my math is right."

Bruder nodded.

Rison said, "Then we just get in the truck and head for the highway. If we come across the other two, we put them down. Then we can go get a burger at Len's. I'm kidding about that part, but you know what I mean."

Bruder climbed down.

"Let's talk outside. So everybody can hear it."

***

"Ambush," Bruder said.

Rison and Connelly and Nora stood by the tailgate of the truck, listening.

"I've been thinking about it too, looking at the angles. I didn't think about inside the shed. It's a good idea. It might work. I don't like bringing them to the one with the money in it, but maybe the other one."

"It would be harder to hide in there," Nora said. "It's mostly attachments, like discs and plows and sprayers. They take up a lot of room, but they aren't very tall."

Bruder headed for the other shed and they followed.

Nora unlocked the door and sure enough, the floor was packed but Bruder could see all the way across to the far walls. The tallest thing was an orange Kubota tractor that rose just past Bruder's chest.

No good.

Bruder nodded.

"The other one, then. We plan *for* it, but not *on* it. Understand?"

Connelly and Rison nodded and started toward the truck to move more bags.

"Hold on," Nora said. "You guys are going to leave a bunch of dead bodies around my house?"

Connelly said, "Whatever we do, it won't come back on you. We won't leave a mess."

She didn't seem convinced but didn't say anything else

about it.

Connelly and Rison got back to work, leaving Nora and Bruder standing in the doorway.

"Don't get him killed," she said.

Bruder shrugged.

"That's up to him."

"But you're in charge. You're management."

Bruder dismissed that and said, "When Razvan gets here, what will you do?"

"Talk to him, I guess. Shouldn't I?"

"Yes. Will you be able to? By yourself?"

"I'll be fine," she said, and her tone told him she probably would be. "What are you going to do about the truck?"

Bruder asked her, "How deep is your pond?"

***

They got what they needed out of the truck and left everything else inside with the side cap windows and tailgate open.

Rison put all the cab windows down and drove it to the edge of the pond, then put it in neutral and hopped out, closing the door as the truck rolled forward.

The pond was about fifty yards across, mostly round, and Nora had said it dropped quickly to fifteen to twenty feet deep.

The truck slid into the water and kicked up a tan cloud of mud, like a trailer launching a boat, and for a moment it looked like it might hang up there, or even float, then it dipped down and water poured into the open front windows and the truck did a nose dive.

The last they saw of it was the open cap and tailgate, like two tail fins waving goodbye.

A few big bubbles roiled the surface, then some smaller ones rose and burst, then nothing.

"Goddam shame," Rison said.

Connelly patted his shoulder.

"It'll be here. Depending on how things go, we give it a couple days, a few weeks, then pull her back out and see what we can do."

"A whole lotta nothing," Rison said, like he was burying a friend.

Bruder interrupted them.

"This is a problem."

He showed them the tire tracks cutting across the grass from the driveway to the pond. The light dusting of snow had mostly melted in the afternoon sun, but the tires still left a set of railroad tracks pointing right where the truck went in.

Nora looked at the tracks.

"I'll be right back."

She went behind the house and a few minutes later they heard an engine grow louder, then Nora came around the corner driving the Kubota tractor with a bucket on the front and some sort of mower deck on the back.

Kershaw stuck his head out of the wooden barn to see what was going on.

Connelly gave him a thumbs-up and Kershaw went back to watching the road.

Nora moved some levers and the engine climbed and the mower deck dropped. She ran over the spot where the tire tracks started, then cut left and pulled around to come across the tracks at a ninety-degree angle, bouncing a little in the seat.

After the mower passed, that section of truck tracks was gone.

Bruder, Connelly, and Rison stood by the edge of the pond, watching her.

"Is it me," Connelly said, "or is this super sexy?"

Rison said, "It's not you."

Connelly looked over at him.

"Alright, stop staring."

Nora aimed for a pile of dead leaves blown up against

the base of the porch and sent them across the grass like a confetti cannon. Then she swiped across them, again and again, erasing tire tracks and boot prints and working the tractor through an area that looked like a natural section of the yard, not just a narrow runway.

One of her passes sent a shower of grass and leaves onto the three men, peppering their coats and pants.

"We should probably move," Connelly said.

They walked back onto the crushed stone driveway while Nora finished up and followed their path, just to be safe.

She raised the mower deck and sped away toward the first steel shed, which had its door almost all the way open.

Connelly said to the others, but mostly for Bruder, "That was good. She really helped us out."

"We'll see," Bruder said, and went to set up the ambush.

CHAPTER SIXTEEN

It was close to 2:30 in the afternoon when Kershaw saw the trucks.

"Incoming," he said over the radio. "F-250 and another pickup, maybe a Tacoma."

He was out in the field under the camouflage poncho with dirt and corn leaves piled on top, watching the truck through the rifle's optics. They only offered 5X magnification, but it was enough to see two men in the lead truck and one in the second.

They disappeared behind the old wooden barn, and when Kershaw saw them again, they were slowing near the end of the driveway.

"They're here," he said.

***

Razvan drove his truck up the driveway, ducking down so he could scan the windows and doors and the old wooden barn on the right.

"Watch the loft," he told Benj, who had his AK pointed out the window, tracking everywhere his eyes went.

Razvan glanced at the rear-view mirror to make sure Mihail was in place.

He was, parked across the end of the driveway and standing behind the truck's engine with the bipod of his M249 machine gun resting on a sandbag on the hood.

From there, he could sweep the property left to right with bullets.

When Razvan stopped in the driveway next to the steps to the porch he looked at the long garage and two big barns behind the house.

Those would be blind spots for Mihail.

He called his cell and told him what to do, then waited while Mihail backed up on the road until he could see every structure.

Razvan said, "You can see the front of the barns? The steel ones?"

"Yes. The wooden one is in the way, a little, but I'm good."

"Any movement?"

"Just the woman."

"Mm," Razvan said, and hung up.

He looked out his window at the woman, Nora, standing on her porch in a sweater, looking like someone had just killed her dog.

Razvan smiled at her.

"Good afternoon, Nora."

"What do you want?"

"I want you to hold still."

He lifted the gun, a Pistolul model 1998, also called a Dracula, and pointed it at her face.

It was a fully automatic machine pistol about the size of a Colt 1911, but had a spare magazine fitted to the rail beneath the barrel to use as a fore grip.

It was a nasty looking thing, and it had the effect Razvan wanted.

Nora took a step back and put her hands out in front of her.

"No, wait!"

"I said hold still."

Razvan kept the machine pistol on her while he opened the door and unfolded himself from the truck.

Benj got out the other side and walked toward the wooden barn to check it.

Razvan could hear him talking to Mihail over the phone, keeping each other updated in case Mihail saw movement, and so he wouldn't shoot Benj if he happened to poke his head out a window.

Razvan asked Nora, "Is anyone else here?"

"No. Put the gun down, please."

"You first. It's in your pocket, yes? I can see the bulge."

She brought her right hand toward the pocket.

"Slow," Razvan said. "I know you're not going to shoot me, but my men are a little upset right now. They might not be as trusting."

She used her forefinger and thumb to lift the compact pistol out of her pocket and let it dangle out at her side.

"I'm coming to take it from you," Razvan said.

He climbed the steps and stood next to her for a moment, forcing her to crank her neck up to look up at his face.

The Dracula pistol was still pointed at her face.

He took her gun away and stuffed it into a back pocket and stood there, staring down at her.

She looked away and tried to take a step to her left but Razvan hooked her arm with his free hand.

"Do you know why my men are upset?"

"No."

"We found a truck, north of here. Grigore's truck."

"So?"

"Grigore and Pavel were with it. Both of them shot dead."

She blinked but wouldn't look up at him.

He said, "And we haven't heard from Claudiu for hours now. He's just vanished. What can you tell me about these things?"

"Nothing. I don't know anything about them."

"No? You didn't shoot them with this gun of yours?"

"Of course not."

Razvan took her gun back out and sniffed the barrel.

"No, not with this one. Maybe another gun you have here?"

"No."

"You tried to shoot Grigore once already."

Nora shook her head.

"That's…no, I didn't. I was defending myself. I just wanted to leave."

"Just defending yourself," Razvan echoed. "You and,
who was it…ah, your boyfriend. What's his name?"

"Adam."

"Adam. You were defending him, yes? Because he was
about to get his ass beaten. Because he was causing trouble."

"I didn't shoot anyone," Nora said.

"Is your boyfriend here now?"

"No."

"Where is he?"

"I don't know."

"No? Why not? Did he leave you?"

"He's just not here."

"Hm."

Razvan looked at the house, the wooden barn, the front
yard.

He studied the fresh tracks and sniffed the air, noting the
smell of cut grass and wet leaves.

"He should be here to help with the work."

"I don't need any help," Nora said.

"Then he should be here to make sure you are safe. There
are dangerous men on the loose."

She cast a glance his way.

"I'm fine. I'm safe."

Razvan said, "Are you?"

***

Connelly whispered into the mic, "What's happening?"

No one answered.

"Can anybody see?"

Rison said, "I can't see shit. Just the doorway. Now shut up."

He was in the back right corner of the shed, in almost complete darkness, standing behind the cab of a tractor.

Connelly said, "Turkey hunter, what do you see?"

No response.

Connelly was in the front left corner of the shed, tucked under a trailer with an empty fertilizer tank on it. His line of sight paralleled the front door of the shed, so he'd have a good shot at anyone who stepped inside, but other than that he was blind.

It was driving him crazy.

"Turkey hunter, status update."

He willed Kershaw to answer.

After a moment, he did, and he sounded unhappy about it.

"One guy in the wood barn, AK-47, knit cap, beard. Second truck out on the road. One shooter there, long gun on the hood, possibly an M249, giving overwatch."

Connelly said, "A fucking machine gun? What about Nora?"

"Front porch. Talking with Razvan, based on his height."

"She's okay?"

"Yes. Fine."

"What's Razvan doing?"

"She's fine," Kershaw repeated. "Now shut the fuck up."

"What—" The large hand clamped over Connelly's and held it while the other hand plucked the mic away from him.

Connelly looked up and saw Bruder kneeling over him, his eyes grim inside the balaclava.

Bruder yanked the mic cord out of the radio, leaving Connelly with just the receiver and earpiece, then disappeared into the gloom of the shed, back to his spot in the rear left corner.

In the earpiece Bruder's voice said, "No more chatter."

Connelly fumed in silence, glaring at the patch of sunlight coming through the doorway.

He begged Razvan to step inside and catch half of a magazine from all three shooters inside the shed while Kershaw opened up on the man on the road.

The one in the barn, they'd just shoot him through the cracks when he moved.

Connelly watched the patch on the floor, waiting for a shadow to fall across it.

Rison or Kershaw would let him know if it was Nora coming in first.

Bruder could see as well, but Connelly didn't think he'd mention it.

The prick.

Connelly wiped the sweat out of his eyes and compelled Razvan into his line of fire.

Then Kershaw's voice said, "Nora and Razvan are going inside the house."

***

Razvan took Nora into the house through the side door and stopped and listened.

The door led into the kitchen, a large square with white cabinets and black countertops.

The light fixture hanging from the middle of the ceiling was low enough to hit Razvan in the face, so he stepped around it and tilted his head like he was feeling the vibrations in the house, the sounds.

The ugly pistol was still in his hand, hanging down by his leg.

Nora watched him, waiting, wondering if Adam—or whatever his real name was—and the others knew they'd gone inside.

The one with the glasses was out in the field somewhere, so he probably knew.

The question was, did he care?

"The house is empty," Razvan said.

"Yes. Like I told you."

He nodded.

"I'll check anyway. Give me a tour."

Then he grinned at her, his hollow cheeks and sunken eyes making her stomach turn.

"Your parents never offered."

She grimaced and led the way out of the kitchen into the dining room, then the family room, then the home office with stacks of papers and equipment catalogs that she'd sorted and stacked but really ought to toss out.

She showed him the downstairs bathroom and he checked behind the shower curtain, leading with the pistol.

He asked her, "Have you gotten any good offers?"

"No."

"A shame. This is a very nice home. When I get my money back, I'll buy it from you."

"No," she said again.

He looked at her, the skin on his face stretched into a concerned frown.

"You shouldn't hold a grudge about what happened between me and your mother and father. It was business, just like selling a house is business. I make you a good offer, you accept."

"I'll burn it down myself before I let you have it."

He shrugged and walked toward the stairs leading to the second floor.

"Burn the barns too. More farmland for us to use. Is your boyfriend coming into town soon?"

The sudden pivot caught Nora off guard.

She waited too long to answer, and Razvan started to smile again.

She tried to turn it around on him.

"Why do you want to know?"

He stood there at the bottom of the stairs, smiling at her like he knew something she didn't and wanted to savor the moment.

As he climbed the stairs, the gun still hanging at his side, he said, "Do you know a man named Charles Larson?"

Nora stayed at the base of the steps.

She knew Charlie, but had no idea where this was going.

"Yes, why?"

She could hear his footsteps as he moved from room to room above her, and doors opening, and his voice.

"One of my men, Luca—you know Luca, of course—stopped Charles Larson as he drove his truck into town. This was after we saw the white truck coming out this way, and Charles Larson came from the same direction the white truck had come. So Luca wanted to know if Charles Larson had seen anything."

Nora gripped the wooden newel post at the bottom of the stairs.

Razvan's voice fell on her from above.

"From what Luca told me, Charles Larson seemed nervous. Possibly even guilty. So Luca stuck a knife under his kneecap, and do you know what Charles Larson told Luca?"

Razvan appeared at the top of the stairs, just his legs and torso and the gun visible from where Nora stood.

"He told Luca that he saw your boyfriend, the guitar singer, in the white truck."

***

Bruder crouched behind the seat of some sort of tractor in the back left corner of the shed.

The tractor was high enough to see between the cabs of the larger machines in front of him, but not high enough to highlight his spot, make it a focal point.

He waited, watching a narrow strip of light along the edge of the shed door, about thirty yards away.

Scanning to the left, his view was blocked by some chutes and smokestacks, then he could see all the way to the other side of the opening.

He could hear Connelly in the front corner, shifting around and cursing under his breath.

Bruder let it go.

He'd tell him to knock it off when someone approached the shed.

The Romanian in the wooden barn had come back out to stand by the pickup truck. He was watching the sheds, apparently waiting for Razvan to come out of the house before checking them.

The man with the machine gun was still on the road.

That put a small wrinkle into the plan.

That, and Razvan having Nora inside the house.

If the man from the barn poked his head inside and got it shot off, Kershaw would have to take out the man with the machine gun.

Then, what?

Razvan takes the woman hostage and calls for backup?

They storm the house and get into a firefight?

No.

Bruder's choice would be to pack the money into the pickup and drive away.

But he didn't like leaving Razvan behind him to make calls to whoever he had left and the crew coming in from Chicago.

Or go to work on the woman, getting what little information she could offer.

Whatever she told him, it would be too much.

So Bruder sat and waited.

He had one of the remotes for the explosives tucked in the hopper with the duffels of money.

Kershaw had the other two.

So if it came down to it and Razvan took her as a hostage, they had a hostage of their own to negotiate with.

Until somebody got a chance to shoot Razvan, hopefully.

It was all a mess, and unnecessary, but there wasn't any point in dwelling on it or getting frustrated.

He just looked at what was in front of them and how to get around it or through it.

Over the radio Kershaw said, "Razvan on the second floor, looking out the window. AK still by the truck."

Bruder heard an irritated sound from Connelly's corner, like he wanted to know more.

Too bad for him.

Then Kershaw said, "No sign of Nora," like he thought it would soothe Connelly's nerves.

"Goddam it," Connelly whispered.

Things were quiet for almost a minute.

"Razvan and Nora back on the porch," Kershaw said. "AK starting toward you. He's not in a hurry."

Bruder sat and waited.

He kept still when Connelly pulled himself out from under the trailer and stood up, in full view of anyone who looked around the door.

Bruder keyed his mic.

"Get back to your spot."

Rison and Kershaw were both in their spots, so they knew who he was talking to.

Instead, Connelly picked his way through the machinery and equipment toward Bruder.

Bruder watched him coming, making noise and inviting fire from the AK when it arrived, and decided he'd had enough.

Connelly was a good breacher, a good thief, but he was going to get them all killed.

Bruder touched the mic and whispered, "Are we still clear?"

Kershaw said, "AK by garages. He's waiting for Razvan."

Too close for anything that made noise.

Bruder pulled the knife out of the horizontal sheath on the back of his belt and waited for Connelly to get close enough.

Kershaw said, "Nora is on her phone. Not talking, I think she's making a call. And, ah, Razvan has the gun in her face."

Connelly stumbled over a bundle of hydraulic hoses and leaned up toward Bruder with his arm outstretched, making it easy.

Bruder would grab the wrist and pull him onto the blade, up under the chin, then drop down and wrap an arm around his face and keep him quiet while he sawed around.

Connelly was three steps away, then two, when he said, "Nora's calling me."

Bruder saw the phone in the outstretched hand.

It vibrated and the screen was lit up.

"She's standing out there with Razvan, calling me. What do you want to do?"

***

"Don't answer," Bruder said.

He kept the blade ready while they stared at the phone until it went silent, the call kicked into voicemail.

"She's talking," Kershaw said in their earpieces.

Connelly could hear, but not respond.

He whispered to Bruder, "What about Razvan? The gun?"

Bruder ignored him.

After a few seconds Kershaw said, "Phone call's over. She handed the phone to Razvan."

Bruder said, "Where's the AK?"

"Looking in the garages."

Bruder told Connelly, "The message."

Connelly hit some buttons and made sure the volume was low before he put it on speaker.

Nora's shaky voice said, "Adam, it's Nora. I need you to call me back as soon as you get this. I, um...just call me. Please. It's important. It's about today. Call me."

The message ended.

Connelly's eyes were fierce inside the balaclava.

"We gotta go kill that fucker."

"Give me the phone."

"What for?"

Bruder held his hand out. The one without the knife in it.

Connelly slapped the phone into his palm and Bruder slid it into a pocket.

"Let's go," Connelly said.

"Not yet."

"Why the hell not?"

Bruder touched the mic and asked Kershaw, "Do you have a shot on the gunner?"

"Nope. He's hunkered down behind the engine block with the gun in front of his face. I don't even have a clear shot on Razvan, unless we're okay with Nora getting hit too."

Connelly shook his head.

Bruder didn't care about that, but he didn't like the machine gun out there, untouchable and free to hose the landscape down.

Kershaw said, "AK going between the garages and the first shed, checking behind. I can't see him."

Bruder and Connelly both turned their attention to the other side of the back wall, listening for movement.

They heard nothing.

Kershaw said, "Wait, he's back. He's moving. Razvan too. They're all heading toward the sheds."

"All?" Bruder said.

"Yeah. Razvan has the gun on Nora, holding her close. AK is at the first shed. He has his phone out. Talking to the machine gunner, my guess."

Bruder told Connelly, "Get back to your spot."

Connelly stood there and tapped his trigger finger against the side of his rifle.

"If she gets shot," he said, "I'm going to be a problem."

He turned and crept back to his corner.

Bruder put the blade away and flicked the rifle's safety selector to single shot and pointed it at the opening, listening to the approaching footsteps.

***

"Open it," Razvan said.

He kept the pistol aimed between her shoulder blades while she stepped forward and opened the sliding door to the first metal shed.

Razvan walked with her, keeping the door and her body between him and anybody who might be inside.

Benj was off to the right of the opening with his gun ready.

His phone was in his breast pocket with Mihail listening on the other end.

When the door was all the way open Razvan studied the interior from the left side.

He saw an orange Kubota tractor with wet grass and leaves stuck to its wheels and attachments.

A bunch of other farm equipment meant for bigger tractors.

Belts and hoses and chains hanging on a pegboard along the back.

He pushed Nora into the opening and followed, crouching behind her with the gun pointing over her shoulder. It was hard on his back but better than getting shot.

Benj came in from the right, tracking with the rifle, and it was clear there was no white truck hidden among the equipment.

"Check the floor," Razvan said.

Benj knelt down, then got on his belly and looked under the equipment.

He moved around until he was satisfied, then stood and shook his head.

"Nobody."

"Next one," Razvan said.

***

"Coming to you," Kershaw said. "I have a shot on AK. Razvan, maybe, but he's keeping Nora in tight. Machine gunner...still no shot."

Bruder whispered, "If we shoot, do what you can on the gunner. And nobody shoots before me."

The criteria for him pulling the trigger was a clear shot on both AK and Razvan.

If they only killed one of the Romanians, they risked getting into a shootout with the gunner out there and another one running around the property, either or both of them calling in backup, even if it was just two more guys.

Who knew what kind of firepower they might bring, including cops?

If they could take AK and Razvan down it would still be bad having the gunner left out at the road, but between the four of them they could keep him busy and away from the phone, hopefully, while somebody flanked him and ended it.

Also, hopefully, without anyone getting shot by the M249.

If they got spotted inside the shed before Bruder fired, he would call out about the explosives in with the money.

Then the negotiations would begin, and they'd probably be trapped inside the shed until the crew from Chicago arrived in—Bruder glanced at his watch—two or three hours.

At that point, things would have officially gone to hell.

A shadow leaked into the sunshine outside the doorway.

Bruder put his optics at the edge of the door, where the owner of the shadow's head would appear, and waited.

***

When the face came around the door Bruder had it centered in his rifle's holosight.

It was Nora, her mouth set in a flat line and her chest lifting and falling from short, tight breaths.

Razvan was tucked in behind her, as much as he could be.

His pistol was pressed under her left ear.

The one with the AK stepped out from behind Razvan and swept the inside of the shed with his barrel, his eyes bright and ready.

Bruder reminded himself they were looking for a white truck full of men, not just the men.

Not yet, anyway.

Razvan risked a peek over Nora's shoulder and scanned the shed's contents.

They moved to their right, blocked from Bruder by the chutes and stacks.

He eased the rifle to his left, the other side of the obstruction, and rested the sight's red dot on AK's forehead.

He touched the mic and barely breathed the words.

"Anyone have Razvan?"

"No," Kershaw said.

Rison didn't answer and Connelly couldn't, except by firing.

Bruder whispered, "If you have Razvan, take him."

He kept the dot on AK and waited.

Nobody fired.

Kershaw said, "He's staying out in the driveway, behind Nora. If he takes her inside you might have a shot from the front corner."

Which meant Connelly.

Bruder didn't know if he'd take the shot.

Movement brought him back to the holosight and he watched as AK stepped forward, crossing the threshold into the shed, directly into Connelly's sights.

If Connelly shot him, it would be a mad scramble to get at Razvan before he had a chance to make more trouble.

It wouldn't end well, Bruder knew.

He waited for the shot, for everything to start happening quickly with more shots coming from Kershaw and the machine gunner, people yelling and dying.

AK moved deeper into the shed, out of Bruder's view, then popped on the cab of the combine, craning his neck to see over and past the other machines.

Bruder kept still, a dark lump among the shadows in the back corner.

He didn't move the rifle, wary of any reflection coming from the optics lens.

He looked just to the left of the man with the AK, not wanting him to feel any eyes.

After a moment the man shook his head and said something to Razvan in Romanian, then disappeared behind the combine.

Bruder watched him walk past the far side of the opening, heading for the other front corner of the shed.

"AK is checking the back side," Kershaw said.

It was where the truck had been parked before they put it in the pond, but the crushed stone left no tracks.

He wouldn't find anything.

When Bruder brought the rifle back to look for Razvan, he caught a glimpse of him and Nora moving to the right, blocked now by the shed's door.

Kershaw said, "I have Razvan. Nora is close but I have the shot."

"AK?" Bruder asked.

"Behind the shed, no go."

Bruder searched the back wall, knowing there weren't any doors or windows, but maybe there was a crack or hole or seam, and when a shape moved past he could put a burst through the steel and Kershaw could take Razvan.

But there was nothing, just ribbed metal and wooden posts and crossbeams.

Rison whispered, "What about when he passes between the sheds?"

"Bad angle, I can't see all the way through," Kershaw said. "If he comes out to the front, maybe."

Everyone waited.

Then Kershaw said, "Razvan is at the truck. He's putting Nora in. No sign of AK."

Bruder heard Connelly moving, scraping along the floor to get out from under the trailer.

Kershaw said, "Razvan is in the truck, he's backing up. Nora is in the front with him, in the middle. I—wait, AK is there, he went all the way around the house. He's at the corner of the porch, looking down at the pond."

Bruder dropped down from the tractor and worked through the equipment, catching up with Connelly at the edge of the doorway.

"We can't let them leave," Connelly said.

He had his balaclava off now, and his hair was matted with sweat.

Rison stepped out of the shadows on the other side of the opening.

"What's the move?"

"Nothing," Bruder said.

Connelly glared at him.

"Nothing? We can't let them take her."

"They want her to get to you," Bruder said. "She'll be fine until then."

Connelly turned and pulled a fist back, ready to pound it into the steel door, but kept himself under control. He sucked air in through his teeth and let it out in a low, seething growl.

Kershaw told them, "AK is getting into the truck, passenger side. Backing up, turning around on the grass. At the road. Turning north."

Rison said, "North?"

"Machine gunner is packing up," Kershaw said. "He's following them. They're gone."

***

They waited a full minute, then Kershaw walked into the shed with the poncho over his shoulder. His face was sweaty and streaked with dirt.

The four of them met in front of the combine.

"We let them take her," Connelly said.

Everybody knew that already, so nobody responded.

Rison said, "Why go north? There are other properties south of here."

"They don't have to search anymore," Bruder said, looking at Connelly. "They have the woman. They think we'll come to them now."

CHAPTER SEVENTEEN

Razvan drove with Nora wedged between him and Benj, who had his rifle butt-down between his knees. He was twisted to the left so he could look back at the house and barns.

He frowned at them and breathed loudly through his mouth, blowing air against Nora's right ear.

She stared straight ahead through the windshield with her arms crossed, and Razvan thought she had the look of a long-suffering wife.

Benj said in Romanian, "Something's going on back there."

Razvan grunted and kept their native language going.

"Oh, she's up to something. We'll get some details when her man calls us back."

"What if he doesn't?"

Razvan grinned and glanced over at Nora, who met his eyes for a moment then went back to scowling out the window. When he smiled, the thin flesh around his eyes piled up and made his sunken sockets look even deeper.

"Then we'll see what she knows. I suspect it's nothing— she's been a pawn for the thieves, I think—but maybe he'll call us back if we leave him another message with some real motivation in it."

Benj nodded.

Standard practice, about what he'd expected.

He looked back at the woman's place, becoming a group of boxes in the surrounding flatlands.

"Why don't you let me out here? I want to see what happens."

"Like what?"

Benj shrugged.

"Maybe they're watching the place, and they come crawling out of their holes when they see us leaving. If I spot anything, I'll call you back in."

Razvan thought about it, then shook his head.

"Costel and Luca are at the intersection up here. Anyone comes or goes, they will see them. I need both you and Mihail at the compound."

"For her? She'll be easy. The hard part will be making sure she doesn't just die on you."

"Not for her," Razvan said. "For the thieves, when they come with the money. And for the men from Chicago."

"Ah, shit. Them."

"Yes, you see? We're going to be very busy soon."

He grinned at Nora again and pushed the truck faster.

***

"Give me the phone," Connelly said. "I'm calling her back."

"What for?" Bruder said.

He didn't reach for the pocket with the phone.

Connelly's mouth flapped.

"Uh, to make sure she's alive?"

"And if she isn't?"

Rison and Kershaw watched the conversation, back and forth.

"Then we go to war."

"And what if she just doesn't answer? What if Razvan

does?"

"Okay, fine, calling is a bad idea. You got anything better?"

"Yes," Bruder said. "They're distracted by the woman—they think they found something useful, a tool they can pry with. We have about two hours until the crew from Chicago gets here, probably less. Maybe it's two guys, maybe it's twenty. We pack the money into Nora's car and take our chances with whoever they have between us and the highway."

"Are you kidding me?" Connelly said.

Bruder ignored him.

"I figure it's two guys, three at the most if they dropped one off on the way out."

"What if it's the machine gunner?" Kershaw said.

"Like I said. We take our chances. It's only going to get worse, and we have a short window to jump through."

Kershaw nodded.

"Let's get a look at that trunk."

Connelly took a step backward, putting himself between them and the shed's opening and spreading his arms.

"No."

Bruder checked his watch again, then kept it brief.

"You want to go after her, that's your call. We'll hold your share until you reach out or we hear you're dead."

"Hold up," Rison said. "What if they get a hold of him and start asking questions about us?"

"Oh, fuck you very much," Connelly said.

"Hey, I'm just being realistic."

They both looked at Bruder, who shrugged.

"You know names. Or think you do. You don't know how to get in touch with any of us except Rison, so that's his problem."

Rison blinked.

"Yeah, then they come after me."

"So, don't get found," Bruder said.

Rison's brow furrowed while he tried to make sense of it.

"See how it feels?" Connelly asked him.

Then, to Bruder: "What if they had one of us right now? Not a week from now, or a month. Right now, driving us away."

"That's different."

"How?"

Bruder didn't know why he had to explain this.

"We're all still on the job."

"Exactly," Connelly said. "And part of the job is we look out for each other. Right? There's a principle involved. A code. Am I right or not?"

Bruder shook his head.

"There's money involved. You helped us get the money. You earned a chance to spend your cut."

"Fine, that's fucked up, but I'll take it."

"But," Bruder cut him off, "when the job's done, it's done. You go off trying to rescue your woman, you're on your own."

"Yes, of course," Connelly said. "But they have Nora, and the job's not done. She helped us get the money. She earned a chance to spend her cut."

Everyone paused to dwell on that.

"She's not on the roster," Bruder said.

"Yes she is. As soon as we started using her, she was part of it."

"You mean as soon as you fell for her," Kershaw said.

"Doesn't matter. She's part of it. I made her part of it."

"You did," Bruder agreed. "It's called the chump. Chumps don't get shares."

"Don't call her that."

"We're wasting time," Bruder said. "Let's get moving."

He stepped toward Connelly, who didn't budge.

Instead, he said, "You know what? You're so damn busy looking for a way out of this you haven't thought about what you're leaving behind."

"I already told you, she's your problem."

"Not her," Connelly said. "The Romanians. Razvan. The crew from Chicago."

"They won't matter once they're in the rear view mirror."

"But you'll matter to them. We just talked about it. They go to work on Nora, then me, then Rison. You want to walk around the rest of your life double-checking every guy with a beard?"

Bruder shook his head again.

He thought about some of the people who'd like to find him, lay hands on him if they could.

Too many to remember, let alone count.

The most recent were Howell and McIntyre in New York, men he maybe should have killed, but they'd never find him unless they passed each other on the street.

And he hated New York, so the chances were slim.

He told Connelly, "This loose end doesn't lead to me. Or Kershaw. Or Rison, if you stay careful and keep your mouth shut. But if you're saying you won't do that, you might even help them find us..."

"I never said that," Connelly told him.

"...Then the safest thing would be to kill you right here. That cuts the loose end off before it starts."

"I never said that," Connelly repeated.

They stared at each other.

Before Bruder could decide what to do, Rison said, "Ah, shit. Hold on, hold on. I been thinking about it while you two hens clucked at each other, and I think he's right."

Connelly looked at him.

"Who?"

"You, dummy. I mean, she helped with the setup, yeah, but she didn't know what she was doing. Doesn't count in my book. But after we got here, she found us a place to stash the money, she told us how deep the pond was—she could have lied about that and said it wouldn't hide the truck—she covered our tracks with the mower...so, yeah. I flip it around, if I was on a job and reached out to someone I knew, and they did all that for me, I'd cut them in."

Bruder studied him for a moment, then looked at Kershaw, who said, "Makes sense to me. Plus the fact she could have told Razvan where we were hiding, and didn't."

"Good one," Rison said.

They all looked at Bruder, Connelly with that hopeful face again.

Bruder wasn't happy about it, but they were right.

He hadn't taken the time to consider what Nora had done for them.

And it didn't matter if he was happy or not, things needed to get done.

"Her share comes out of yours," Bruder said.

"Of course, fine."

Connelly's head dipped forward, waiting for more stipulations he'd agree to.

"We have two hours to get her," Bruder said. "Two hours. After that, the Chicago crew gets here, and it's every man and woman for themselves."

***

Connelly backed Nora's Lexus out of the garage and up to the shed door, and they made another fire brigade line, with Kershaw tossing the duffels of cash down from the hopper to Rison, and eventually into the trunk and back seat of the car.

Rison kept shucking bags when he asked, "Should we do the split now? Before shit gets hairy?"

"No time," Bruder said.

"Besides," Kershaw added, "what's the point of splitting it four ways when there might not be four of us left?"

"You're a real ray of sunshine," Rison said.

Bruder moved bags and said, "If anyone gets snatched, assume the hotel room in Minnesota is burned. Whoever gets out of here with the money—if any of us do—leave a message with Lola. Everybody else, check in with her when you can. She knows how to make sure you don't have the phone in one ear and a Romanian gun in the other."

"Pause," Kershaw said. "I'm down to the charges."

"You want help?" Connelly said.

"Nah." He toggled the receivers on the charges off and eased the bundles down with the two remotes he'd carried.

When it got to Bruder he added his remote and handed all of it to Connelly, who put it in the passenger seat.

Kershaw pulled the rest of the bags out of the hopper, and when they got to Bruder he set them on the stones next to the car instead of inside.

When they were done Rison eyeballed those bags, then the space left in the trunk and back seat.

"Draw straws to see who rides on the roof?"

Bruder said, "Only Connelly's in this car."

Connelly looked at him.

"This sounds like the start of a plan."

"I wouldn't call it a plan. Not yet."

"Well, step one is I get in the car. Step two?"

"You call Nora back."

Connelly paused.

"Do I want to hear step three?"

"You agree to drive yourself and the money out to the Romanian compound. With one of the explosive charges in with the cash, just in case."

"Fuck me. Okay, then what?"

"That's as far as I got," Bruder said. "Anybody has any ideas, speak up."

***

Luca perked up when he saw Razvan's F-250 and Mihail's Tacoma coming from the south, and when Luca's phone buzzed with a call from Razvan he answered with, "You get the money? The thieves?"

"One step closer," Razvan said in Romanian. This didn't tell Luca anything and was irritating, based on how long they'd been sitting there waiting for something to happen.

He was in the driver's seat with the heat on, listening to a story on public radio about the best way to slice a Thanksgiving turkey.

He asked Razvan, "One step? What's that mean?"

"You'll see when we drive past you."

"Past? We're not following you?"

By then Razvan was a few hundred yards away and had hung up.

Luca rolled his window down and told Costel, "They're coming. Raz is being cryptic."

Costel grunted, unsurprised. He was splayed out in the bed of the truck, enjoying the warm sunshine with the bite of cold wind blowing above him.

They were parked in the dead center of the first intersection coming up from the south, through which anyone trying to get back into town would have to pass.

No one had tried to get through for hours.

Everyone in town knew by now to stay at home, or wherever they were.

Luca and Costel had moved the truck steadily further south and west as Razvan, Benj, and Mihail cleared properties, looking for the white truck and the men from it, but mainly heading to the woman's house because they knew her boyfriend, the Hungary fan, was involved somehow.

When they found Pavel's truck in the ditch, stalled out with both him and Grigore shot to death, Benj and Mihail suggested they start executing locals until someone came forward with information about the thieves, even though they already had the information about the woman.

Luca nodded along with their rage, ready to follow, and Razvan seemed to be warming to the idea.

Finally.

Luca's hatred for the sheep in this cowshit town grew with every person he passed while he sped Pavel's truck back to the compound, the two bodies in the back covered by a flapping tarp anchored by spare tires.

Mihail followed dangerously close to his rear bumper to keep anyone else from getting a good look at the two pairs of boots flashing out inside the missing tailgate.

Luca parked the truck—now a hearse, he supposed—next to the wheelless armored car, squatting on the ground like a garbage bin, hauled there from the tunnel by a wrecker who took his cash payment and knew better than to show any curiosity about the situation.

On the way south again, riding with Mihail, the two of them stoked each other about how they were going to execute a scorched earth policy upon the masses here, an ethnic cleansing on a people who didn't seem to have any ethnicity, but still...

But when they reunited with the rest of the men, the fury that had been building behind Razvan's sunken eyes was gone, replaced by the simmering patience they all knew could erupt at any moment, but it was not the rage felt by Luca and Mihail and Benj.

Costel...he was just an ox, satisfied to pull whatever wagon Razvan hitched him to.

And Razvan told them all, "There's no need for a massacre, boys. We know who is involved, or at least who is associated with those involved."

The woman.

Her boyfriend.

Luca had been with Grigore during the incident at Len's, and he'd noticed how the shitty guitar player moved when he attacked Grigore. It hadn't meant anything at the time—the singer knew how to fight a little, so what?—but when they all heard what the farmer said about him being in the white truck, Luca wasn't shocked.

Maybe surprised, but not shocked.

He looked forward to seeing the singing Hungary fan again. He had some things to share with him in return for the sucker punch at Len's, and for killing Grigore and Pavel.

And probably Claudiu, though they didn't know for sure yet.

And for taking away the widespread bloodletting he and Mihail considered their right.

And for being a Hungary fan.

The turkey carving story on the radio was actually interesting when Luca substituted the thief for the turkey, but he turned it down as Razvan slowed his truck and angled as he approached the intersection so his side would be closest to Luca's door.

The driver's window came down and Razvan leaned out, his gaunt face grinning at them like he had a secret.

Luca saw the woman crammed between him and Benj, wearing a face like she was on her way to a firing squad.

"So she knows?" Luca said.

"Maybe. We'll find out. We left her boyfriend a message."

"What if he doesn't care?"

Razvan shrugged.

"Then we push further out and flush them."

Costel sat up in the truck bed and said, "Why not do that now? We're already here."

Razvan turned and muttered something to Benj, something about how it was easy for them to suggest such a thing, then told them, "Three men isn't enough. The further out we go, the easier it will be to see us coming. They'll be waiting for us."

Luca picked something up in his tone, in the way he squinted through the windshield instead of looking over at them.

He was trying to save face while admitting he needed the men from Chicago.

Luca nodded, helping him.

"Hey, if anyone else has to get shot, it might as well be a city boy."

Razvan smiled again, liking the idea, and said, "You two stay here in case they come chasing after us or try to slip out. They probably don't even know we have her yet, but they will as soon as he calls back."

"Hundred bucks says he doesn't," Costel said, and dropped back into the bed.

Luca said, "Give us Mihail and the machine gun."

Razvan shook his head.

"I need them. I'll check in every twenty minutes. You see anything, call me."

He pulled away and headed toward town with Mihail following.

Luca waved at Mihail, who wagged his tongue and gave him the finger.

Luca rolled his window back up and sulked through the windshield.

So the three of them—Razvan, Benj, and Mihail—needed more men to search for the thieves, but if they came roaring up the road he and Costel were sufficient?

He hoped they did show up.

Let him and Costel drive back to the compound with the four assholes slung across the roof like the deer they saw around town or stacked up in the bed like they used to do back home with the people going into pits.

Like Pavel and Grigore were, in the truck parked out at the compound now.

Let Razvan and the crew from Chicago suck on that for a while.

Luca stared down the road, willing the thieves—wherever they were out there—to come his way.

***

They had a plan.

Or, according to Bruder and the others, something close enough to a plan to get moving.

Connelly stood next to Nora's car and called her phone on speaker.

The other three men watched the road and fields and listened to the ringing.

She answered after the second one.

"Adam?"

There was engine noise and airflow, telling him she was on speaker too.

"Hey, what's up? Are you okay?"

"I—"Razvan cut her off.

"Hello, asshole. You know who this is?"

"Uh, no," he said, playing stupid. "Nora, what's going on?"

Razvan said, "You're not talking to her anymore, you're talking to me. You know what's going on, and so do we. We talked to the farmer you ran into north of town."

Connelly looked around to see if Bruder was giving him an *I told you so* face, but he still gazed out at the horizon, watching.

"I know you have my money," Razvan said. "And I know you're still here. And now you know I have your woman. Here's the deal: Bring me my money, you get her back un-harmed. Do not do this, you do not get her back, and she gets harmed. Very much. Now, where are you, and where is my money?"

Connelly paused.

They'd all agreed to string it out for as long as possible—maybe the Romanians weren't certain about anything—but if it became clear they knew the situation, continuing to play dumb would just waste time they didn't have.

"Okay, you have a deal. Money for her, and I drive out of town with her."

Razvan laughed.

"I did not mention what happens to you and your friends."

"No need," Connelly said. "I just told you what happens. And my friends are gone."

"Oh? They left you and my money behind?"

He didn't sound convinced.

"They didn't like how things were going."

"Better to live to steal another day, eh?"

"Something like that," Connelly said.

"Well, they didn't drive out of town, I can promise you."

Connelly didn't say anything.

Razvan said, "They are on foot? If so, we'll find them. Would you like to take a turn with the knife, let them know how you feel about being abandoned?"

"The money for Nora," Connelly said, getting back on track. "And she and I drive away."

"Okay, okay, we'll discuss your friends when we meet. Where are you?"

"I'll come to you."

"Why is that?"

"Because we're meeting on the highway, east of town. I'm tired of being boxed in."

"I see."

Razvan was quiet for a moment, then said, "No. You'll come to our compound."

"Not a chance."

"Then she's dead. And so are you, eventually. You have to know we'll find you."

Connelly looked at Bruder.

They'd expected something along these lines and were ready for it.

Bruder nodded.

Connelly told Razvan, "Okay, okay, fine. Your farm."

"Compound."

"Whatever. But listen up—I have explosives tamped in with the cash. I see anything that looks like a trap, or you do anything I don't like once I get to the meet, I blow the money."

Razvan processed that.

"With you standing next to it?"

"If the alternative is letting you go to work on me, hell yes. And there's enough boom in here to flatten everything for fifty yards, so I'll probably take you with me."

"Hm. All of this—losing the money, willing to explode yourself—all of this for the woman?"

"I'm not interested in your opinion on it. Are we doing this or not?"

"All business, I like it. You know where the compound is, I assume?"

"Yes," Connelly said.

"You can be there in ten minutes?"

Putting him on the spot, trying to gauge where he actually was.

"Make it thirty," Connelly said.

"Half an hour, then."

"Who am I going to run into between here and there?"

"Depends on where you are," Razvan said, teasing.

"I don't want anybody shooting at me."

"My men will know to bring you, no shots fired. I'll tell them about the explosives too. Oh, have you counted my money yet?"

"I haven't really had the luxury."

Razvan laughed.

"That's true. I'm just curious, it will be interesting to find out exactly how much this whore is worth to you. See you soon."

The call ended.

Connelly put the phone away.

"Too easy. They're going to kill me at that compound."

Bruder nodded.

"Nora too. But he'll make an example of you first, for his

men and the people in Chicago. So, we'll have time before he kills you."

"How much time?" Connelly said, keeping his voice level.

"As long as it takes," Bruder said.

***

Razvan killed the call as he pulled into the compound. He kept Nora's phone in case the boyfriend called again.

Nora watched him drop it into his breast pocket but didn't say anything.

The driveway into the compound went through an open, hinged gate attached to an eight-foot chain link fence with barbed wire along the top. The fence wrapped all the way around the few acres of house, silos, and outbuildings.

The silos and conveyors and the metal and concrete buildings dedicated to them were on the right side of the driveway, just inside the gate, acting like another barrier between the house and the road.

Razvan turned and drove along those with the silos looming over the truck in the afternoon sun, which was already dipping toward the western tree line at four o'clock, then he cut left and pulled in close to the front of the house.

They'd ripped out the landscaping and tilled the grass under years ago and now just had a flat lot of crushed stone inside the fence, making the place look and feel more like a way station than a homestead.

On the other side of the fence to the west and south was flat, plowed cornfield, smelling faintly of fertilizer and waiting for the spring planting.

To the east, back toward Pine Street, was the tree line serving as a wind and snow break for the compound. Razvan and his men had cut into the trees thirty yards or so, creating a no-man's land between the fence and remaining trees filled with stumps and trunks that had been cut and stacked but not yet split.

Nothing about it was fresh or recent.

Razvan got out of the truck and waved his fingers, telling Nora to follow him.

Benj got out the other side and went up the steps into the house, a two-story rectangle with yellow siding and brown shutters. It didn't have a nice porch, like Nora's, just a set of poured concrete steps leading up to the door, which had a small canopy roof jutting out of the house's face to offer a bit of shelter from rain and snow.

Nora got out of the truck and moved past him to stand near the tailgate.

He asked her, "Would you like a coat?"

"No."

She was being stubborn and pouty, so he didn't ask again.

Mihail pulled through the gate and trotted over to close it, then took the Tacoma in a tight circle and put the front bumper against the inside of the gate, blocking it. He hauled the M249 and sandbag out and carried them into the metal and concrete building closest to the gate and shut the door behind him.

Razvan knew he'd be setting up in one of the windows with an angle covering the gate and looking east along the road, where the boyfriend would come from.

Nora seemed to know this as well. A line appeared between her eyebrows.

He told her, "When I bought this place, I stood upstairs in the master bedroom and looked out the windows at these fields, almost as far as I could see, and I thought, 'How depressing.' Then I realized, for you people, it was like looking out at fields of money. Like a man who owns a diamond mine looking out at sand and rocks. And for me, it was the same. For different reasons, obviously, but the same. Money, almost as far as I could see."

She didn't respond or act like she'd heard him at all.

"Did you know your boyfriend was planning to steal it

from me?"

Now she heard him.

"No."

"But you told him some things about me, didn't you? About how we operate."

She shook her head.

"I think you did," he said. "Even if you didn't know it, he was finding things out. Otherwise, how would they know to hit the truck at the tunnel? And when to be there?"

She said, "Maybe one of your men has a big mouth."

It made him laugh.

"Well, yes, they all do. But only with each other. Certainly not with a shitty singer who showed up in town a few weeks ago."

She went back to silence.

Razvan said, "You told him about your parents, I'm sure. Do they like it in Arizona?"

She looked at him, the line between her brows deeper now.

"I've heard it's nice," he said, "especially this time of year, when the heat is finally bearable. You should know, if something happens to you because of your boyfriend—like if we have to kill you—I will deliver the news to your mother and father myself, in person."

It hung between them, unaffected by gravity.

"So, make sure he doesn't do anything stupid, okay? For your sake, and theirs. Just do exactly what I tell you to do and everything will be fine."

***

He was lying, Nora knew, but her brain tried to convince her otherwise.

It kept telling her to go along with it, be polite, follow the norms of society even though this was as abnormal as it could get.

If she behaved, like Razvan said, she'd be fine.

But no, that was a lie.

He was going to kill her and Adam—that was his name until she learned otherwise—as soon as he got the money back.

But her brain wouldn't accept that, so it tried to construct a narrative in which she and Adam drove away from this tiny prison yard, unscathed and free to go, left to sort out their future with this insanity lingering like a bloodstain on the infancy of their relationship.

Like something they'd tell their kids about, years down the line: *The crazy time your father stole some money from Romanian gangsters and I got held hostage until he gave the money back. Oh, it was such a hoot...*

There her brain went again, wandering off into a future she knew did not exist.

She looked at the flat black armored car, which now had no wheels and looked like a boxy, beached submarine. And next to that, a pickup truck with four boots sticking out where the tailgate should be, and the legs attached to those boots.

Dead bodies.

She saw all of that and tried to put it into context with the man she knew as Adam, who was funny and enjoyed making her laugh, who put too much sugar in his coffee, who kept trying to convince her *Die Hard* was a Christmas movie and they should start a tradition to watch it every year on Christmas Eve.

To picture him doing any of this, to think he was capable of it...it disturbed her, but what was even more troubling was how much it pleased her.

To have someone in her life who was that capable—who came across a situation like Razvan and his men, then set about making a plan and executing it to come out on top—it ought to terrify her.

But it didn't.

The idea of being next to a person like that for the rest of her life made her think of one word: Peaceful.

She didn't need anyone to take care of her.

No, the thought of that was chafing.

It made her bristle.

But to walk through the world knowing she didn't have to worry about people like Razvan anymore...

And there she went *again*, thinking she and Adam were going to walk away from this.

The pragmatic side of her brain, the one she used at work—and now that she was forced to examine it, just about every other part of her life—figured it was a survival response.

A coping mechanism meant to keep her from panicking.

She noted the irony.

Panicking and doing something drastic, instead of cooperating, was exactly what might keep her alive.

But so far, her brain wouldn't let her.

It kept telling her things were going to work out fine, and maybe this would be a story she and Adam would tell her parents when they met this Christmas.

CHAPTER EIGHTEEN

Connelly pulled out of Nora's driveway at 4:15 and turned left, north.

Even though the sun hovered just above the western edge of the field off to his left there was still plenty of light to see, since there were no shadows or trees forming a darker canopy along the road.

Still, he found the headlights and turned them on.

He didn't want anyone ahead of him to get the idea he was trying to sneak around.

All in all, he gave it about a fifty percent chance this was all going to work.

He would have put it at less, but Bruder had come up with the rest of the plan, and the man never seemed to do anything unless he was clear on the outcome, or at least clear on the contingencies if that outcome didn't, well, come out.

So Connelly was either driving towards rescuing Nora and getting the hell out of town with the cash and crew, or he was driving towards his own torture and execution, alongside Nora, while the rest of the crew slipped away thanks to his distraction.

Fifty-fifty.

A coin toss.

For Connelly, the risk was worth the reward.

He just hoped everybody else felt the same.

***

Connelly came to the first house north of Nora's and said, "Neighbor is two point seven miles from the driveway. Vehicles in the driveway but nobody moving around."

He didn't bother to turn his head when he spoke—they'd tested the radio with the mic locked open and the sound came through just fine with him looking forward.

The radio was inside the partially open zipper of the duffel bag in the middle of the back seat floor, likely to be one of the last bags Razvan and his men got to, if they got that far.

The explosives were tamped between bags in the trunk.

The remote was in Connelly's hand.

So far, the hand wasn't sweating.

***

He was still a mile out when he saw the truck waiting for him in the middle of the intersection.

When he got closer, he glanced at the odometer and said, "Five point six miles from the driveway. I can see two men standing behind a truck in the intersection, the first one coming north. Both have long guns, pointed at me. They've been waiting."

Nobody could respond with the mic locked, so he had to assume they'd heard everything and would act accordingly.

He closed the last mile and dropped the driver's window, then coasted to a stop just before the intersection.

He lifted his hands to show the left was empty and the right held the remote.

"Hey guys. Easy with the guns."

The one behind the hood yelled, "Get out!"

Connelly got out.

He used slow, deliberate movements, watching the men as they came around opposite ends of the truck to flank him from both sides.

"Arms out," the one from behind the hood said.

He was wiry with a cropped black beard and seemed to be in charge.

The other one was bigger, with a reddened face like he'd been exercising or standing in the sun and wind.

They both kept their rifles pointed at him.

Connelly spread his arms.

He told the one in charge, who was on his right, "Don't touch this hand, please. Razvan told you about that, right? The explosives?"

"Yes, we know. I think you're bluffing—nobody would blow up this much money—but you stole it from us in the first place, so maybe you are stupid enough to destroy it too."

Connelly shrugged.

"I'm more than stupid enough."

"I agree. I was there when you sucker punched Grigore. That was very stupid."

Connelly watched the big one, on his left, stepping all the way behind him.

"Hey, that wasn't a sucker punch. He was standing right there, ready to fight."

"No, no, you had the woman distract him. Then you hit him. A bitch move, my friend."

Connelly scoffed.

"Bullshit, pal. But all that is ancient history."

He glanced over his left shoulder.

The big one was at his eight o'clock, out of sight and out of the line of fire if the other one decided to shoot.

The one in front of him said, "Yes, history. Because now Grigore is dead—did you kill him?"

"Nope."

He lifted the rifle, moving the barrel from Connelly's chest to his face.

"I think you did."

"Is this what Razvan told you to do? Threaten me and scare me into blowing the cash? Because it's working."

The man behind him said something in Romanian, making the one in front blink a few times.

Making a decision.

"Hold still," he said.

Connelly heard adjustments and footsteps behind him, then large hands checked him for anything other than the remote.

They didn't find anything because he didn't have anything.

"Where is your phone? The one you used to call the girl?"

"In the car, the cup holder."

The big one looked inside to confirm this, then stepped behind him again.

"We're going to check the bags," the man in front said.

"All of them?"

He stopped after one step toward the car and looked at Connelly.

"Do we need to?"

"No, it's all there. It would just take a long time to check them all. And I don't want you jostling the explosives."

"Jostling?"

"Fucking with."

The man glanced at the other one and said, "Where are the explosives?"

"Packed in the trunk, buried under a couple of the bags. You know, for maximum damage."

"Just open the door. And the trunk."

Connelly did.

The big one unzipped a few of the top bags in the back seat and stuck his hand in, pawing around to make sure the cash went all the way to the bottom of the duffels, then went to the trunk and looked in at the pile.

He told Connelly, "Pull them out."

"Which ones?"

The man pointed.

"This one. That one. And that one."

Connelly pulled them out one at a time with his left hand and set them in the road.

"Open."

He unzipped the bags—slightly difficult with the remote clutched in his right hand—and made a show of the bundled money inside.

"See? No magazines, or newspapers, or whatever else we might have found to replace the cash. Soybeans? Who knows."

The two men were only half-listening, both of them peering into the trunk at the sliver of explosives showing between two of the bags. It was just a black satchel, but Connelly had pulled the flap open a bit to show some wires, knowing those had a tendency to freak people out.

He waited while they silently freaked out.

If Connelly had a weapon stashed on him, it would have been the perfect opportunity to use it and get rid of both of these clowns.

But that wasn't the plan.

If these two went radio silent and Connelly showed up at the compound alone, he probably wouldn't get the warm welcome Razvan had promised.

So he waited for them to turn and acknowledge the money, then closed the bags and eased them back in the trunk one by one, playing up the possibility of the explosives accidentally going off, which was actually zero.

The two men stepped away while he worked.

He closed the trunk and back door.

The one in charge said, "I'm driving this car. You're riding with me."

"Okay."

"I want to be sure, if you decide to blow me up, you die too."

Connelly went around to the passenger side and got in. He looked over at the man, standing outside the open driver's door, sweating.

"Seat belt," the man said.

Connelly fumbled it into place with his left hand.

"Now put your left arm under the belt, like that. Yes, tuck it in so it's strapped against you. Your right hand, keep it up where I can see it."

Connelly said, "I'm not going to blow us both up just because we almost got into a bar fight. So come on. Hop in."

The man handed his rifle to the big one and pulled a flat black pistol from his waistband.

He kept that in his left hand, away from but pointed at Connelly, as he got in and closed the door.

"If you blow us up, the woman dies. You know that, right?"

"Thanks for reminding me."

They led the way out of the intersection with the truck following.

Connelly checked his mirror and saw the big guy was hanging back, just in case the Lexus exploded.

He looked over at the driver, who had a drop of sweat hanging off the end of his nose.

"You guys aren't leaving anybody here?"

"Shut up."

"It's just, I was kinda hoping you'd find my friends. Well, my former friends. They left me hanging."

"We'll find them, don't worry about it."

He glanced over at Connelly and didn't say anything, but his face told the story.

He was supposed to keep up the charade about Connelly and Nora being safe, reunited, allowed to go on their merry way once the cash was handed over.

But the look told Connelly the Romanians were going to do whatever they wanted and needed to in order to find everyone responsible.

"I hope so," Connelly said.

Then, knowing Bruder and the others on the other end of the radio had the information they needed, he said, "So you're a soccer fan, huh?"

***

Jim Thorensen watched the Lexus drive past his house, going north with its lights on, and frowned at it.

His house was close enough to the road to hear and sometimes feel every vehicle that went past, and it looked like the Albrecht girl's car, but there was a man in the driver's seat.

In addition to that oddity, nobody was supposed to be out driving around until this madness with the Romanian fellas and the sheriff and whoever the heck else was involved got settled.

Jim almost called Sheriff Wern to report it, but decided it was a better idea to mind his own business and go back to trying to fix his chainsaw while listening to the boys on AM radio and their commentary about how the Hawkeyes were getting screwed once again in the national rankings.

He wandered back into the dining room, a small space with a small table and four chairs next to a sliding door overlooking the property out back.

The chainsaw parts were spread across the table on top of a few layers of newspaper.

Carol was in the kitchen, just on the other side of a breakfast bar countertop.

"I heard right," he told her. "It was a car."

"Oh? Who?"

"Don't know, don't care."

Carol knew that tone and accepted the end of the discussion.

She and Jim weren't farmers and never had been, unless you counted Jim's endless harvesting of firewood for their stove. The fields around their home were owned and managed by the Schillers, the next house to the north, and while the Thorensens knew of the Romanians and the sketchiness around them, their lives had never directly crossed.

"Chicken and green beans for dinner," she said.

Jim grunted and went back to being miserable about his chainsaw and a bunch of college kids playing keepaway with a football.

***

Razvan led Nora into the house, which smelled like fried food, beer, and wood smoke. She'd taken a tour of a fire station in Minneapolis once, and this place looked and felt like a contaminated version of it.

The living room just inside the door was large and square with wood paneling and a massive television on one wall.

A black wood stove in the far corner glowed with embers, and next to that was a ragged stack of wood piled right on the shabby carpet.

Mismatched couches and chairs all faced the TV, which showed a movie with the volume off.

The kitchen was to the left. Dirty pots and pans covered the stovetop and a commercial-sized trash can overflowed with paper plates, dirty napkins, and food boxes. Another can held empty beer bottles, with more empties stacked in cases and six-pack boxes around it.

Razvan said, "Can I get you anything?"

"No."

"Do you need to use the bathroom?"

She shuddered at what that room must look and smell like.

"No."

"Fine. Sit down then, the remote is right there. Find something you like while we wait for your boyfriend to—"His phone rang and he looked at the screen, then grinned at Nora.

"Let's find out if he's behaving so far."

He switched to Romanian while he spoke into the phone, then listened.

Back and forth, watching Nora the whole time.

Nora didn't blink, trying to glean anything she could from this end of the conversation.

Was Adam okay?

Was he alive?

Was he really coming?

And where the hell were the other three men?

Razvan hung up and put the phone away.

"Good news. You'll see him again in a few minutes. He's being very cooperative. Except for the explosives, but I can't blame him for it, I suppose."

"When he gets here and gives you the money," Nora said, "we leave. Right?"

"Sure," Razvan said. "After we count the money, of course, to make sure it is all there. I'll need your help for that part."

"I'm not counting your money."

"No, no, of course not. But to count the money, we will need to move the explosives he put in there."

Nora frowned, still not sure what he was getting at.

Razvan said, "So when the time comes to move them, that will be your job. Pick the bomb up and hold it while we count the money. You can do that, right?"

***

Connelly had given up on conversation and rode in silence as they took the turn on Pine, angling northwest away from the highway.

Traffic was normal now, no more checkpoints necessary, and he felt slightly miffed about how everyone else in the world just went on with their lives while Nora was out here in the growing darkness with a Romanian thug and his men.

But they didn't know, or didn't care, and it didn't do any good to hold out hope for a posse of townsfolk finally ready to drive the invaders out.

When they approached the tunnel, Connelly saw the tarp on the southern side was still there, pulled up and to the side to let traffic through.

The armored car was gone, but the Lexus' headlights showed fresh scorch and gouge marks in the battered asphalt.

The driver looked over at Connelly as they bumped along the ruts made from the wrecker dragging the armored car out.

His hands flexed on the steering wheel.

Connelly stared straight ahead, not wanting to antagonize him any more than he already was.

They came out the other side and the man pushed the Lexus to what Connelly felt was an irresponsible speed, given the possibility of ice and wildlife, but he kept his mouth shut and they survived to make the left turn onto the dirt road leading to the compound.

Connelly saw the silos far ahead, lit from below by harsh white security lights.

He glanced over his left shoulder at the following truck, which also made the turn, and used the motion to check the stretch of Pine they'd just covered.

No other vehicles, headlights or not, that he could see.

But they wouldn't be that obvious about it, would they?

Assuming they were coming...

It was all technically still a coin flip, but he didn't feel that confident anymore.

**

Jim and Carol had a compost pile that was really just a mound of stuff for the possums and raccoons to eat, and when he carried the bowl of green bean stems and chicken skin around the back corner of the garage it took him a few seconds to realize something was wrong.

It was almost full dark, but part of the driveway was visible off to his right and there was too much space over that way, too much peripheral view of the road and harvested field beyond.

He turned to frown at the driveway.

The Cherokee was gone.

He stood there with the empty bowl dangling from his hand, sorting it out.

Did Carol pull it into the garage?

No, she couldn't have, the table saw was set up in there on sawhorses, like it had been for the past four months.

Did she move the saw?

Shaking his head and grumbling, he went over and peered through the garage window.

In the green light from a battery charger, he could see the sawhorses were still there, taking up enough room to block both parking spots.

"Well, what the hell then?"

Jim walked around the front corner and stared at the spot where the Cherokee should be.

Had Carol left while he was taking out the compost?

No, she would have taken the Ford.

He looked north, toward town, and saw nothing.

He looked south and saw a tractor parked on the side of the road, about a hundred yards away, an angular lump in the settling gray of night.

Well, that hadn't been there before, when he looked out and saw the Lexus going by.

He went inside and got the deer shiner, forgetting to put the empty bowl down.

Carol was just putting the rolls on the table.

She picked up on Jim's focus.

"Coyotes?"

"The damn Cherokee is gone," he said.

She blinked a few times.

"What?"

But he was already out the front door and she followed him, across the yard to the south.

She glanced at the driveway and sure enough, the Cherokee was missing.

"Jim?"

He got to the edge of their grass and hit the spotlight and put it on an orange Kubota tractor squatting in the field, just off the road.

"What's that doing there?" Carol said.

"No idea. It's the Albrecht's, right?"

"Oh, I think so."

Jim moved the beam to point toward the Albrecht property, much too far away to be seen, even in broad daylight.

"What the hell is going on down there?"

"Jim, the Cherokee's gone."

"I know, I know. Where's the damn phone?"

***

The Romanian driving Nora's car pulled into a short driveway blocked by an eight-foot gate.

A pickup truck faced them from the other side, its bumper touching the gate.

In case anyone tried to ram their way through, Connelly supposed.

The driver opened the door and put one foot out, just enough to stick his head above the roof and yell something.

Another man—Connelly thought he might be the one from the road, with the machine gun, but couldn't be sure—came around the corner of a squat block and steel building to the right of the gate.

He laughed and said something in Romanian, then backed the pickup away from the gate.

By then the truck behind Connelly had arrived, and the bulky driver shuffled past to push the gate open.

As they pulled through the driver pointed through the windshield.

"You recognize those?"

Connelly looked at the armored car, dumped next to the pickup truck they'd sent rolling across a field. The two bodies were still in the bed.

"Yeah, I do."

No point in lying about it.

They sat there while the other pickup came in behind them, the two men outside the car talking and glaring in at Connelly while they closed the gate and put the truck back in place against it.

The driver pulled to the right and drove toward a bland house in the back left corner.

He said, "You shot them?"

Connelly shook his head.

"No, not me."

"What about Claudiu? Did you kill him?"

This, maybe he could lie about.

"I don't know who that is."

"No?"

The driver was getting antsy, pulling on the steering wheel.

Connelly got the feeling the guy knew these were their last moments alone before Razvan took over, and he might be working himself up to get some shots in before it was too late.

He turned toward the driver and scratched his chin with the hand holding the remote for the explosive charge.

"No, who is Claudiu?"

The driver glanced at the remote and gave a sour grin, knowing what Connelly was doing.

"You're going to be sorry, my friend."

"Sorry? Why? I thought we were doing a trade here, nobody gets hurt."

They stopped in front of the house, next to the truck Razvan had used to drive Nora away.

The front door opened and Razvan was there, ducking down to look out at them.

The driver said, "Sure, you're right. Everything is fine."

He popped the trunk and got out.

Connelly leaned over to unclip his seatbelt and said, just loud enough for the open radio, "Hurry hurry hurry."

CHAPTER NINETEEN

Sheriff Wern was eating a cold takeout dinner from Len's in his office and thought he was at the end of a long, insane day when he heard Dispatch put the word out about Jim Thorensen's Jeep Grand Cherokee going missing.

Dispatch, currently a woman named Beth, went on to say, "Jim also told me he saw a man driving Nora Albrecht's car, the Lexus, but she hasn't reported that stolen."

Wern thought about that.

Jim Thorensen, who lived next to Nora Albrecht, who seemed to be the focal point of Razvan's efforts to get his property back.

Wern had gathered that much when Razvan told him he didn't need the checkpoints at the crossroads and along the highways anymore, and if anyone around the Albrecht property called in about noise, he should ignore them.

"What kind of noise?" Wern had asked.

"Just ignore them," Razvan told him.

And now Jim Thorensen's Cherokee was missing, and some guy was driving Nora's car around.

Should he ignore that?

They didn't get many stolen vehicles around town.

The ones they did get were almost always a misunderstanding or a dumbass kid trying to impress a girl or prove a point to their parents.

But this was different, he knew.

He got on the radio.

"Copy that, Dispatch. One-two, what's your twenty?"

This was Officer Hennig.

"One-two, I'm at the motel, domestic disturbance."

Again?

If they weren't careful, Ed and Barbara were going to burn that place down someday.

He told Hennig, "When you're done there take a drive out to Jim Thorensen's and take a look at the Albrecht place."

"What am I looking for?"

"Oh, just trouble of any sort."

"Plenty of that to go around today."

"I'll sign off on that, for damn sure. One-four, what about you?"

Unit One-Four, Donaldson, came back: "Two miles west of town, speed trap in the median."

Wern said, "Do me a favor, take a look up Pine, to the intersection with 64th. Keep an eye out for the missing Cherokee."

Donaldson had been out there with one of the Romanians during the whole lockdown and had told Wern he wasn't going to shoot anybody, no matter what the Romanian said, unless his or another resident's life was in danger.

Meaning, if the Romanian got into trouble, that was his own damn problem.

Donaldson was a combat veteran and hadn't been shy about telling the Romanian the same exact thing.

Wern winced when he heard about that, but it hadn't amounted to anything serious.

Now Donaldson said, "You think they stole Jim's Jeep?"

"Apparently somebody did. Don't make the turn, now. We don't want anybody getting more riled than they are. Just take a look up Pine and see what you can see."

"What if I see the Cherokee?"

"Uh…let me know, I guess."

"Copy that."

***

Connelly stood with the remote in his hand and watched while the two Romanians who escorted him to the compound eased the duffel bags out of the Lexus' trunk and lined them up on the ground.

The silos loomed behind him, about twenty yards away, which seemed an odd thing to walk out of your front door and see, but maybe not in Iowa.

He looked at the front door, Razvan standing there with an arm around Nora's shoulders, the hand resting on her upper arm.

His other hand held a mean-looking pistol with the barrel pointed at Nora's stomach.

Nora stared back at Connelly, her chest rising and falling rapidly.

But her mouth was a straight line, determined to keep it all together until this was over, and he felt bad for her, getting sucked into this nonsense between the two groups of rough men.

If it got her hurt, or killed, he didn't see much point in working the rest of his life to get over it.

The man who'd driven the Lexus said something to Razvan, who told Connelly, "They've uncovered the explosives. Now, slowly, bring them to her."

He gestured with the pistol.

"No," Connelly said. "They stay with the cash."

Razvan nodded, then dragged Nora down the concrete steps over to the bags on the ground.

Now they were about five yards from Connelly.

"She is with the cash," Razvan said. "Put the explosives in her hands."

Connelly was stuck.

He considered Razvan for a few moments, the two men staring at each other, then looked at Nora again.

"Just give them to me," she said.

Connelly stepped over the bags and went to the trunk.

The driver moved ten yards away and used a blinding flashlight to illuminate the inside of the car, spotlighting the satchel of explosives and making sure Connelly didn't have a flamethrower or anything else stashed in there.

The other Romanian stood next to him, both of them looking uneasy.

Connelly lifted the satchel by its strap and let the weight swing a bit while he turned.

He couldn't see the men standing behind the flashlight now, but the beam did move back a few more steps.

He carried the satchel to Nora and laid the strap across her outstretched hands.

"Hold it close," Razvan told her. "Hug it to your chest."

She did, staring straight ahead with her jaw muscles working.

"This is the only one?" Razvan said.

Connelly nodded.

"You have the money. We're leaving now."

"Not until we count it."

"It's all there."

Razvan shrugged.

"Maybe. Also, not until you tell me how to find your friends."

Connelly expected this but tried to look caught off-guard.

"That's not part of the deal."

"The deal is, you give me what I want and the two of you get to leave."

"Unharmed."

"That's subjective. I think we have different definitions for it."

"No, it means you keep your hands off us."

Razvan smiled but didn't respond, so Connelly said, "You said you wanted the money. It's here."

"And your friends."

"They aren't my friends. They left. And I don't know how to find them myself, so how can I tell you?"

"Figure it out. You have until the money is counted."

"This is bullshit," Connelly said.

"Then blow us all up. That will teach me, no?"

Another man came out of the house.

Connelly recognized him as the one who walked into the shed at Nora's, the one he'd almost shot.

He picked up two of the duffels and carried them past Connelly to one of the low concrete and steel buildings.

Connelly watched while he dropped the bags at the door and went through.

When the lights in there came on Connelly saw a very clean space, white walls with no furniture except tables and folding chairs. The tables were set up with cash-counting machines.

The man carried the bags inside and came back for the next pair.

The other two, Connelly's escorts, moved faster now that the explosives were out of the car. They opened the back doors and yanked the duffels out, carrying them all the way to the counting room.

Connelly figured they wouldn't notice the partially open zipper with the radio inside if they kept up their current pace, but eventually someone would find the gear.

When it happened, things would change.

Razvan said, "The bomb stays with the money, right?"

He pulled Nora and the explosives toward the counting room.

Before he ducked inside he told Connelly, "Start thinking. And don't make me ask again. This won't take long."

***

Donaldson drove his cruiser northwest on Pine, splashing the cornfields with his spotlight because who knows what the hell he might see on a day like this?

He stopped at the sign before the railroad tunnel, where all of the horseshit allegedly started.

Well, today anyway.

The Romanians had started it years before, and now things had taken a turn on them.

There weren't any headlights coming toward him so he pulled through the tunnel, thinking about the crew who'd somehow found out about the armored car and decided it was something to try and take.

Part of him hoped they got away with it.

Teach Razvan and his cocky boys a lesson, maybe pull them out of town on a manhunt.

But what he thought would happen, and dreaded, was some sort of vengeance upon the town and its people. Payback for the humiliation and perceived conspiracy against them and their enterprise.

Donaldson had seen it during his time in the sandbox, and it was infuriating to imagine it happening here at home.

He didn't think the sheriff would allow anything like that to happen, but he wasn't certain of it.

Donaldson shook his head, finding it hard to believe.

How, if it came down to backing his officers or the Romanians, he wasn't sure what Wern would do. Wern was a good man, trying to do what he thought was best for everyone, but even so it was horseshit, all around.

Donaldson was about a mile away from the dirt road leading to the damn compound they had out here, caught up in a fantasy about going in all by himself and cleaning it out, when the taillights reflected back at him.

He sped up.

At first, he thought the vehicle was pulled off the left side of the road, but when he got close enough to hit it with his spotlight he saw it was parked across the dirt road leading west, toward the compound.

The vehicle was dark, shut off, with no sign of anyone around it.

Donaldson got on the radio.

"Sheriff, you should ask that crystal ball of yours about some Lotto numbers. I just found the Cherokee."

Wern came back with, "Is that so? One piece?"

"Looks like it. Parked across 64th, like it's blocking the way in or out."

The radio was silent for a moment.

Then Wern said, "Anybody around it?"

"Negative. And, if I may speak freely here, I think the folks out here in the compound finally came across somebody a little badder than they are."

"Seems that way," Wern said.

It wasn't meant to be a slight against the sheriff, but Donaldson couldn't help it if he took it that way.

"Well," Wern said, "if the Cherokee's not hurting anybody or messing with Pine, let's leave her there until morning. I'll let Jim and Carol know, and they can either come and get it or we'll have it towed out to them."

Donaldson said, "So, do nothing?"

"Maybe put a reflective sticker on it, for safety."

"Sure, copy that."

Donaldson grinned, pleased about the sheriff's willingness to step back and let these two groups have it out, if that's what was going to happen.

He didn't think it was quite to the level of 'the enemy of my enemy is my friend,' but it felt close.

He kept the spotlight on the Cherokee as he opened his

door and stepped out, then instinctively dove back into the
car when the gunfire started.

***

Bruder heard voices coming from the far side of the house
but he couldn't make out the words.

Nobody was screaming yet, which was good.

He focused on the voices and sounds coming through
his earpiece.

The voices spoke Romanian and the sounds were things
being moved, slid around, dropped, then loud mechanical
chattering, like something being dispensed.

Or cash being counted.

Bruder switched his radio to the channel he and Kershaw
and Rison were using.

"Go."

Stealing the same money twice from the same people
wasn't something Bruder found appealing, especially when
those people seemed to be expecting it.

But the money was right there, on the other side of a
fence along with Connelly and the woman, Nora.

And the men protecting the money were the sort to hold
a grudge, and Bruder didn't want to worry about anybody
with a grudge and the means to track him down.

He stood outside the southwest corner of the fence,
shielded from the rest of the compound by the two story
house. He was just beyond the halo of security lights coming
across the fence, watching the windows of the house and
everything else in front of him while Kershaw worked on the
chain link with the cutters on his Leatherman.

When Kershaw pulled the flap open and slipped through
with his rifle and took up a spot at the near corner of the
house, staying below the windows, Bruder moved forward
and used the same opening. He went to the other corner,
where he could see the pickup truck and armored car parked

near some piles of junk.

He leaned the rifle against the wall and went flat on his stomach, not caring about the marks he left in the snow and crusted ice. He slid his head forward an inch at a time, easing his eyes to the corner and looking at the scene in front of the house.

Two men, one lean and one big and wide, carried duffels past Connelly into a bunker-like building with bright lights coming from inside.

Bruder caught a glimpse of Razvan in there, and an elbow and shoulder that had to belong to Nora.

That was three, plus the one they'd spotted on the way in from the Cherokee, the one moving around inside the building next to the gate with the machine gun sticking out of the window.

That left one missing Romanian, who could be right on the other side of the wall from Bruder.

The men made another trip to the trunk and only brought out two bags—the last two, apparently—and the big one carried them away while the lean one closed the car doors and lifted a rifle out of the bed of the truck parked next to Nora's car.

He kept the rifle on his hip but pointed it at Connelly, who said something Bruder couldn't hear.

It was probably wise, and it would be just like him to get shot right before the plan went into full swing.

The man with the rifle had his left profile to Bruder.

It was an easy shot, but beyond the man was the bunker with the men and money inside, and Nora, and Bruder didn't want any bullets to pass through the guy's body and go through the metal siding if the concrete blocks didn't go all the way up.

He pulled back from the corner and met Kershaw near the middle of the house, to the side of a back door that looked like it hadn't been used in a decade.

They spoke in low voices and agreed on the next steps, and just in case Bruder reached up and tried the back door.

Locked or nailed shut with no keyhole on the outside.

Either way, too loud to open.

Bruder nodded and they went back to their corners.

He stayed on his feet this time and counted to ten, then slid his right eye past the corner.

Same arrangement, only now the door to the counting room was closed.

It didn't matter.

He said, "Hey," just loud enough for the man to hear.

The man turned his head, startled, and frowned at the shape of Bruder's head leaning around the corner.

He opened his mouth and started to turn his body, bringing the gun around, and as soon as his attention was away from the front of the house Kershaw's shots came, three of them, knocking the man against the truck and dropping him near the front tire.

They were suppressed but still loud, unmistakable as gunshots, and Bruder moved around the corner with his rifle up, zeroed on the doorway of the counting room.

He got to the front corner and found Kershaw covering the front door and windows of the house, waiting for the fifth man to come out.

Connelly was already moving toward the counting room.

"They're all over here!" he said. "And watch that one, that door, the machine gun is inside!"

"We know," Bruder said. "Get back here, get down."

Connelly turned to say something else and the M249 machine gun—as if it knew they were taking about it—opened up from inside the building, ripping through the sheet metal like a buzzsaw.

Connelly ducked and kept moving toward the counting room and got around the corner near the door.

"Nora, get down! Stay down!"

Bruder knelt next to the dead Romanian, putting the pickup truck's engine block between him and the gunner.

Kershaw moved up to the Lexus and returned fire, though the man with the M249 didn't seem to notice.

Bruder got onto his stomach again with his sights on the door of the gunner's bunker and waited for it to open.

"Front gate, go, go, go," Kershaw said.

Bruder heard him through the earpiece as well.

Rison came back: "Keep your heads down."

Kershaw yelled at Connelly, "Down! Down!"

They couldn't see Rison or the explosive charge labeled with *******4 come over the fence and land on top of the gunner's nest, but they heard and felt it when Rison pressed the remote.

The door in Bruder's sights disappeared in a wave of splinters and dust and smoke.

Pieces of roof and concrete fell around and on top of him, and when he stood up a shape stumbled out of the doorway clutching an arm that seemed to be attached by a few threads of a smoldering coat.

Bruder put three rounds into the shape and saw it fall back into the dust.

He pressed the mic.

"Gunner's down. We have a hole in the fence behind the house."

Rison said, "Nah, I'm good."

A moment later they watched him jog toward the gate with two rifles slung across his back—his and Connelly's— then scale the fence, straddle the barbed wire, and come down the inside without getting hung up.

"Damn," Kershaw said.

Rison peered into the mess made by the explosives and shook his head, then met Bruder and Kershaw in front of the pickup truck.

"You guys had to cut a hole? Impound lots have better

fences than these guys."

Connelly poked his head around the corner of the counting room building.

"Hey guys."

Then, toward the counting room door: "Nora! You okay?"

No one answered.

Rison gave the door a wide berth and handed the extra rifle to Connelly, who checked it and said, "Listen up in there. We got four men out here with automatic weapons. You have a few pistols, maybe, and a big ass pack of explosives. Do the smart thing and send Nora out, then we'll talk about how you guys walk away from this."

There was no answer for nearly a minute, then Razvan yelled, "Fuck you. You open that door, she dies."

***

When Razvan heard what he thought were gunshots he told everyone to shut up and turn off the counting machines.

They did, and Benj and Costel picked up on Razvan's posture of looking at nothing in particular while he strained to hear what was happening outside.

Nora looked between all of them, trying to interpret this new development while her arms shook from holding the explosives.

Razvan had tried to reassure her, saying there was no way her boyfriend would blow her up, or the money. This was all just an insurance policy to make him behave while they counted the money.

And, because there was no way for her to send a warning, he also showed her the knife he was going to use on Adam to make sure he told them everything.

That was to make her behave.

Get her thinking about the knife being used on her, and how it would be better to just come out with it.

But now something was happening outside.

Benj frowned at the door and said, "Was—"Then the unmistakable sound of the M249 ripping through a belt of ammunition made them all duck.

"What the fuck?" Benj yelled.

Costel pulled his pistol out of his belt and pointed it at the door.

From outside the door a man—it had to be the boyfriend—yelled, "Nora, get down! Stay down!"

No shots were coming their way, so far, and Razvan was reaching for the door when something very close exploded, impossibly loud, knocking him to the ground and silencing the machine gun.

Now there was just ringing in his ears as he tried to sort out what was happening.

And it was fairly clear.

The whole thing was a setup, and he'd jumped right into it.

Well, sort of.

The good news was, now he wouldn't need to work to find the thieves.

They'd come right back to him.

He pointed at Nora and told Benj, "Put a gun to her head."

Then he called Chicago.

When the old voice answered Razvan asked in Romanian, "How long?"

The answer was good news.

Razvan said to the old voice, "Wait, please," because a man—the boyfriend again—was hollering through the closed door, telling them about the predicament they were in and how they might get out of it.

When he was done, Razvan went back to the phone.

"Give me the direct number to the crew."

"You don't need to talk to them," the old man said. "They talk to me."

Razvan didn't have time for it.

"Look, you want your money? Give me the fucking number. Now. The thieves are here, we have them trapped. You'll only get in the way."

After a moment of shocked silence, the old man gave him the number. He sounded disgusted about having to do so, but that was for another time.

Razvan called the number and told the man who answered what to do.

Then he ended the call and told Benj and Costel, "We hold out for ten minutes. Maybe less."

They nodded.

Nora hadn't moved since Benj pressed the gun to her temple, and now the only thing moving were her eyes, wide and searching for help.

Razvan grinned at her, piling the flesh around his sunken eyes, and yelled to the men outside, "Fuck you. You open that door, she dies."

***

Donaldson stood in the open door of his cruiser, gaping down the dirt road at the fireworks show coming from the Romanian property.

The sounds were a bit behind the flashes of gunfire, all of it unmistakable and taking him straight back to his time in combat, surreal and not anything he wanted to experience again.

Then a big flash and a second later the crack and boom of a large explosion, and Donaldson ducked back into the cruiser and got on the radio, fighting the urge to call for air support.

"Sheriff, it's insane out here. I've got shots fired and bombs going off."

Sheriff Wern said, "Bombs?"

"Affirmative."

"Well, who's out there? Just the Romanians?"

"I have no idea. I assume it's them and the guys who went after the armored car this morning."

Wern was silent for what seemed an hour, then said, "Any sign of Nora Albrecht or her vehicle? A Lexus?"

"What? No. Why?"

"Well, she's not exactly missing, but Hennig didn't find her out at her place. And Jim saw a man driving her car…"

Donaldson shook his head, marveling at the sheriff locking up the radio while he thought out loud.

When the line was open again he said, "I don't know about any of that. But we got big problems out here, and I mean big. We—"Then he stopped and listened.

"Hold on sheriff, it all went quiet just now."

"Can you see anything?"

"Just the silos poking up over the street, and the lights, and what looks to be smoke. I can't see anything on the ground."

"No vehicles moving around?"

"Negative. I'm gonna drive closer for a look."

"You damn well will not, Donaldson. You stay put."

"Sheriff, they—""Whatever is going on out there is between them. None of my people are getting hurt over some dirty money getting tugged on by two gangs of scumbags."

Donaldson was a little ashamed of the relief he felt at being ordered to stand down, but he couldn't give up that easily.

"You said the Albrecht girl might be out here."

"No, I said she's not at home. You get confirmation she's out there with the Romanians, that's another story."

"So, I ought to take a look."

"You ought not! Stay put or I'll call your butt back to the station."

"Fine, copy that. But—hold on, I got headlights approaching from the southeast. Any units coming my way?"

"No," Wern said, "is it the Lexus?"

Donaldson waited until the vehicle got closer. It had those bright LED headlights with the blue tint, painful to look straight into, but he could tell it was too big to be the missing Lexus.

"Some kind of SUV or larger," he said. "Standby."

He put the radio down and walked around the hood of the cruiser, where he was illuminated by his own lights and felt safe with the buffer of the car between him and the approaching vehicle.

He put his left hand up, telling the driver to stop.

His right hand was on his service pistol.

The vehicle came on, slowing as it got closer, and when it stopped Donaldson was going to tell them to keep going straight toward home or turn around, depending on who it was.

But it didn't stop.

It rolled right past the cruiser and Donaldson, who glared at the heavily tinted passenger window and couldn't see a damn thing inside.

It was a Suburban, long as a ship as it rolled by, and he thumped on the back door.

"I said stop!"

The Suburban ignored him.

It got to the intersection with the Cherokee parked across the western stretch of 64th Street and bumped into the ditch, the engine clearing its throat when the big tank climbed out the other side and kept rolling down 64th toward the compound.

Donaldson was angry enough to send a few warning shots over the roof, but instead made note of the Illinois plates and shared the situation with Sheriff Wern, who went quiet again for a few moments, then said, "Okay, get out of there."

"Say again?"

"Pull back. I don't want you sitting between whatever

comes out of that place and the way out of town. Go north, far enough they won't see you, and make sure this thing doesn't spill out."

Donaldson didn't know what to think of this plan, if you could call it that.

"Well, what the hell should I do if it does spill out?"

"I'll probably call the National Guard, but I'd rather not. Now get moving."

***

Bruder listened to the channel with the open microphone, inside the counting room with the Romanians, but they were speaking in Romanian and offering zero insight for what they were planning.

Connelly paced the width of the pickup truck, back and forth along the front bumper.

"They can't kill her," Rison said, to calm him down. "If they do, they're dead."

"Yeah, but are they too stupid to know that? I mean, they won't even say what they want. Like, a truck and half the money. They won't say anything."

Kershaw said, "They're just killing time. Stalling until backup arrives."

"Which we can't allow to happen," Bruder said.

Connelly shook his head.

"Well, we can't just bust in there. Razvan has that gun on her, and those other two are armed. We kick that door once, she's dead."

"Tell them you're gonna blow the charge," Rison said.

"They won't buy it. Not for a second. Not with her in there holding it."

Rison shrugged.

"Worth a shot."

"No, I'll go talk to them," Connelly said. "I'll get them to come out."

"Don't bother," Bruder told him.

They all looked at Bruder, then followed his gaze toward the road, where they saw bright LED headlights coming their way, strobing through the tree line.

***

Bruder asked Rison, "You have number five?"

Rison brought the explosive charge with ******5 written on it and handed it to Bruder along with the remote.

Bruder looked at the clumps of soil and scraps of corn leaf stuck to the bundle.

Rison shrugged again.

"I kinda tossed it away from me before I hit the button on number four. Just in case."

He looked at Connelly.

"No offense."

Connelly didn't notice. He was watching the headlights coming closer, probably seeing them as the end of his chance to get Nora out of that room with Razvan.

Bruder asked Kershaw, "You got the door?"

He nodded along his rifle.

Bruder pointed to the pickup blocking the gate and told Rison, "Move the truck."

That snapped Connelly out of it.

"No. What? You're letting them in?"

Bruder and Rison were already jogging to the truck.

"Keys are in it," Rison said, and started it up and bumped backward over chunks of rubble from the gunner's bunker.

When he had enough room Bruder swung both sides of the gate open and spent a few seconds studying the mess on the outside of the fence, then dropped the explosives next to a piece of tarpaper with a ragged scrap of plywood still attached.

He and Rison hustled back to the front of the house and got behind the vehicles parked there.

"Door," Kershaw called out.

Bruder looked over and the door to the counting room was opening.

Nora appeared first.

She had a long, thin arm tucked under her chin like a snake and the satchel of explosives clutched against her chest.

The arm belonged to Razvan, his left, and he followed her through the doorway.

Even with her throat in the crook of his elbow, Razvan's arm was still long enough to use that hand to press a phone to his ear.

The other hand held a pistol with a fore grip, or extra magazine, hanging down below the barrel.

The gun dug into her ribs hard enough to curve her torso.

Rison and Kershaw and Connelly tracked him with their rifles and Connelly said, "Stop. Gun down and move away from her."

Razvan ignored him and spoke Romanian into the phone.

His eyes glittered in their sockets and he grinned out at Bruder and the others.

"What a long day, eh boys? You can relax now, it's done. It's over."

He moved out of the doorway so the other two men could get past. They tried to aim their pistols at everyone at once, and the one Bruder recognized from Nora's shed approached Connelly with one hand out.

"Give me the rifle."

"Stop right there," Connelly said.

"Come on, asshole. Look, you see those headlights? That's your doom."

After a few seconds of looking around, Razvan's eyes landed on Bruder and stayed there.

He called across the lot, "You're the boss. I can tell. The only one not bothering to point a weapon at us. The General."

Bruder checked the headlights, coming up on the tree

line now, and didn't answer.

"The cavalry," Razvan said, gesturing with the phone as well. "They want to have you drawn and quartered. You know what that means?"

"Claudiu didn't mention that one," Bruder said.

The smile fell off Razvan's face, but his eyes still glittered back in their pits.

He stared at Bruder but spoke for everyone to hear.

"The boss will get what's coming to him. The rest of you fucking thieves, put your guns down and behave, and I'll give you quick deaths. After you watch him die."

"Let Nora go first," Connelly said.

Razvan sneered at him and nuzzled his chin across the top of Nora's head.

"We're way past that, boyfriend. It was never going to happen anyway. You were both dead the moment you arrived. You were *all* dead the moment you touched my money."

He stretched tall, unconcerned in his moment of victory about exposing himself to the rifles, which were now dipping toward the ground as the vehicle rolled into the reach of security lights and became a blacked-out Suburban.

It slowed for the turn into the driveway and tried to weave around the larger bits of concrete and metal.

"Welcome to Iowa," Razvan said into the phone, and Bruder hit the remote.

***

The explosives lifted the back end of the Suburban off the ground, making it look like a bucking horse for a second, and blew the windows out and doors open.

Bruder and his crew were ready for it, though it still made them flinch.

Razvan and his men were not, and they ducked and twisted and spent too much time trying to figure out what happened.

In that time, the rifles came back up.

Kershaw put five fast rounds into the big Romanian, who fell face-down into the stones.

Rison shot the one reaching for Connelly's gun twice, center mass, and once more in the head as he sagged.

Connelly dove for the gun in Razvan's hand and Razvan, who probably had time to shoot Nora, panicked and brought the pistol toward Connelly and fired as Connelly dropped away from the barrel and yanked the wrist down with him.

Bruder shot Razvan once under the right collarbone, then again, just below the first shot, when Nora spun away.

Razvan's head was there the whole time, floating like a balloon above Nora, but Bruder didn't want to risk a miss.

Connelly pulled the gun out of Razvan's limp hand and tossed it away, then shoved the Romanian in the chest to speed his collapse against the wall next to the counting room door.

Kershaw kept his rifle pointed at Razvan and said, "You hit?"

"I'm fine," Connelly said, and rushed to Nora.

Rison glanced at Bruder to make sure he was good, and said, "Looks like we're all keeping our blood inside today."

Then he looked at the smoking Suburban with its doors hanging open like loose teeth.

"Them, not so much."

"Come on," Kershaw said, and he and Rison went to see if any more work needed to be done.

Bruder walked over to Connelly and Nora and pried them apart to get at the satchel.

"Gimme that," he said, and took the explosives from her and the remote from Connelly.

He crouched next to Razvan and shoved the satchel under his damp shirt, then checked him over.

He found Nora's phone and kept it, and Nora's gun stuck in his waistband, and he took that too.

Then he looked at the phone Razvan had been using to talk to the Suburban.

That call had ended abruptly, but the phone was still unlocked.

"This other Chicago number. This is your boss?"

Razvan groaned and coughed blood.

Bruder said, "What did you say about us? About Nora and her boyfriend?"

Razvan showed him bloody teeth.

"Everything. I told him everything."

Bruder considered that.

"Him? It's just one man?"

The grin faltered.

"No, dozens of men. Hundreds."

"I don't buy it," Bruder said, picking the ugly pistol up. "What's the address?"

Razvan laughed and coughed.

"Fuck you."

Kershaw and Rison strolled back.

"It's a genetic blender in there," Kershaw said.

Bruder showed him the phone.

"You can find the address for this number?"

"Sure. Just a matter of time and effort."

Razvan looked between them, his bluster fading to confusion.

"You're going to see him?"

"No, you are."

The confusion turned to surprise when the bullets hit him, then the surprise turned to nothing.

***

They put the loose cash back inside the duffel bags and loaded them into the bed of Razvan's pickup truck.

When that was done, they dragged Razvan's body into the counting room, then the others from the lot and the dust-covered machine gunner, stacking them on top of Razvan and the explosives.

The bodies in the Suburban stayed where they were.

Connelly kept a close eye on Nora, who helped load the cash but didn't want to touch the bodies.

She was a little shaky, which was understandable, but seemed to understand and accept what had happened, and what needed to happen next.

All in all, his opinion of her continued to grow.

Rison checked the house to make sure no one was locked or hiding inside, then opened the wood stove and stuck the corner of a blanket in. He dragged the opposite corner to a couch and dumped the barrel of dirty paper plates and napkins over all of it and walked out.

They all met at the Lexus and agreed it was time to leave.

Rison drove Connelly and Nora in the Lexus through the gate and around the Suburban.

Kershaw and Bruder followed in Razvan's truck.

They got to the tree line and stopped and met between the two vehicles.

Smoke began to lap out of the house's open front door.

"I just realized I'm starving," Rison said. "Who wants a burger?"

"Maybe down the road," Bruder said.

He had the remote labeled with ******3 in his hand.

"I think Connelly should have the honors," Kershaw said.

Nora said, "Who's Connelly?"

Then, when Bruder handed the remote to the man next her, "Oh."

CHAPTER TWENTY

Donaldson heard the booms and the shots, then another big boom, then he watched the car and truck roll down 64th Street toward Pine.

He was north of the intersection, like the sheriff wanted, pulled off the road and close enough to be seen from the intersection in daylight but invisible in the dark.

He got out and rested his elbows on the cruiser's roof to look through the binoculars he'd gotten from the trunk.

The second vehicle's headlights showed him the Lexus in front, and he figured the second one for a pickup by the height and shape of its lights.

He radioed Sheriff Wern.

"I got a Lexus and a pickup truck, maybe a Tacoma, going east on 64th. Probably headed towards town."

"Who's inside?" Wern said.

"I'm too far north, I can't tell. Hold on, they're coming up on the Cherokee."

He watched a man get out of the Lexus and start the Cherokee up and drive it onto the shoulder, then get back into the Lexus and turn southeast on Pine.

The pickup followed, and Donaldson used the binoculars to check the silhouettes created by the head and taillights.

"I can tell both vehicles are full of people, too far away to recognize, with plates too far away to read. I can say, with some degree of certainty, there aren't any tall Romanian assholes among them."

"Huh," Wern said. "Are they shooting at anybody?"

"They aren't even speeding, sheriff."

Wern was quiet for a moment.

"Well, okay then. Come on in and clock out. We'll call it a day."

***

Rison drove east through the main crossroads, where they should have been about ten hours earlier in the white truck before everything went to hell.

He looked though the front windows of Len's as they passed and saw Marie in there, standing next to a table full of people with her hip cocked, laughing at something.

"She seems happy," Connelly said from the back seat.

He had his arm around Nora, who leaned into him and wouldn't let go of his hand.

Rison said, "Of course she's happy. She doesn't have to listen to *Little Pink Houses* anymore."

***

They all met again an hour and a half later at the motel off of 90 in Minnesota, and Bruder backed the pickup as close to the room's door as he could get.

They moved the duffels inside and Bruder and Kershaw used the showers in the adjoining rooms to rinse the day off before changing into clean clothes.

It had taken Kershaw most of the drive, working on his laptop with a hotspot, to find the address connected to the phone number in Chicago.

They ate some protein bars from the room's stocked provisions and stuffed more in Kershaw's bag, along with bottles of Gatorade, and got moving again.

Bruder drove the Romanian pickup truck and Kershaw followed in one of the cars Rison had staged at the motel, a Ford sedan.

They got back onto 90, headed for Chicago.

***

It was close to 3:30 in the morning when Bruder walked up the concrete stoop to the door on Halstead Street.

Razvan's pickup was parked illegally along the curb with the keys in the ignition.

Kershaw waited a hundred yards down the silent street while Bruder called the number from Razvan's phone and put his ear to the door.

After a moment, he heard the ringing inside.

He let it ring and went to work on the locks, which were old and a bit sticky from a lack of maintenance but opened for him in less than a minute.

He went inside and closed the door behind him.

The phone was also old, with an actual bell somewhere inside the housing, and he crept down a long wood-floored hallway with a dark staircase on his right.

An opening on the left showed a shabby living room with sagging furniture and stacks of old newspapers.

The ringing kept going, deeper in the building, and between rings Bruder heard the creak of feet on floorboards coming from the same direction.

The hallway emptied into a kitchen, and when Bruder looked through the opening he saw an old man, once strong but now stooped, dragging an oxygen tank behind him for the last steps to the phone.

He wore an open bathrobe over pajamas that might have been silk at one time but had lost the shine.

He picked up the phone and barked a question in Romanian. "What?" or "Yes?"

Too short to be "Who the hell is calling me at three thirty in the morning?"

So he was expecting some sort of news.

He didn't see Bruder until the ugly pistol was already up in his gloved hand.

Bruder squeezed the trigger and the gun spat half of the magazine out at once, a shocking noise in the small kitchen that, outside the brick walls, would sound like somebody nudging furniture across the floor.

Bruder looked at the gun for a moment, a nasty, unsettling little thing, then dropped it on the floor and walked outside where Kershaw was waiting.

He got into the car and they drove away.

Let the Romanians—whoever was left—waste their time figuring that out.

***

On the way back to the motel room Kershaw said, "I didn't figure Connelly for a romantic."

"Surprised me too," Bruder said.

They had coffee and breakfast sandwiches from a 24-hour fast food drive-through.

The radio was on low, a news station, and so far there was nothing about the compound in Iowa or dead Romanians.

Kershaw said, "You know, romantics, they buy into stuff like honor, and debts of gratitude. Stuff like that."

Bruder knew where this was headed.

He chewed his sandwich and waited.

Kershaw said, "And I figure Connelly was a stand-up guy before all of this. A solid crew member. But now, I'm not worried at all about him saying anything to anybody. Same goes for Nora. Not after what we did for them."

"We didn't do it for them," Bruder said.

"Doesn't matter to a romantic."

"Good point," Bruder said.

Then, "They need to get their own room."

***

Thursday morning at 10:30 they got back to the motel in Minnesota and found the new luggage lined up along the front wall of Rison's room with small gaps between each share.

Bruder looked into the adjoining room and found it empty, the beds undisturbed.

"Where are they?"

"Got another room," Rison said. "We didn't know when you'd be getting back, figured you might want to crash."

Kershaw told Bruder, "See?"

Rison waited for an explanation about that, and when he didn't get one said, "You can use this room too. I'm heading out."

Bruder pointed at the suitcases.

"How'd we do?"

"Just under three million apiece. Less than the fourteen total we'd hoped for, but not too shabby."

Kershaw nodded.

"Connelly say how he's going to split his with Nora?"

"Tell you the truth, I don't think they'll split it at all. I think it's their nest egg. Or, what do you call it? A dowry?"

They thought about that for a moment, how it might turn out and if it meant anything to them.

Finally Rison said, "There's a diner on the other side of the parking lot, I think they serve breakfast all day."

They shook hands and Rison carried his luggage to the car he'd staged for himself, another forgettable sedan, and drove away.

Bruder was thinking about another shower when someone knocked on the door.

Kershaw checked through the front window, then opened the door for Connelly and Nora.

They looked fresh and well-scrubbed, Nora wearing the same clothes and without any sort of makeup or work done on her hair.

They looked, Bruder decided, like a young couple excited for whatever the day brought.

Picking apples, maybe.

Kershaw closed the door and asked, "How you two doing?"

He was being polite, but also checking in with Connelly, not wanting to come right out with it in front of Nora, just in case.

"We're good," Connelly said, and gave small nods to both Bruder and Kershaw, letting them know it was true.

"Heading to Minneapolis?" Bruder said.

"Not sure yet," Connelly said, looking at Nora.

It was the right thing to say.

Whether Bruder was just making conversation — unlikely — or looking to find out where they'd be if he needed to find them sometime soon, Connelly was smart to keep their next stop to himself.

Nora said, "I had a few voicemails on my phone, from Helen and Donna, a couple others. Mostly checking in on me, but also saying the place out on 64th pretty much burned to the ground. The fire department went out but couldn't do anything. They found a license plate from Illinois, and now everybody's talking about some kind of gang war."

Kershaw smiled.

"You call them back?" Bruder asked.

"Not yet. I will, just to let everyone know I'm okay, but I don't think I'll see them again. That part of my life is done."

Bruder believed her.

Connelly picked up their share of luggage.

"I'm set for a while, but when I'm ready for work I'll reach out to Rison and leave a number. So if something comes up and I can help, you know..."

Nora didn't seem surprised by this, so they'd either discussed it or there wasn't any need to.

They turned and walked out, and Bruder noticed something heavy pulling the pocket of Nora's sweater down.

Her pistol.

Kershaw saw it too and shook his head.

"Romantics."

A LOOK AT: THE WAKE: A BRUDER HEIST NOVEL

Bruder doesn't kill anyone unless he has to, but for some people he's willing to make an exception...

When a past job comes back to haunt Bruder, a man he should have killed forces him to pull off what seems like a simple errand—steal an impounded yacht and deliver it to its owner in the Gulf of Mexico—but the heist quickly gets complicated when he finds out who the luxury craft belongs to and meets the ruthless crew he's supposed to run.

On top of it all, Bruder doesn't know a damn thing about boats, or enjoy any time on them, and when he discovers the yacht is much more than just a floating status symbol, the stakes turn more dangerous than a shark in bloody water. But Bruder is dead set on pulling off the job and getting free of the man he should have killed, and this time around, he's not leaving any survivors in his wake.

The Wake is the third book in the gritty Bruder Heist Novels. If you like professional hard case criminals with a relentless focus on pulling off the big heist and getting away with it, join the crew and buckle up.

AVAILABLE JUNE 2021

ABOUT THE AUTHOR

Jeremy Brown is a novelist working in many genres, including crime thrillers, murder mysteries, and military thrillers. He has worked as a narrative designer and lead writer for a massively popular video game and enjoys kettlebells, stockpiling firewood, and using coffee as a delivery system for cream. He lives in Michigan with his wife, sons, and various animals.

CPSIA information can be obtained
at www.ICGtesting.com
Printed in the USA
LVHW042300040521
686548LV00016B/1373